New Generation **Publishing**

THE 'REVOLVING PLANETS' SERIES IS ABOUT DIVERSE AND ALTERNATIVE PERSPECTIVES OF HISTORY AND GEOGRAPHY.

'A COPPERS LOT' IS THE 2ND IN THE REVOLVING PLANET SERIES AND INSPIRED BY THE AMERICAN POLICE SERIES *'LAW AND ORDER'* AND THE POST WAR BRITISH POLICE FILMS *'THE BLUE LAMP'* AND *'THE LONG ARM'*. EACH CHAPTER OF THE BOOK IS HEADED BY A SONG TITLE AND STARTING WITH *'UNION CITY BLUE'* THE STORY IS SET IN 2006 AND 2007 AND WHERE MODERN POLICING HAS RETURNED TO THE MAVERICK STYLE POLICING OF THE 1970's WITH GREAT USE OF THE WAYS AND MEANS ACT. POLICE OFFICERS DISCREETLY PLAY AWAY WHILE THEIR GIRLFRIENDS STRAY WITH FEMALE PARTNERS, MANY OF WHOM ARE MANAGEMENT OF LICENSED, UPMARKET BROTHELS AND GIRLIE CLUBS LIKE THE PENCIL SKIRT, THE BLACKBOARD JUNGLE AND THE MASCARA'. THIS IS THE WORLD OF SAFFRON FRISCO KANE' AN 'ALFIE' STYLE POLICE OFFICER WHO ENDURES A ROLLER COASTER OF EMOTIONS, WHILE ENJOYING A COLOURFUL LOVE LIFE WITH A STRING OF BISEXUAL AND MURDEROUS FEMALES. AS HE AND HIS FELLOW OFFICERS AND THEIR VICE WORLD PLAYMATES DOUBLE DEAL WITH MURDEROUS VILLIANS AND CROOKED COPS. AS THEY PLAY THE 'RAG TRADE' (STREET SEX) AND THE SARABAND (PIMPS) AT THEIR OWN GAME IN A PROLIFIC INVESTIGATION OF SEXUAL MURDER, MURDER AND ARMED

ROBBERY THAT TWISTS AND TURNS BETWEEN WOLVERHAMPTON, SOUTH STAFFORDSHIRE AND LONDON.

CHAPTER 1

UNION CITY BLUE

Narrated by Frisco Kane

" 'If your standing on the corner all alone and feeling low,

Liver Birds will come and get you, singing E.I adio.'

"Oy, Frisco, are you going to help me with my bra, or what?"

"Only, if you get out the car love. I tell you now there's nothing worse than a wet n steamy panda car, in fact any car, after a bit of nookie on the back seat. As for me my name's Saffron Frisco Kane a twenty seven year old Special Constable with the City of Wolverhampton Constabulary and it's a warm Friday evening in September 2006 on Penn Common. While the screeching feline is WPC Barbara Windsor who has the voice to match, but thirty years younger than her namesake"

The police radio then crackles 'Golf Four Control to Zulu One' and I receive a message that my presence is required back at the station... "Received Zulu One out" There are nine 'Z Car' class panda cars that make up Wolverhampton's police force and part of a national police force of borough and shire constabularies. With its own Deputy and Chief Constable and the only ranks after Chief Inspector while the West Midlands has reverted to its original three counties of Worcester, Warwick and Staffordshire with a new Stafford and the Black Country BBC Radio Station. So we're no longer talked down too, by BBC Radio Birmingham and the Ivory towers of Lloyd House or the *Blue Lamp* meets

Police Academy. Policing like the whole country has changed to reflect style, so now it's *Hill Street Blues* style uniforms and the motto 'To Serve AND Protect'...or *Kojak* meets *the Sweeny!*"

"Here is my uniform straight' WPC Windsor asks as she joins me beside the panda car. 'I've managed to get my bra on, no thanks to you"

"You'll do, unless you to want take your uniform off and start again"

"Cheeky, but you could check my skirt zip" she replies

'Which way, up or down'

'Behave I'm dying to go to the loo here, where the nearest toilets' she asks

"There's a pub just over there, the Turf Tavern, it's mainly used by golfers as an alternative nineteenth hole to the clubhouse. I think the car should be dried out by the time you get back and while she's gone I'll take a short stroll and read what the jokers have written on that disused bus shelter.

'Sex is like baseball, if you run a finger down the small of a bird's back and she sighs, go to second base then if you don't get an angry stare or your face slapped then it's a home run'

"Here do you know what? There was a kid in there, who thought I was his eighteenth birthday strippergram". WPC Windsor tells me, as she returns "He even tried to pull my uniform off, so I took him outside and belted him around the back of his head and sent him home crying to his mum.'

"Welcome to policing in the twenty first century!" I muse.

The drive back to Golf Four takes in the leafy suburbs of Penn before hitting the bright lights of Wolverhampton or 'Rampton' as the locals call it. The station is in the red light district of Horsley Fields' a Victorian crossroads of shabby housing and shoddy industrial street corners and where on one corner stands Golf Four, a former Victorian lockup and Edwardian pub and where sits twenty nine year old Special Constable Dominic Vegas and in what passes for a police canteen

"Greetings" Vegas says and who looks like Montel Williams, as I enter the almost empty canteen.

"Alright, so what's happening then? Why have we been called back to the station?" I ask, as I make myself a drink and join him, where he is sitting, nursing a mug of tea. "Has our beloved Staff Sergeant been at it again, you know, threatening to teach a drunk the difference between a special and a regular?"

"Ah the station motto, Brute Force and Ignorance" Vegas quips as we sing "There's a hold up in Bilston, Blakenhall's broken out in fights. There's a traffic jam in Wednesfield that's backed up to Heathtown heights. Dunstall's caught on fire and Whitmoreans is running riot...Uniform Golf where are you?"

"Ah good old Wolves and its motto of 'Ecstasy and Apathy" I say

"In answer to your question, the answers no, our glorious leader's been transferred to the Deltas!" Vegas says

"And that's about his barrow, on all fours on a collar and lead!" I laugh, as we are joined by Jesty Dollamore our thirty year old coy, cat Special Inspector and feisty as the female sergeant in *Hill Street Blues*, while looking like Nicole Kidman with the figure and long legs of Paris Hilton.

"And how's the world of Cowboy Coppers this evening?" Jesty says.

"Better now we've got rid of those fire service

insignias like Section Officer and Sub Divisional Officer." I reply.

"Ah the Goons, Blue Watch, Blue Watch to your duties fall out" Vegas quips before adding. "And speaking of goons have you heard about the American vigilantes that are patrolling London's underground in sky blue berets decorated with badges n fur tails and white T-shirts with American police badge logos".

"I've heard about them on the news, they call themselves Gabriel's Angels, they're led by a native New Yorker named Spiro. I'll tell you what it's going to be fun during the football season, with the Beverly Hills Cops on duty". I laugh.

"Well what about that new British version of *Jailhouse Rock* that's just been released. It's called the *Wandsworth Stomp* with all the corny American characters replaced by British criminals like the Kray Twins and the Train Robbers instead of the Purple Gang" Jesty says.

"The *Wandsworth Stomp*, it sounds like a punk rock record?" Vegas says

"It's by a band called Moolah and the Spondulicks?" Jesty replies

"I'll bet that's gone down well with the Elvis fans, they'll all be going round dressed like something out of *Porridge*!" I laugh.

"Anyway, shall we get down to business?" Jesty says, before realising what she has just said.

"What here in the canteen…it's a bit public isn't it?" I reply

"Second thoughts don't answer that, I've just pictured myself standing here in all me glory…and it's not a pretty sight" Vegas quips

"Behave!" Jesty says with a smirk. "What I meant was that your promotion to the part time regulars has come through, so Vegas, you're a new Squad Sergeant while you Frisco have been seconded to CID... so well done you two."

"And now I'm part time regular squad sergeant, I can wear a crown above my stripes and my ASPOM badge." Vegas says proudly

"You mean Avon and Somerset Police, Operation Miner?" Jesty asks

"Or Arthur Scargill Pays Our Mortgages" Vegas quips

"But you were never on the picket lines, were you?" Jesty asks

"Listen. Its amazing what good stories you can learn off the coppers who were on the picket lines, to make any bullshit sound convincing." I reply.

"Come on *Starsky n Hutch*, its time for you two to be hitting the streets and Frisco don't forget to pick up your detective shield." Jesty says, as she plays footsie with me under the table.

Vegas and I stroll around the beat and down Minerva Lane which is a real, rubbish tip: needles, condoms and litter everywhere and where the toms come in two kinds. "Not bad from a distance." I remark about a girl in a t. shirt, shorts and sun visor and who is chatting through a rolled down car window to a punter."

"And bulldog chewing a wasp." Vegas added, as we pass a chubby tart with the words 'Fat Slag' on her pink T shirt. "While the supermodels have to be over twenty one years old and licensed like Domino Dancer who looks like Ginger Spice while being mad about the Petshop Boys, hence her name."

Vegas then flags down a panda car that is driven by a rookie wooden top and hitches us a lift back in to town.

"Then there's French Angel aka Blue Angel, a classy soft porn show girl with a punchy American

9

drawl!" I say as I relax in the back of the Police car.

"With the body of Britney Spears...and the jugs to match" Vegas quips.

"Trust you to say that." I laugh.

"And speaking of class acts, there's always Amazon?" Vegas muses'

"I've heard of her?" The rookie wooden top says before adding. "I've been told that she looks like that model in the High Karate adverts and wears a perfume called Scentabell that smells just as sweet as Saint Bruno"

"I thought you were going to say Frank Bruno?" I laugh.

"But honestly don't go there mate" Vegas adds. "By the time she's finished with you, you'll be lucky to go home in just your helmet and boots...with your whistle and truncheon handcuffed to your bollocks."

Vegas and I jump out at the Art Gallery and where Vegas reminisced about Scotch Jimmy and his funeral. "It all started here in St Peter's Gardens, when he got drunk and rolled around the fountain, trying to fight a set of bagpipes that he swore was an Octopus, trying to strangle him. Then he caught flumonia and wrote that poem for his funeral –'I've drowned my sorrows in drink and found solace in the devil's brew. I've drunk myself to death and died a lonely man!"

Vegas and I reflect on Scotch Jimmy's words until I ask Vegas if he's heard about the plans for Wolverhampton's new millennium city centre.

"Why, what they going do, model us on Bilston?" Vegas says

"I bloody hope not, we've only just got divorced!" I exclaim. "No...you know that film *Dick Tracy*...well there going to use the coloured city from the film as a blueprint and name the buildings after some of Wolverhampton's original pubs   like a Reindeer

Centre shopping mall, a Chequer Ball barbers shop café, a Limerick milk bar, Guys n Dolls coffee bar and a combined 'Bull and Mouth' town hall and Magistrates court"

"The Bull and Mouth, which ones which..?" Vegas quips

"Well you haven't heard the best yet, you know Wolverhampton's new

Lord Mayor had to hold his civic reception at Posh Ada's." I reply

"What the smallest pub in town?" Vegas says

"The very same...anyway this guys a class act and the town halls got the decorators in, you know, the same ones who painted the Olympia art deco cinema, like a Wrigley's spearmint gum wrapper. Well, anyway, the Mayor has to use Posh Ada's and ends up tripping up on the edge of the pub stage and tearing his red robe on a loose nail, before throttling himself, when the mayoral chain swings around his neck and hit's him up the face. Then as the mayor begins his inaugural speech with the words' No way, No way! Under no circumstances! Mind you fair comment!' The stage gives way and our beloved mayor disappears through the floor!"

Vegas and I envisage the mayor's predicament, as a real piece of slapstick and almost fall about with laughter as we make our way through Queen Square and down Victoria Street to Skinner Street and where, as an alarm rings, three masked robbers dash from the doorway of the LA Cafe Bingo Hall

"Police, Stand Still!" Vegas shouts at which one of the robbers shouts back "Fuck off Coppers!" But the words are simultaneously drowned out by the blast of a sawn off shotgun that leaves Vegas collapsing with a bloody chest wound.

CHAPTER 2

DUB BE GOOD TO ME

Narrated by Frisco Kane

Vegas was dead before he hit the pavement while I felt numbingly scared as the robber pulled off his ski mask and grinned at me, as he waved the shotgun in my face. The robber then laughed and jumped in to a waiting car that sped off while I stood over Vegas's body and shouted in to my radio for assistance.

Blue's and Two's screamed through Wolverhampton City Centre and armed police officers beat down doors and threatened gangland style executions, to any villains with any connection to armed robbery and violent assault and who could not genuinely account for their movements over the last few hours.

It was then the middle of the night and I suddenly found myself, suffering from delayed shock, feeling all of a shiver and sick in my throat, as acute cold pains pierce my stomach. I was in bed. I switched the light on and off, it is too bright and I am scared of seeing Vegas's ghost before I throw back the covers and sit on the edge of the bed with my head in hands. Then in the darkness I stumble about, grabbing my bathrobe and a baseball bat that I keep to guard against intruders and make my way downstairs, where I nervously shiver and run my fingers through my hair, as I sit in the darkness, crying with fear and anger and lolling my head against the back of an armchair

"Vegas's dead and they're going to bloody blame me for it, they're going to do me for his murder...but I didn't kill him, it wasn't my fault, I didn't pull the fucking trigger. I don't won't to go to gaol for something I haven't done!" I scream, as tears stream from my eyes, before I get up from the chair, clutching the baseball bat, a comforting weapon against the forces of darkness that I imagine are out to get me. I stand behind the chair and cry in to my arms that are folded across the top of the armchair, before shouting out loud. "Fuck it! No bastard copper is going to take me down for murder, not without a fucking fight ...fucking wankers!"

I then stomp off down the hallway, while keeping the baseball bat in my hand and after opening the front door, I sit on the doorstep and stare in to the night sky, as the tune *The Ice Cream Man* begins to play in my head. I start to remember about returning to the police station and making a statement and looking at mug shots, but after which it's all a hazy blur. I sit on the doorstep and stare at the night sky and wish I was up there and not down here on earth with this madding crowd, before ringing Jesty on my mobile, even though it's the middle of the night and just saying 'Vegas's dead' when she answers the phone.

Jesty found me, sitting on the doorstep of my house in Wheatville Terrace at the Chapel Ash end of the West Park, I was shivering and snivelling with shock and cradling the baseball bat that I gripped tightly when she came near. I then relaxed when I saw no police uniform, only a coat over her pyjamas and so she made two mugs of hot sweet coffee and joined me on the doorstep while the tune *'The Ice Cream Man'* still kept playing in my head. I finally fell asleep, just as dawn was breaking on a sunny Saturday morning and when I awoke, I was back in bed but still feeling nervously sick. Jesty had also climbed in to my bed and so I kissed her on the head as she lay across my chest. Jesty just being there had eased the pain then as I got washed and dressed, she slipped on her coat and quietly left the house.

I decided to go walkabout and followed the smell of bleach and chlorine that enshrouds the Olympic central baths in Aquarium Street. The tune *Crunchy Granola* played in the background, as I sat in the public gallery and where a tall and well built biker in black leathers and who had the words 'Teddy Boys' tattooed across his knuckles, gave me a swift look up and down before grunting something incomprehensible. I felt warm and safe and stare at a coloured, window of Dolphins at play and think about how Chapel Ash has been revamped. The spit and saw dust Alexandra was now the real ale pub of Polly Garters where *Seaside Shuffle* boomed out, in the summer months. The former Lloyds bank was now Swanny's Lounge, a tartan bar and grill that specialised in Celtic foods like haggis, tatties n neeps and Celtic ales like Tam o Shanter and Swansea Jack. While on the corner of St Mark's Road stood the American style Popeye's Bar, a former car showrooms that retained its 1960's diamond style neon, roof sign that said Vauxhall. I was then jolted back to reality by Domino Dancer and French Angel who having seen me sitting in the gallery, while they had been swimming, now squeezed my hand and expressed their sympathy about Vegas. While I just smiled and nodded thanks, as Domino said. "Right you're coming home with us"

The smell of disinfectant greeted us, as we entered Graisley Court and got the lift to reach the girls high rise flat that was reasonably clean and tidy and where I sat on the sofa, as Frenchy took my coat and Domino made coffee. The two girls then changed in to housecoats and furry slippers, before Frenchy knelt down beside the sofa and unzipped my jeans, her gentle touch arousing me, while she softly said "Let Mummy see"

Frenchy and Domino then got frisky while I suddenly fell asleep and had a rather funny dream. I visualised Captain Scarlet being kidnapped by two cartoon style little green men who laughed, as their cartoon style flying saucer whizzed off in to outer space. The dream then changed to the surface of a planet and so close to deep space, you could literally touch the stars as they twinkled. The only thing on the planet's surface was Captain Scarlet's uniform while the little green men laugh, as they whizz off in a flying saucer, to that whirling fizz at the end of the Captain Scarlet theme tune. When I awoke about a hour and a half later I was stark naked and in bed with an equally naked Frenchy and Domino who were sharing a French Kiss as they leaned across me, with only a single sheet covering our dignity. I tell Domino and Frenchy about my Captain Scarlet dream, to which Domino said "I bet the reason the aliens kept on laughing was, once they'd stripped him bare and found that he was a dickless wonder, just like Action Man, they shafted him doggy style. Before rubbing his body with some sort of hormone cream and turning him in to a woman and shagging him properly and whisking him away as a sex slave!"

"Just like you're our sex slave" Frenchy laughed, as she handcuffed me to the bedpost while Domino giggled and gave me a sexy French kiss.

Domino said that she wanted to massage my bum with talcum powder and Frenchy said she wanted to shave my pubic hair in to a heart to show how much she loved me. But instead, they kept me a prisoner of love until about 5.p.m. and when they finally let me go with a pulsating kiss, but once I was back out on the street I began to feel like a Zombie. I could see what was going on, but I just wasn't there, as I walked via the windswept market patch, in to the Mander shopping centre and where I stood on the gallery. I kept imagining that I was going to fight the centre's security guards, during which I would throw at least one of them over the balcony.

I then made my way to Skinner Street where I ignored Police calls to stop as I ducked under the Police cordon tape and sat down with my back to the wall of the bingo hall. I was given a cup of tea by a uniformed bobby, for which I said thanks, as I stared at the pavement that was covered in bouquets of flowers, where Vegas had died. I sat outside the bingo hall for what seemed like ages, as I could not be bothered to move, I just wanted to be left alone. My legs became cramped and I was dying for a James, so I walked to the car park behind the dark and imposing Darlington Street, Methodist Church and where in the shadows I relieved myself, as its better out than in. I then ambled back home through the bright lights of Chapel Ash to Wheatville Terrace, where I closed the curtains, unplugged the phone and in the silence and darkness, lay in a sleepy, secluded state, until a quarter to one on the Sunday afternoon. Someone had knocked hard on the door at around 10.a.m. but I could not be bothered answering, instead I had just sworn in to the darkness. "Why don't you just fuck off and leave me alone!"

I later found a note pushed through the letterbox from Jesty who asked me to call her, but I just shoved it in my pocket, grabbed my coat and went walkabout. I went wherever the footpath took me, while feeling sick with hunger, yet feeling too sick to eat, so I just bought and drank a bottle of milk that settled my stomach, as my aimless wander led me to the West Park. I stood on a Victorian Bridge and gazed at the boating lake where the small wooden boats were strenuously rowed by colourful crews, in what seemed like a modern version of Boulters Lock. I watched the sailing melee and felt at peace and all alone in the world, before loudly breaking wind and walking off the bridge and around the edge of the pool and where I heard the words "Do you want business?"

The question I felt was directed at me and which made me turn and spy a young woman, who looked in her early twenties, sitting on a park bench and patting the bench space beside her. Although I was not really in the mood for company, I sat down beside her, as she said in a quasi American accent "The name's Norma Jean...I'm not really on the game. I just wanted to see what'd happen if I said it, when a guy passed by?"

Norma Jean then passed me a bottle in a brown paper bag and giggled when I wiped the glass rim with my coat sleeve and took a swig of Thunderbird. I then passed the bottle back, as Norma Jean said "I bet we must look a right couple of Wino's? I'm really a student nurse, its' my day off and I've just broke up with my boyfriend. He's, actually gone off with my roommate, so here I am drowning my sorrows, still not to worry, plenty more fish in the sea and if you're wondering about the American accent that's phoney. I'm actually from Birmingham but my name's real enough, I was named after Marilyn Monroe. I thought it might be fun to speak like an American, so I bought some language records from a charity shop and been practising ever since. That's why I can't stop talking. I must sound like Ruby Wax or Joan Rivers?"

I smiled to myself, as Norma Jean who was casually dressed in a sweatshirt and jeans, only stopped talking when she took a swig of Thunderbird and asked me, her new found drinking partner my name.

"Frisco" I told her. "It's short for Saffron Frisco Kane. I was named after San Francisco, where my parents spent their honeymoon and yes you do sound like Joan Rivers and Ruby Wax, but you look more, like Sandy from Grease."

At which Norma Jean began to sing *Summer Loving* and which I applauded before Norma Jean challenged me to sing. Although I'm not a brilliant singer I had been practising to sing like a crooner and sang Johnny Ray's, *Build Your Love*. I also felt the sensation of the delayed shock leave me, as I sang and was so relieved, the last thirty six hours had been a nervous hell. I stood up from the park bench and began *Singing the Blues*, as I walked off and left Norma Jean finishing off the last of the Thunderbird.

My appetite had also returned, I felt as hungry as a horse and headed for the nearest chippy that had just opened at 4.p.m. in time for the Sunday night trade. I ordered a large cone of chips with salt and vinegar and a pickled egg, before I stood in a doorway to eat what seemed, like a feast fit for a king. I then reprised *'Singing the Blues*, as I crossed myself in a thank you to God, as I made my way back home. Then as I opened the front door and went inside, it suddenly began to pour with rain and I got the feeling that someone was following me. I quickly locked the porch door and dashed to the bathroom, as nature called, before taking up sentry duty with a mug of coffee at the front windows. I was undecided which window to use to stand guard, the downstairs or the front bedroom and in the end I chose the latter. Then with my baseball bat at hand, I lounged by the window and watched for my shadow to appear. I was half expecting it to be the smirking face of the villain who had shot Vegas, but I was surprised to see Norma Jean suddenly appear from behind a large tree and look like a drowned rat. Norma Jean then looked the house up and down, as the rain eased off while I could not help but laugh, as I grabbed my bathrobe off the bedroom door and raced downstairs, unlocked the porch door and shouted. "Do you want a drink …tea or coffee?"

Norma Jean smiled in acceptance, as I beckoned her inside before locking the porch door and closing the front door and ushering her in to the kitchen. "Don't worry your safe. I always lock the porch door to keep out unwanted guests. So I take it you have been following me ever since I walked off and left you in the park and now your all dripping wet." I said as I handed her my bathrobe and a big towel.

"Thanks" Norma Jean said as she dried her face and hair and stripped naked and slipped on the bathrobe and handed me her wet clothes to dry. "I hope you don't mind me following you, but I just wondered why you just walked off like that."

"I'm sorry about that but it was nothing personal, I've just had a bad couple of days and all that singing suddenly released a great pressure from shoulders." I said.

I then invited Norma Jean to sit down at the kitchen table and where over a mug of coffee I told her about suffering from delayed shock, ever since Vegas was murdered and which had caused me to act out of sorts. It was only when I had started singing that I began to feel the delayed shock leave me.

Norma Jean just smiled and squeezed my hand, before taking a drink of coffee and saying. "Do you still want business?"

"I thought you said you weren't a Tom?" I laughed.

"No I'm not, honest, but listen I'm sorry maybe it would be better if I just get dressed and go." Norma Jean said

"No you won't, you'll stay and finish your coffee and let your clothes dry, so sit back and relax." I replied

Norma Jean smiled and said "You know what I'd rather look at your bedroom ceiling than watch the telly."

Then as I led Norma Jean upstairs, I stopped halfway and said "Listen love, if you say no and change your mind, then I'll back off, it's down to you."

To which Norma Jean made a play for the belt on my jeans and said. "Thank you...but do I have to undress you on the stairs to prove that I'm game?"

I then grabbed her hand and led Norma Jean to my bedroom and where we collapsed on my bed, in a heap of smouldering passion. My delayed shock had been replaced by impromptu lust that Norma Jean sensually reciprocated, until quite late in the evening. I don't recollect what time it was when Norma Jean finally left to go home, except it was dark and while she waited for a taxi, she slipped me a piece of paper with her phone number on it. I stuffed it in my pocket, as she thrust her hand down the front of my jeans and we shared a passionate kiss on the doorstep.

I then went back to bed and had a peculiar dream. I was lying in a single bed at the far end of a big yellow room that was devoid of any other furniture and with a door in the far corner. Through which strode an attractive Dusty Springfield who tucked me in, while a rotating glass case of cakes stood at the end of the bed.

The dream then changed to a sky blue kitchen where I saw myself climbing on top of a young female. I couldn't see her head, but she wore navy blue jeans and a white bra and lay on a grey and white check, oval table and just as I was about to kiss her, the dream ended.

When I awoke it was a sunny Monday morning and I vividly remembered the dreams and this made me think about my nickname of 'Alfie' and of all the birds that I knew. What if I had to pick one to be my wife? Who would I choose Frenchy, Jesty or even Norma Jean? Then after a hot shower, I decided to skip breakfast and report to Golf Four to see what progress had been made with regard to catching Vegas's murderer.

CHAPTER 3

TRANSLYVANIAN TWIST

Narrated by Frisco Kane

After catching a bus to town which was busy with market day shoppers, school kids and pensioners, I took a steady walk to Golf Four where I stood outside and took a deep breath, before entering the fray. I found the local constabulary busier than usual and nodding politely, as though they didn't know what to say, when I walked through the Police station and made my way to CID.

The detective in charge of the murder investigation was DCI James Bernard Netherbourne, a breezy Scotsman with a trademark trench coat and pipe that earned him the nickname of Maigret, who sharpened his train of thought by reading his favourite novel *Whiskey Galore*. The salvaged brand names of which, he had framed between a colour photocopy of the book's paperback cover on his office wall. DCI Netherbourne looked up from his copy of *Whiskey Galore* when I knocked on the office door and upon seeing me, said "That man there!"

"Detective Constable Frisco Kane sir...I just came to see if any progress had been made, with regard to the shooting of Squad Sergeant Dominic Vegas?"

"No nothing...we've turned over most of the usual suspects and possible contenders, even threatened them with court martial but nobody's talking or has an alibi that checks out. The staff at the bingo hall can only remember seeing, armed robbers in dark clothing and balaclavas. Even old faithful here has failed to inspire any sort of lead." DCI Netherbourne said as he patted the book *'Whiskey Galore'*

"I suppose I could always try watching the film *The Long Arm*?"

"Well I don't remember much about the robber's face, I saw, except he had a craggy grin like Charles Bronson. But I'd like to take another look at the mug shots...just in case I missed anything?" I said.

"Okay, give it a go...and by the way I've paired you up with a DS Jubilee Christian. She's not exactly a conventional copper, in fact she's more like a hippy, but she knows her job that's the main thing. You'll find her in the cubby hole, just down the hall." DCI Netherbourne replied, as he rummaged through his desk for the video of *The Long Arm* that he placed on his desk along with a small bottle of scotch, to lace his tea.

"Thank you sir...and your right about *The Long Arm*, it's a good film, Jack Hawkins was well cast as being a sort of *Gideon of the Yard*. It's a pity they don't remake it in colour that and the *Blue Lamp* and use the cast of *The Bill* with the characters of Jack Meadows and Mickey Webb as the lead detectives".

"This is a police station Constable not Pinewood" DCI Netherbourne said with a smile, as I made a swift exit.

I searched along the corridor for a door that was marked Golf 4 CID and found a broom cupboard, size room, where a framed poster of the American Police Shield from The Prodigy album adorned the office and the fragrant aroma of Euphoria emulated from a tall and slender female with long shiny black hair.

"Sorry to disturb you but I'm looking for a DS Jubilee Christian?" I said, as the female stared at me through gothic, black eye shadow that made her look like a darkly seductive, post teens 'Morticia Addams' in black Doc Martens with Union Jack toe caps and a long, black, woollen coat and woven with large red, yellow, blue and green cannabis leaves.

"Well you've found her and I take it you are DC Frisco Kane?" DS Jubilee Christian said as she stretched out her hand that I shook, while wondering if I should mug up on knowing the prayer for the dead as she added with a wry laugh.

"You seem a bit taken aback by my appearance, well don't worry, I don't bite on the first date...and only then when there's a full moon!"

I found her perfume and dark eye shadow rather enticing and expected to see fangs when she cracked a smile, as I made the sign of the cross with my right hand, just like the Pope at Mass and said. "Anno Domino, Spiritu, Sanctu!"

"I think you and me, will get on fine" Jubilee laughed "Now give me a kiss!"

"You what" I said rather surprised, as Jubilee then backed me in to a corner by the door and kissed me, while turning the lock on the office door.

"It'll be even better when I've got you chained to our marital bed, twenty-four...seven!" Jubilee whispered.

"Blimey! Talk about love at first bite!" I said as Jubilee then backed away and laughed "I thought I'd just turn the tables, just to see what happened? You see I already know about your nickname...and reputation"

I then pulled Jubilee towards me and fumbled for the silver cross that hung around my neck, before placing it in her mouth. She looked frightened, as I kissed her on the forehead and blessed her in the same way that a vicar would baptise a child. I then took the cross from Jubilee's mouth and pressed on to her forehead, before saying. "In the name of the father, the son and the holy toast ...amen."

I then put the silver cross back inside my shirt and

kissed Jubilee on the forehead, before whispering "You alright?"

Jubilee murmured, before forcing me across a desk, scattering the contents everywhere. Jubilee then used all her might to pin me down, as she straddled me and stared in to my face and gently whispered "Sorry! But you don't win that easy constable, even with the ritualistic engagement!"

"Blimey! You do believe in love at first sight." I said

"And I'm still going to marry you" Jubilee smilingly whispered, before she unzipped my jeans and waited for my reaction. She then zipped up my jeans and dismounted, before helping me up, off the desk with a gentle pull and said. "Now do you want to carry on...constable?"

I smirked at the corny remark, as I regained my composure and gently held her hand, before pulling her towards me and holding her tight, before kissing her and pulling her black coat off her shoulders. We then fell back across the desk and engaged in a very passionate embrace until the door knocked, which caused us to jump up and straighten ourselves, before Jubilee unlocked the door. I combed my hair, before picking up the spilled paper work that was on the floor and when I came across a photograph in a folder and recognised the face of Vegas's killer, as it stared back at me from behind a droopy Mexican style moustache.

Reno Dunster was a fifty seven year old hardnosed villain and former boxer with a five year conviction for manslaughter, a four year conviction for robbery and convictions for violence, theft, drunk and disorderly that included him climbing on to a Black Maria and leaving a dollop of excrement on the van's roof, then after his arrest after a scuffle, during which Reno had his hands stamped on to try and stop him fighting.

Reno refused to get out of the van at the police station, so a Police dog was sent in and the door closed, but when it was reopened, Reno threw the dog's dead body out and entered the station of his own accord. Reno even refused to wear prison uniform when he first went to gaol and would walk about the wings in just a blanket.

I passed the file to DCI Netherbourne who shook his head in disbelief.

"What it doesn't tell you is that Reno was also suspected of raping a WPC probationer across the bonnet of her panda car. But we couldn't make it stick, as the WPC had been made to take a date rape drug while her masked assailant used a condom that was never found, so she couldn't remember much about the incident. A prison psychiatrist deduced that Dunster was a psychopathic schizophrenic who when inside should be on prescribed medication, to keep him docile. Mark my words Reno Dunster's a regular section eight! He'll get life for sure, for this caper and end up in Rampton...or with any luck Broadmoor."

"So where do we start looking then, sir? Reno's one of those that we've been unable to trace since the murder." Jubilee said with a wince, as I stood beside her and slid my hand down the back of her trousers.

"Try the third rock from the sun." DCI Netherbourne sarcastically replied.

CHAPTER 4

WIVES AND LOVERS

Narrated by Frisco Kane

Reno Dunster's description and minus the droopy Mexican moustache was circulated, while a press conference, offered a £25000 reward for any information that would lead to his arrest and conviction for the murder of Dominic Vegas. I meanwhile had to contact Amazon who could be a mind of information, so that meant a drive around the beat zone with Jubilee Christian.

"So what's this then *The Italian Job?*" I said as we climbed in to Jubilee's black and white Mini Cooper that really was a bit too low for my liking.

"Well how about you, putting your hand down the back of my trousers ...and in front of the DCI as well." Jubilee laughed.

"Did it make you jump then?" I asked.

"I know who I'd like to jump?" Jubilee replied

"So do I that DCI Sam Nixon out of *the Bill*...she's a corker. While the best romantic movie I've ever seen is *Renta Cop*" I said

"So she's your fantasy queen? Well you'll have to make do with me from now on." Jubilee said softly with a passionate kiss, as she played a CD *'The Best of the Honeycombs'*.

I left discreet messages that I wanted to see Amazon at variety of places I knew she frequented and warily visited various battle cruisers that Reno haunted. I then finished my tour of duty at four that afternoon, so I could get ready for work as night security at an incorporated Econo Lodge Motel, Ramuda Coffee Shop and Dairy Queen Diner. Jubilee dropped me off at home and promised to be in touch. Then as I walked through my front door, I heard a voice say "Good Afternoon" and nearly jumped when I found Amazon, sporting a black tracksuit and donkey jacket, sitting in the lounge and drinking coffee.

"Well don't look so surprised, I wasn't always on the game, I used to be a cat burglar!" Amazon laughed, as she clutched a set of skeleton keys and a credit card in her hand. "Anyway you wanted to speak to me, but if it's about Reno...I don't know a thing." Amazon added defensively

"Not even for a shake of twenty five grand?" I said.

"Keep talking" Amazon said, as she stood up, proffered her empty coffee mug for a refill, slipped off her coat and followed me in to the kitchen.

"Well that's the reward. And if you help me catch him, a hefty chunk of that is yours?" I said as I made more coffee, while Amazon stood behind me and sized me up and down.

"Sugar...or are you sweet enough?" I then said, as Amazon unzipped her tracksuit top and lolled against the kitchen work surface, before licking her lips, as she took the coffee mugs off me, placed them on the side and pounced like a tiger. 'So this is the great Amazon' I thought 'Great perfume and drop dead gorgeous just like that bird off the High Karate adverts!'

"Reno's a bastard! He almost did for three of my girls, not long back. He's a rough diamond, make no mistake!" Amazon growled before gently saying. "But I was sorry to hear about Vegas, you know I gave him his twenty first birthday treat and he said then that you and I should meet up some day, for a loving spoonful ... now get your kit off and let me take you to bed!"

I didn't need asking twice and by eight thirty that

evening, Amazon left me basking in the exuberance of the experience, while she got dressed and tucked £30 from my wallet in to her bosom, before zipping up her tracksuit top, as 'Time was money.' Amazon promised to let me know if Reno made more than just a fleeting appearance and told me to lookout for a long legged hooker named Lusty Jewson, who Reno had a thing for. Then as she was closing the front door on her way out, Amazon called back and told me to keep the bed warm and which made me smile and raise my eyebrows in anticipation.

When the time came to go to work, I felt as happy as sandboy and wondered if I would get any nocturnal visitors, like the motel manager Babs whose pussycat eyes espoused love and warmth like Samantha Janus. The night shift though passed peacefully, until I got back home at about 8 a.m. on the Tuesday morning and was about to turn the key in the door, when I heard a female voice say 'Hello trouble!'

"Blimey you're an early bird. I was just about to go to bed." I said to Norma Jean, as she followed me in to the house, where I ditched my coat and we went into the kitchen, where I asked what she wanted to drink, tea or coffee.

"Coffee please and you're a quick worker wanting to go to bed, as soon as

I walk through the door...you must be pleased to see me?" Norma Jean said

"I've just come off nights, so I want to get my head down...but aren't you supposed to be at work?" I asked.

"I'm also on a nights, so I thought I'd come and pay you a visit... but don't you notice anything different about me?" Norma Jean said, as she gave twirl in her long black great coat and red woollen scarf, to match her new bubble cut haircut.

"Oh yes, you look like that Dawn Hope out of *Emmerdale*, but don't take your coat off, just let me look at you...your beautiful." I said

"Thank you kind sir, now can I take my coat off...or can't I stop?"

Norma Jean said, while sounding a little disappointed.

"Of course you can stop I just wanted to kiss you...just as you are!" I said, as I gave Norma Jean a great big kiss and yawningly added. "Right I'm going to bed, make yourself some breakfast if you want, there's some bacon in the fridge and I'll see you later."

The smell of frying bacon soon wafted up from the kitchen and I suspected that Norma Jean would be looking around the house and deciding that it needed a woman's touch. Norma Jean then came upstairs and sat on the edge of the bed, as I felt her stroke my head and heard her say. "Someday I'm going to be your wife."

Norma Jean then climbed in to bed, where I felt her naked body snuggle up against me, so I turned to face her and hold her tight. I slept through to about four in the afternoon and when I awoke I found that I was alone in bed, Norma Jean had gone or so I thought, until after getting washed, dressed and going downstairs I found Norma Jean lying on the sofa and watching the telly.

"Afternoon...anything good on" I yawned and stretched.

"Hello big boy want a drink?" Norma Jean said, as she stood up and made her way to the kitchen.

"I wouldn't mind a mug of tea and I've still got to get my dinner yet." I said as I followed her in to the kitchen and stood watching her make me a drink.

"What d' you want, I'll cook it." Norma Jean said as she handed me my tea.

"Whatever you can find, there's some spuds and

stuff in the cupboard and some Chinese style barbecue ribs in the fridge. But isn't this all a bit momiscal, you wanting to cook for me and all that?" I said

"Not momiscal but wifeseical, as wifesical is as nicesical as twiceiscals."

Norma Jean said while sounding like an advert for Rice Crispies. "Oh did I tell you, I'm doing an arts and drama course at college, two days a week. There's a girl there you might know, Jubilee Christian. She's a copper as well, part time regular, she's a bit off the wall in her style, but she's nice all the same."

I retired to the hallway and stood on the front door step with my tea, this was getting like the play *Boeing, Boeing*. Frenchy was in love with me, Jubilee wanted to marry me and Norma Jean wanted to be my wife. Then there was Jesty but she was in the middle of getting divorced and what about Thursday and Vegas's funeral. They were all going to be there Frenchy, Jesty, Jubilee and what if Norma Jean came along as my partner? The problem is that I fancy and would marry all of them if the law allowed, but I don't fancy becoming a Mormon so I can have four wives and I can't see Norma Jean wanting to share and I definitely didn't want to get done for bigamy. No this is really, going to take some thinking out?

After dinner Norma Jean rested her head on my shoulder and we both went to sleep, only to awake, to find the place was in darkness and the clocking saying it was almost eight oclock. I had the Honeycomb's song *Colour Slide* playing in my head, as I fumbled for the light switch, while Norma Jean made a quick drink and put on her coat, as she had to go home and get ready before starting work.

"Next time I'll bring my uniform with me." Norma Jean said. "Better still, what if I move in?" she added and a proposition that left me perplexed.

I left at 9.p.m. for work at the Econo Lodge that was part of an American chain, with the coffee crème coloured motel, coffee shop and diner, originally being a petrol station and two houses that had initially been converted in to a pub called 'The Old Bull and Bush.' The coffee shop shut at 10.p.m. while the diner continued to serve until midnight, after which, I pretty much had the place to myself. Then after making sure the place was secure by locking the Econo Lodge's front door, so that any late arrivals used the night bell, to awaken me from my regular catnaps. I switched on the radio to stop myself from getting bored and allow the time to pass more quickly, while allowing me to think in peace. I was warming to the idea of Norma Jean becoming my wife, but I didn't want to hurt her, by seeing Frenchy on the side, while Jubilee was another problem. She also wanted a ring on her finger, a wedding ring, or so she said…as for the rest it would be a case of when discretion allowed?

The night passed relatively peacefully and after jumping off an early morning bus, I walked home and scoured the horizon for any signs of Norma Jean or Jubilee Christian prowling about. I then dashed inside, locked the door and went to bed. Although I liked having a bird to share my bed, I needed to sleep on the problem of my complex personal life. After which, it was pretty much the same, as usual, bar the fact that I refused to answer the door when someone knocked and I snorted. "If its Jehovah's Witnesses, they can bugger off!"

CHAPTER 5

SEASONS IN THE SUN

Narrated by Frisco Kane

I stood on the Econo car park and looked up at the sky. It was going to be a dry night, so I got my all jobs done as quickly as possible, as the weather was right for unexpected visitors. The first was a drunk on a push bike and who having tried the coffee shop door, peered through the lattice style shutters, only to get a shock when I suddenly appeared at the window, wearing a Scream mask. The drunk, just as though he was having a seizure, clutched his chest before pedalling away on his bike like mad while I burst out laughing.

"Oh there you are?" Babs said, as she stood in the doorway of the darkened coffee shop, with her sudden appearance making me jump.

I was pleased to see Babs who was a cute and cuddly, petite, blonde who had entered through the back door and heard all the laughing, before I explained to her about the drunk, to which she laughed "Your' wicked, you are?"

"Not as wicked as I'd like to be?" I mused as I walked across the room and stood in front of her, while the moonlight reflected on Babs face and black business suit. I then draped my arms around her neck and looked down in to her face, before giving her a gentle kiss that she didn't try to fend off.

"I know it's wrong, as I'm married and everything...but please don't stop!" Babs said, as I broke off the kiss, so that I could just hold her close and look at her warm smiling face in the coming winter moonlight.

"Take me to bed!" Babs said while not wanting to move, as she felt so cosy and snug, while I smiled and gave her another gentle kiss as I held her tight.

"Only, if you really want me too" I said while gently kissing her nose

Babs shook her head and said "Maybe next time."

I carried a sleepy Bab's upstairs to a vacant bedroom where I laid her on the bed and covered her gently with a blanket, while giving her a goodnight kiss on her forehead that made her moan and turn her head on the pillow. I then crept out of the darkened room and stole away, this was not the first time I had been frisky with a manager, but Babs was the best.

Then at 7.a.m. after awakening Babs and explaining to her about what had happened, after she fell asleep and for which she thanked me for being so kind with a gentle kiss. I left work and was nearly run down by Jesty in her car, who shouted. "Come on jump in... I've come to give you a ride home."

Jesty took a detour to my house and drove off the main Penn Road via the steep and winding Vicarage road to the narrow Chamberlain's Lane and Fergies Common that ran back to the countryside surrounding the Econo Lodge. Jesty then backed the car along the common's rough, single track that had no place to turn and parked up, before unpacking a flask of coffee and nudging me awake.

"Oh Cheers." I yawned and sipped the coffee. The heat almost burned my fingers through the plastic cup. "I meant to ask how's' the divorce going?"

"As well as can be expected, my decree nisi comes through in December, the problem is and I don't I know how to say this? You know I like you, in fact I love you. Well I also fancy one of the girls as well. The one they call French Angel ...but I don't know if she's interested?" Jesty said.

I looked at Jesty with disbelief and sighed. "As, if things aren't complicated enough...oh she'll be interested alright, who wouldn't be. Frenchy shares a flat with Domino, they are both bisexual, they don't fancy each other, but they will share the odd kiss out of mischief. My problem is that Jubilee Christian says she wants to marry me, you say you love me. Frenchy says she loves me. A student nurse named Norma Jean wants to be my wife. On top of which you say you fancy Frenchy, well all I can say is good luck. But what's made you suddenly get the hots for Frenchy? I never took you for batting for the other side?"

"Well...and please don't shout but of late I have found some of the girls let's say more than just attractive and so just out of curiosity I decided to surf the Internet and see what websites there were for bisexual females and lesbians like Dirty Hot Love and Lustful Bobcats." Jesty said slightly bashful "When I came across a web site for lesbian lap dancers called Buck Bubbles, so I decided as the registration was free, to take a look and there was Frenchy...La Mar as she called herself...in all her glory."

"You didn't use your right name did you?" I asked in disbelief.

"I'm not that daft. I used the name Foxy Mink." Jesty said "It went well with my topless photo of me playing with my nipples."

"Blimey I wouldn't mind seeing this site myself...and these topless photos of you?" I cheekily mused "But I like your name Foxy Minx. It suits you."

"Why thank you." Jesty replied with a sultry smile. "Now as reward for such a compliment, would you like the pleasure of my minx...across the backseat?"

"And later I'll speak to Amazon about Frenchy. They'll be at the funeral with Domino...unless that is you want to go, round to Frenchy's flat now?" I replied while subtly smiling at the prospect of having Jesty for breakfast.

Jesty shook her head, this afternoon would be fine, for now she just wanted to christen her car and relax in the countryside and watch the morning sun come up. Then when we finally arrived back at my house I was just in time to see Norma Jean walking away, but I didn't call out. As to explain things at this stage would cause more problems than it was worth, so I went to bed and set the alarm for 1.pm. I eventually awoke to the sound of the alarm ringing and then lay in bed to half past one, before stirring myself to have a shower, while Jesty who had already used the bathroom after leaving my bed, had laid out my black suit, before cooking lunch, just like a prospective wife.

I was then giving my suit a final brush, when Jesty stood behind me and said "Look me up and down kid." as she gave a twirl.

"Blimey you really are dressed to impress best Police uniform with a black midi skirt that shows just enough...but not too much" I said, as I gave her a kiss.

"Thank you kind sir...I made a special effort. I just want to do Vegas credit and make you proud?" Jesty whispered in an affectionate tone.

"Listen love you always make me proud...in fact I'd marry you tomorrow. Just remember you're Frisco's girl and you can tell that to Frenchy, if you two hit it off, that'll wind her up. What I'm trying to say is that I hope you get the result you want this afternoon. But if it doesn't work out with Frenchy and she doesn't want to know and I can't see why not, as Foxy and Frenchy does have a certain style to it then as Jackie Wilson said Come Back to me!" I said with a wink and let her in on a secret. "Frenchy's models her American accent on punchy American broads, like Lucille Ball and Shelly Winters. Though that should be Bernie Winters,

36

considering that Frenchy used to perform on stage under her real name of Bernice Winters, a Sally Bowles style stripper with a St Bernard... but don't ask which was the dog?"

Jesty looked amazed at what I'd just said and replied "Frisco Kane your' awful! But there's one thing that worries me, that is I've heard that Frenchy likes to spank girls who displease her...put them over her knee. But I don't fancy Frenchy putting me over her knee, especially in uniform and spanking me like a naughty schoolgirl. I'd feel humiliated."

I had to laugh and held Jesty's hand to reassure her. "Oh that's just Frenchy making smoke and if she does play up...then she'll have me to deal with!"

When we arrived at St Peter's church, everyone from the Chief Constable through to what looked like the whole of Golf Four Control were waiting outside the church for the hearse to arrive, so after joining the patient throng Jesty struck up a conversation with Domino to see if she could provoke a reaction from Frenchy. And who was talking to Amazon who in turn was flitting about, dispensing advice and gathering information, while DCI Netherbourne and I chatted about the murder and I learned that Reno had been busy again, but this time down in London.

"So that's why Jubilee Christian isn't at the funeral...she's gone to see what she can gleam about the two armed robberies in London. But don't worry she'll be back before you know it...I spoke to her this morning and she sends you her love and will see you when she gets back...so are you two an item then or something?" DCI Netherbourne asked.

"It's a little bit more complicated than that?" I said and briefly explained about the situation with my love life, while leaving out the bit, about Jesty fancying Frenchy.

"What is it with you and women?" DCI Netherbourne asked?

"Don't ask me? I'm only a cop trying to do a job." I laughed, as Amazon interrupted our chat and took me aside' for a quiet word.

"Listen...I've spoken to Frenchy and told her about Jesty and I noticed that when she saw Jesty talking to Domino without realising that it was her, she was like a bitch on heat!" Amazon's comment made me laugh, as she then said. "So I'd say that she's up for it, except now Domino fancies me, but I'm not that way inclined and speaking of sex...I hope you've kept that bed warm for me?" And to which I gently laughed as she squeezed my backside.

I watched Jesty take a seat in the same pew as Frenchy who looked up from bowing her head in prayer, but as for what happened next Jesty would tell me later after Vegas's funeral that was a Golf Four drumhead ceremony with the theme tune from *Beverly Hills Cop* and Vegas laid to rest, wearing his Axle Foley style bomber jacket. That had an oval and black badge with silver stitching and the words 'Police Officer' and two white American style police shields that said 'Route 66' in orange stitching. The Chief Constable said a few words on behalf of the local constabulary, after which there was the hymnal *Lead us, heavenly father lead us* which was the same tune as *Softly, Softly*. But it was Domino who had taken it upon herself' to be chief mourner and for very special reasons that came to light during her eulogy. Vegas and Domino had been brought up in care, but where as Domino had turned to vice and adult entertainment and chosen the professional name of Domino Dancer. Vegas had followed law and order until their paths crossed again and since when they had secretly been courting and set a date to get married in the New Year, with Domino expecting Vegas's child. Domino then played the saxophone, as I sang *Sixteen Tons* by Tennessee Ernie Ford. It was a song that Vegas and I often sang together at karaokes.

The church service ended on a high note after which I took a photo of Domino, Amazon and Frenchy, as they stood together on the steps of St Peter's Square like 1940's damsels of the Rue Morgue, in black pencil skirts, black V- neck sweaters, seamed stockings and stilettos, long black trench coats, red neckerchiefs and black French berets.

Domino then invited Amazon, Jesty, DCI Netherbourne and me back to the flat, once she and Frenchy had said a final goodbye to Vegas at a private cremation at Bushbury Cemetery. But in the meantime we retired to the cruise ship bedecked interior of the Royal Wolverhampton Bar that stood next door to the art gallery.

"So how'd do get on then...did you get the result you wanted?" I asked Jesty at the first opportunity to get her alone.

"Now you know a girl doesn't like to tell secrets...but when Frenchy caught a glimpse of my legs and heard me whisper 'Hello', Frenchy replied "Hello yourself sugar...the name's Frenchy."

"I know...my names Jesty...Jesty Dollamore" I said

"You're the cop? The cop who fancies me? Gee whizz doll I don't know what to say, you're a real dish. But I didn't realise ...I saw you talking to Domino, but I didn't realise? Talk about femme fatale female love at first sight, I can't wait to stroke your pussy." Frenchy whispered excitedly. "But listen sugar we can't talk here...how about after the funeral, there's a few of us, bailing back to mine and Domino's flat so why don't you come along and we can get to know each other better and sister I can guarantee you won't be in that uniform for long."

"Frenchy though could not resist the temptation of getting naughty in church, so after patting the seat for me to sit closer and making sure we had privacy in the pew, a sexily excited Frenchy subtly caressed my knee and under my skirt before she nimbly fingered my racy panties in flirtatious foreplay." Jesty said with a cheeky smile.

"So Frenchy's invited you back to play...it'll be knickers off for Xmas then." I teased. "She'll soon have you stripped down to your lingerie ...and less?"

"Don't be cheeky!" Jesty said and gave me a playful swipe. "But, you know when we go back to the flat...Frenchy be gentle with me, she won't try to rape me or anything will she? She'll understand that I'm still a vestal virgin when it comes to femme fatale?" Jesty worried

"You a vestal virgin Foxy Minx and her topless charms that's a good one" I cheekily said, to which Jesty gave me another playful swipe. "But listen Frenchy will be gentle, as a Lamb otherwise she'll have me to deal with? But I'll make sure she knows you're fresh off the boat when it comes to femme fatale...and I'll be there to make sure your safe...so don't worry. But I want you to tell Frenchy that you're my girl, Frisco's girl, not just the property of some happy slapper named Frenchy La Mar...the dumb broad!" I laughed.

"I can't say that...what if she slaps me?" Jesty said

"Don't worry she won't...she'll just laugh and spark off at me and if it does work out between you, I might know someone who can polish up Frenchy's phoney American accent?" I said while thinking about Norma Jean and her collection of American language records.

CHAPTER 6

SWING OUT SISTER

Narrated by French Angel

Frisco I later, learned had told Amazon about me getting naughty in church with Jesty while admitting to sending the wreath with the banner 'To Don De Vegas with deepest respect from 'The Five Families of New York.' But not the wreath from 'Johnny Law and The Mob' that he guessed was from DCI Netherbourne and Golf Four Control with the DCI leading the toast to Vegas. After which Amazon, Frisco and Jesty walked to the flat I shared with Domino and where I gave Jesty a kiss on the cheek and whispered "Hello love" while squeezing her hand.

I hoped that my warm welcome along with the sandwiches and bottled beer as canned beer seems to taste tinny and flat, would help relax any apprehension. As Amazon and Frisco discreetly watched Jesty, Domino and me, revel in each other's company until I took Jesty by the hand and led her out of the room while mouthing "Come with me"

I couldn't believe that I was about to bed an attractive female copper like Jesty who I guessed was a bisexual virgin when it came to femme fatale, while my Ivory Lace with a hint of Tuscany bedroom with its illuminated French film poster of a topless and strikingly sexy *Emmanuelle*, sitting in a wicker chair and wearing only Parisian frills and lace was to be a voyage of discovery for Jesty. I stared in to her deep eyes, gave her a sensual kiss, unbuttoned her tunic and held her by the waist inside her jacket, before stroking her face and whispering "Relax, sugar it's just like turning tricks, just don't let fear get in the way of love!"

"You don't mind me being a Policewoman…do you?" Jesty asked

"Not if you don't me being a madam?" I replied.

"You a madam…I knew you were licensed to thrill, but?" Jesty said

"Gee thanks, you make me sound like James Bond" I laughed "But I thought Frisco would have told you, Domino and me have been granted a licence for the Clarence Hotel, we're going to call it the Pencil Skirt with a Madison lounge bar and colour drawings of girls in silk stockings and high heels, just like the Fratellis albums and a large stencilled 'Mistresses of Burlesque.' You see me and Domino, have got tired of turning tricks and so we thought we'd run the business ourselves."

I slipped the tunic off Jesty's shoulders and unclipped her chequered Police scarf, before undoing the top three buttons of her blouse and kissing her from her neck to her bosom. This was the first time I had seduced a female cop, a girl in blue, oh I had flirted with one or two in the past, but this was different, Jesty was no vice sting and I was no hooker. I was her seductive beau with my touch making her purr, as I unzipped her skirt and reassured her with a kiss, when she slightly shivered, as she stepped out of her skirt, before I gently held her hands and admired her legs and teased "Stockings and suspenders…you certainly know how to please a woman… you naughty girl!"

"I put them on…just in case?" Jesty replied, as I tenderly put a finger to her lips and said "Shush…from now on, it's going to be silk stockings everyday for my girl and direct from Paris, France, nothing but the best!"

"That's what Frisco said that I'd always be his girl,

Frisco's girl, not just the hot property of some happy slapper named Frenchy la Mar, the dumb broad!" Jesty said.

"That sounds like Frisco…the rat! So what else did he have to say?" I asked

"He also told me about your act of being a punchy American broad and your real name. Bernice Winters, a Sally Bowles style cabaret stripper with a St Bernard, only he joked, he didn't know which one was the dog?" Jesty said.

"So he told you all about me eh. Well never mind you'd have to know the truth sometime." I replied, while noticing a look of anguish in Jesty's eyes. "Listen sugar…there's no need to look so worried you've done nothing wrong, it's that big moose Frisco who should be sorry…using my girl to try and wind me up The strange thing is I love him, in fact I'd marry him tomorrow but don't ask me why, because I honestly don't know. I just love him that's all and have done since we first met, do you know that Frisco was the first bloke to ever show me any real kindness, without asking how much, I suppose that's why I love him."

Meanwhile back in the lounge Frisco, Amazon and Domino were guessing over what was happening in the bedroom "Well there's been no screams and folk running out in their underwear crying rape, so Frenchy is behaving herself…if that's at all possible?" Frisco said with mischievous sarcasm

"Well if the sound of the Shirelles and *Baby it's you* is anything to go by they must be getting pretty close to having sex?" Amazon replied, to which Domino laughingly smiled and nodded in agreement.

Meanwhile back in my bedroom, my gentle touch continued to make Jesty smile, as I finished unbuttoning her shirt and slipped it off her shoulders, until she stood before me in just her lingerie which I fingered and said 'Penny Royal?'

"Winchelsea" Jesty whispered

"Good choice." I said. "But I'll have to get something risque for my special girl, because from now on that's what you are, Frenchy's girl. I know a good thing when I see it and I'm not going to let you slip through the net."

"Make love to me?" Jesty replied as I as her mistress stripped down to a rich lingerie of black seamed silk hosiery and gave her a French kiss before rolling down her briefs, sensually stroking her pussy and strapping on a rubber cock to fuck Jesty, missionary doggy and cowgirl style and which she enjoyed, as we lay on the bed. I then put on Jesty's Police tunic, donned a black fedora that I pulled down to a rakish slant, straddled Jesty and sang *Hey Big Spender* as I caressed her curves, after which I threw off the fedora and tunic and said "Hey sexy give us a kiss!"

Sexual intimacy with a female was a new experience for Jesty and who was hesitant at first, as I pulled a duvet over us and in the dark warmth engaged her in a smouldering French kiss, as I slipped off her bra and kissed her pussy and nipples. I then had Jesty remove my bra and the rubber cock so that she could stroke my pussy and nipples, as we made love in alternating positions, 'it felt great fucking a female cop' before I gave her a playful smack on the backside and said. "Time to rejoin the others"

The sudden rush of cold air made Jesty shiver, as I pulled back the duvet and we stared at each other's nakedness and the big rubber cock and we knew that there was no going back, as I said "You know what they say about vaudeville, as we call it?"

"A dishonourable profession run by honourable people and the law is an honourable profession run by dishonourable people!" Jesty said, as I gave her a kiss, walked over to my wardrobe, tossed her a long, slinky grey silk nightgown and said. "Here's a present for you sugar. When I go to bed I like something a bit classy lying beside me!"

Jesty didn't know what to say except 'thank you' in a soft tone, as I said "Ah think nothing of it sugar, but before we announce our engagement, I want to spark off at Mr Frisco Kane call me a happy slapper of a dumb broad will he...the rat!"

"Why what are you going to do?" Jesty asked, as she looked for her lingerie "Just watch and wait sister...just watch and wait!" I replied

Jesty, just put on her uniform shirt over her lingerie while I donned her tunic and pulled her close, as her eyes softly cried 'Please Mistress...shag my pussy.'

"From now on it's just silk stockings and suspender belts when were alone and perhaps just your uniform shirt, as I want to admire your beauty and fuck you at every given opportunity" I said with a laughing smile.

I then opened the bedroom door and walked in to the hall and shouted "Hey Frisco you dirty rat! I want a word with you, so get here now!"

"Awe knock on, knock on, you dumb broad!" Frisco retorted before putting a finger to his lips, as he smirked. While a puzzled Amazon and Domino looked on and heard me yell as I stormed in to the room. "Who you calling a dumb broad, you dumb smuck! I'll give you a crack round the ear in the minute, brother! And don't get calling me a happy slapper and telling my girl that she's your girl?"

"Why you dumb broad I should put you over my knee and spank you!" Frisco jested

"You wouldn't dare!" I snapped

"Who wouldn't, you Broadway Hooker" Frisco yelled back.

"Listen you Harlem Pimp, I aint no Broadway Hooker and Jesty here's my girl and don't you forget it!" I retorted.

"Well call out the cavalry! So French Angel has finally landed herself a tame cop" Frisco laughed, as he raised his glass. "Congratulations baby! And here's to you...and Bernice?"

"What! You rat!" I snapped.

"Jesty's both our girl...and you're beautiful when you're angry!" Frisco teased

"Frisco Kane, I love you...you big moose!" I laughed before I stood back from our confrontational stance and put my arm under Jesty's shirt and around her waist and kissed her and spanked her bum to signify personal ownership before she whispered 'I'm hungry for sex'.

"Anything for my best girl" I said but just as I took her by the hand to stroke her pussy, Frisco stepped forward and took Jesty to one side.

"I thought you didn't want Frenchy spanking you in Police uniform?"

"Listen I'm sorry but don't be cross...but I never thought so either, it's just that I like being fucked by another female and its only here in private." Jesty replied

"Well just remember you're only on loan to Frenchy?" Frisco said smilingly. "Oh she can be a crafty fox, but I'm the wolf in the hen house and she knows it. But I am glad you're happy and I promise I will spoil fuck you just to show how much I love you."

'And strike one for the Gipper!' Amazon smilingly mused 'Jesty's bisexual curiosity has got Frisco and Frenchy fighting over her and they will do whatever it takes to keep the upper hand

CHAPTER 7

IT'S ALL IN THE GAME

Narrated by Frisco Kane

Frenchy and Jesty's raunchy ardour brought a cheery end to Vegas's wake, while I was not alone with my thoughts on how to resolve my problematic love life. I walked home from the wake, accompanied by Amazon and Jesty who nervously realised when I was ready to leave the flat that she was about to be left, fully alone with Frenchy. It wasn't just some flirtatious fling with me waiting in the lounge to take her home afterwards. She was now Frenchy's live in bisexual partner and so I had a word in Frenchy's ear to cut Jesty some slack, so she kissed her and said. "Go and get dressed love and walk Frisco home...and I'll see you later."

As for Amazon when we reached a taxi rank, she whispered that she would be paying me another house call soon. I expected to come home and find Amazon waiting for me in bed and Jubilee and or, Norma Jean waiting on the doorstep.

Jesty had left her car at the former Red Lion Street police station that was used as a lock up, before going up the steps to the Magistrates court. While at night the solitary car park was a dark and eerie place and where I thought I saw ghostly movements, as I gave Jesty a hug and a gentle kiss on her forehead. While she lay, her head on my shoulder, as we sat in her car and talked. "It's not that I've gone off Frenchy, far from it, but it's been such a whirlwind of sexual activity since Vegas's funeral that I haven't had time to think straight. I think that Frenchy wants more than just girly playtime...she wants a mopsy and I'm not sure if I'm ready for that?"

Jesty said.

"Just take it easy and stop worrying, Frenchy's a good girl and she'll look after you and she won't do anything that you don't want to do. And if things go to plan then all well and good, but if it all goes wrong I'll always be there for you."

My reassuring words made Jesty gently cry. "I would like a happy ending to all this uncertainty, but I'm scared of jumping in to bed in haste and then repenting in leisure and getting badly hurt just like in my marriage."

I gently kissed Jesty, hugged her and said "Listen love, I told you earlier that Frenchy wouldn't hurt you and I know she cares for you. I know I'm your comfort zone and this is all something new but your new romance with Frenchy is going to be something as amorous as the beautiful south, you can always get married later on down the line. All three of us can exchange the same vows at a blessing ceremony …if that is what you want!"

Jesty's fears seemed to diminish, as I gave her a gentle hug, dried her tears and said. "Right I need to go to work, but first I want to go home and get changed, as you are not going home tonight. You can sleep in my bed or you can come with me, you can use the bed in the spare room at the motel. But first are you fit to drive, seeing as we've both had a bit to drink?"

"I'll be fine and I'll come with you tonight." Jesty replied, as she closed her eyes when I gave her a passionate kiss.

Jesty went to bed late that Thursday night but she couldn't sleep, so with her tunic over her lingerie, she joined me in the subtly lit lobby for frisky reassurance that continued throughout Friday. I also gave Jesty a spare house key, so she could come and go as she pleased and have somewhere to store all her worldly goods, as I didn't readily want to share Jesty with Frenchy and had an idea and prayed that this was to be a short lived, affair of the heart. Jesty stayed at the motel on the Friday night and where once again she got frisky in the wee small hours, while also feeling that she was ready to move on in her life. I later learned that after dropping me off at home, Jesty drove round to Frenchy and Domino's flat and where she surprised Frenchy with a good morning kiss on the doorstep, before Frenchy took her to bed for some feminine comfort to the tune of *The Man with the Golden Arm*.

I meanwhile was ambushed on my doorstep with the words 'Hello hot stuff!'

It was Norma Jean who took hold of my key, opened the front door then made herself at home and camped out at my house until Monday night. And during which time I used a white lie to make my peace with Norma Jean and cajoled her in to agreeing to help polish up Frenchy's American accent. While in exchange I had to agree to a provisional wedding date. This romantic hayride then came crashing to a halt on Tuesday morning when the telephone rang and made me stumble out of bed, after just coming off a night shift and answer the phone with a bleary hello?

"Oh you are in then?" DCI Netherbourne said. "Right, get yourself ready as there's a car on its way to pick you up. Reno Dunster's been seen in Wolves while the love of your life DS Jubilee Christian has subsequently disappeared, so it's fun and games all round!"

I couldn't get much out of the two constables sent to act as my taxi, as the blues and twos heralded the panda car as it sped through the city centre and along Thompson's Avenue to Rough Hill's in south east, Wolverhampton and the Monkey House. That was a pre war red brick pub with a sandy gravel car park that was thick with Police officers, who were combing the area, including an area of rough waste ground at the pub's rear and which made me muse. "Blimey, there's more wooden tops here than in *the Bill*."

"Ah that man there!" DCI Netherbourne shouted as he beckoned me over to the remains of a burnt out car, where Forensic experts were busily examining the boot of the car that was exuding a terrible stench of baked flesh.

"Pardon the smell, but that so we believe is Lusty Jewson, a known rag trade girlfriend of Reno Dunster. DCI Netherbourne said. "Dunster was seen drinking in the backroom of the pub, but he left shortly before closing and he didn't cause any trouble, in fact he bought the landlord a drink. Then at seven oclock this morning, the landlord spotted the car on fire in his car park. I've had the plates traced and it seems that it's the stolen motor that was used in the job at the LA Cafe Bingo Hall. I've got officers looking for Amazon, as she may be the only one able to identify the victim, seeing as Lusty Jewson had no known family. What we do know is that Lusty Jewson was seen getting in to a car that matches this burnt out one here."

I felt my blood run cold, as I saw the baked body and said. "Well what's Dunster doing back here, I thought he was down in London and what's all this about Jubilee Christian going missing?"

"Well it seems that Jubilee Christian left London around three oclock on the Friday afternoon, with her car being found abandoned by a coastal ranger at Beachy Head, late on the Sunday afternoon." DCI Netherbourne said.

"Abandoned at Beachy Head but that car was the love of her life, I can't see her topping herself?" I queried

"Don't panic, I've asked the Met to check their

traffic cameras for any sight of her car and the Sussex police and coastguard are doing a sweep of the area, but so far nothing's come back". DCI Netherbourne said.

"But Beachy Head's bloody miles from London, you sure the car wasn't nicked or it's the wrong car? Then again her car does stand out a bit, but it does seem bloody strange that Jubilee should suddenly disappear, just as Reno Dunster suddenly reappears, I wonder if he made her and hijacked her car." I said with a puzzled look.

"I've already thought of all those things myself and it is her car, in fact it's already at the station." DCI Netherbourne said. "The car was found unlocked with the keys in the ignition. Now I have a favour to ask and I know it's a bit irregular, but could you keep the car at your gaff. As I don't want any light fingered Larry's screwing around with it at the compound and if Jubilee Christian does miraculously reappear then we'll have the car as bait to find out what the hell is going on?"

"What you trying to say? That you think she's turned native?" I asked.

"I bloody hope not, but then again, anything's possible?" DCI Netherbourne said, as he lit his pipe in order to have a thinking smoke.

A panda car then drew up and out stepped Amazon and who didn't say a word but walked straight towards the burnt out Triumph Stag before turning away, just as quickly and throwing up and shouting 'The Bastard!'

Amazon gave her name as Amanda Barrie of Tettenhall, Wolverhampton and identified the baked corpse by its jewellery, as being that of forty six year old Willenhall prostitute Lusty Jewson. The burnt out car was then taken to the pound and Lusty Jewson taken to the morgue for a post-mortem, while back at Golf Four, I examined the inside of Jubilee's car. I could smell her perfume of Euphoria on the upholstery and found the Fratellis CD of *Chelsea Dagger* still in the CD player. I also found Jubilee's, Fratellis CD collection and the Honeycombs CD that she had played when we first met and slipped all the CD's in to my jacket. Then as I looked for anything else of value that might go astray, I heard a dog bark and a voice say "What's this then SPC Kane, you cleaning cars for a living?"

I emerged from inside of the car and saw a lanky and grinning police officer with slicked back hair and a snuff smudge drooping moustache.

"Do us a favour Bradbeer, get in the back of the van and let the dog do the driving, it's much more intelligent than you...and its DC Kane to you sunshine" I snarled, as Leon Bradbeer and I squared up to one another.

Amazon then came out of the station backdoor and walked towards me and which made Bradbeer quip "What's all this then, you screwing the mama brass?"

DCI Netherbourne then came out of the station and snarled" PC Bradbeer... if you've nothing else better to do than gab, then you can scrub the yard with a tooth brush, otherwise fuck off and go screw a sheep!"

Bradbeer jumped in his van and drove off, as DCI Netherbourne said "Don't worry we'll have him one day, on at least one charge or another, oh yes I've heard about his antics outside the Gifford. Do you want me to show you the difference between a special and a regular...the pratt!"'

Amazon then volunteered to drive the Mini Cooper to my house instead of waiting for a Police driver and promptly took the car keys from me and jumped in to the driver's seat and started up the engine as I climbed in to the passenger's seat. Then as we drove through the city centre, I asked Amazon what had she, got up to at the weekend, as I was half expecting a visit. While thinking 'thank God you didn't turn up, otherwise that would have taken some explaining?'

"Miss me did you?" Amazon teased "If you must know I was enjoying the company of a certain mutual acquaintance...a certain DCI Netherbourne in fact.

"The naughty old Policeman" I laughed.

"I gave him my number at Vegas's funeral and he called me up. I mean it's not every day that a girl gets to earn a treble pony on a Saturday and a double pony on a Sunday, just for lying on her back." Amazon laughed.

"What you charged him the full whack?" Frisco said.

"You must be joking, that was my selective Police rates. Full whack would have cost a grand a day" Amazon said "Plus an obliging top notch hotel, complete with room service, dinner out and a swanky night club and only for top class punters who've got more money than horse sense."

"Are you sweet on the DCI then or something?" I asked.

"Well he's an okay kind of guy and as you get older you need a steady, he just need training up and I can see to that." Amazon said.

"Well why doesn't he move in with you, I mean you've got a spare room haven't you?" I said and which gave Amazon something to think about, as I asked "Just out of curiosity, how come you know Bradbeer then...I didn't think he'd be in your league?"

"Our paths have crossed in the past, but before you ask no it had nothing to do with business and definitely not pleasure." Amazon said. "It's just that he likes to cruise the beat looking for female talent, from the better end of the rag trade."

"Oh does he now?" I said inquisitively.

"There is one girl in particular that Bradbeer has

desires on. Abigail's her name, she's just gone eighteen" Amazon said "You can't mistake her she looks like Baby Spice and too good for Bradbeer. Her father's a vicar I believe. Anyway she's run away from home, after seeing that BBC comedy drama, starring the guy who plays Jonathon Creek, about the guy in suburbia who's trying to save his house after a divorce. So he and a neighbour, a suburban housewife, upper class tom, turn his house in to a select brothel while he manages the front of house."

"I know, I saw it and thought about doing the same thing?" I said.

"How about you and me, going in to business together..?" Amazon laughed.

"Oh that'd be fun...going up against Domino and Frenchy?" I laughed.

"Abigail though needs someone to take her under their wing?" Amazon said. "But definitely not Bradbeer he's more like Jack the Ripper!"

"He probably was in another life...it wouldn't surprise me if he didn't kill Lusty Jewson? But with regards to Abigail don't look at me. I've got enough on my plate!" I said in a clear tone.

"I know DCI Netherbourne told me." Amazon laughed. "Oh what a tangled web we weave?"

"I wondered how long it'd be before it all came out." I replied

"Well your secret's safe with me, but what you were saying about Bradbeer, it's made me think about the old saying. 'Many a true word said in Jest.' What if he did kill Lusty, she was a street girl and he cruises the beat?" Amazon mused.

"Well it seems a bit strange that he should turn up just as Lusty Jewson is found dead? Listen I'll have word with the DCI, as it's raised one or two questions. But about this Abigail, I might know someone who can help?" I said while thinking about the probationer that Vegas and I had hitched a lift with on that fateful Friday night. "But tell me how are, the Saraband reacting to this image of glory, working the streets?"

"Well you know the street pimps, like dogs after a bone, even if the law has legitimised the best end of the market" Amazon replied and which made me laugh and suck my teeth and mimic 'Beeze Boy, Babylon, Dog's' Breath!'

Continuous red lights gave Amazon and me the time to talk, until we reach Chapel Ash and where I spotted something and shouted "Stop!"

I then gave Amazon my house keys and said. "Here let yourself in and make yourself at home. I'll be back in bit, I've just seen something I want to get and while you're at it, think about asking Frenchy and Domino about giving Abigail a job at front of house at the Pencil Skirt, now that they've got a brothel licence?"

I then dashed across the road, to a picture gallery, as Amazon drove to my house where a short time later, I carried in two big pictures and shouting 'Gangway' as Amazon opened the front door. I quickly unwrapped, my two new treasures and fixed them to the walls, as Amazon made two mugs of tea and joined me to admire the newly acquired adornments.

The first picture was entitled 'BACHELORETTE PAD' and was a colour sketch of a young girl with long blonde hair and wearing an aquamarine strapless swimsuit, while relaxing in a Leopard skin covered sixties style basket chair, at the side of which sat a record player and a black vinyl single.

"There you are…just the job, seeing as there are usually more birds round here, than in Trafalgar Square, so why not make it more welcome." I said.

"It's a nice touch and thank you on behalf of all, us

girls! While this should go in between the two wall lights...but then again I'm not sure whether it'd look better in the bathroom?" Amazon said as she laughingly smiled

The second picture was a colour photograph of a young blonde female who wore nothing underneath a white Mac that was pulled back to reveal a pair of long legs, while she used a phone booth that was mounted on a pillar box red brick wall.

"I can see what you mean...the call girl picture would look good in the bath room...better still there's one call girl who'd look good in my bed?" I said as I then had a yawn stifled by Amazon who gave me a passionate kiss, before going upstairs to my bed, while I suddenly felt dog tired and collapsed on the sofa and where I fell sound asleep.

CHAPTER 8

DOUBLE BARREL

Narrated by Frisco Kane

September seemed to run in to October and on a Wednesday afternoon, DCI Netherbourne and I reviewed the state of play. We had hit a cold trail with Reno Dunster and Jubilee Christian, we did however have was a spate of armed bingo hall robberies across Northern England that DCI Netherbourne was convinced was the work of the same gang.

The problem was that Reno Dunster only ventured north when serving a stretch in Strangeways or Durham, so it didn't make sense that he would suddenly take a shine to northern hospitality, with his favourite bolthole outside of Wolves being London. At each of the robberies, a striking female with long blonde hair and dressed in a long black, leather coat and dark shades was present, but she never took part in the robberies. All she did was watch and co-ordinate the robbers every move with subtle gestures then leave on a black heavy-duty motorbike that had no number plates. The only thing that stood out was the silver coloured crash helmet that she wore.

"Well the blonde hair could easily be a wig and if that's the case then I think we should take it that it's Jubilee Christian. But I can't see Dunster relinquishing his role as leader of the gang." DCI Netherbourne said while sucking on a dry pipe.

"Unless she killed Lusty Jewson to get close to Dunster and then killed him in order to take over the gang. I mean they've made a tidy haul and no one's been killed during a robbery, since Vegas's murder." I said.

"So what you're saying is that we could have two tom killers running loose." DCI Netherbourne said "Jubilee Christian and Bradbeer?"

"Well to be honest, Bradbeer's activities do make him a likely candidate for the Wolverhampton Prowler...but tell me, how are you and Amazon getting on?" I asked.

"Very well thanks. It's a lot better than sitting in some crummy bedsit and watching the wallpaper peel." DCI Netherbourne whispered.

"Amazon's a good catch and she doesn't mind the pipe." I said.

DCI Netherbourne laughed. He was grateful for the suggestion about him moving in with Amazon, as she had taken hold of his life and turned it around, he had lost weight, had his wardrobe sorted out and been given a new sense of purpose.

"Right" DCI Netherbourne said, as he returned his attention to the matter at hand. "The bodies of the first two toms were found on the outdoor stage at Hickman Park and in a rowing boat that was left afloat on West Park pool."

"It sounds as though our killer's got a taste for the dramatics? Claregate was a case of catch me if you can, as it was on right your doorstep while Hickman Park follows the old saying of dying on stage, The West Park was like the lady of Shallot and remember what Amazon said about Bradbeer being keen on this girl Abigail that she wants better things for. I'd like to do is keep Abigail under surveillance and see what Bradbeer does?" I said.

"You mean the vicar's daughter who calls herself Bootsy Swanscat." DCI Netherbourne said. "It's risky, but it's better than nothing. But just remember the last three toms were strangled with silk ties, just as though the killer is copying the Hitchcock film *Frenzied!* So please let's not have a fourth body."

"And talking of bodies, have I been allotted a new partner yet or am I still a cruising maverick?" I asked.

"No you've got two new partners, the one you know very well she's a newly promoted Detective Sergeant who should be waiting for you in the squad office." DCI Netherbourne said with a grin. "As for the other one, I'll send him up to you."

The conclusion of the meeting left me puzzled as to the identity of the newly promoted DS that I was supposed to know? Then after making my way to the squad office, I was surprised to find not a DS that I supposedly already knew, but a tall, clean shaven and dark hair young probationary constable in his uniform standing to attention and saying. "PC Carrick Macross looking for DC Kane?"

"You found him" I said. "And I've been looking for you...do you remember you gave me and my late partner Dominic Vegas a lift back to the city centre on that fateful Friday night...and we had a discussion about the upper class toms."

"Of course and I'm sorry about what happened that Friday night, it's a bad business. But what do you want to see me for unless you've got me a date with the amazing Amazon, French Angel or Domino Dancer?" PC Macross said.

"Sorry mate you're not that lucky. But I'd like you to help me do Amazon a favour, if you would? Have you heard about a new girl called Bootsy Swanscat, she's supposed to look like Baby Spice and be sex mad." I said.

"Which one...Baby Spice or Bootsy Swanscat" PC Macross laughed

"No, but seriously you've hit the jackpot. You see Amazon asked me to find a friendly wing for Bootsy and since when I've had you in mind." I said with a grin

"Well I'm game, but I don't want to lose my job or nothing. But can I get to see her first, to see if she's as attractive as her name." PC Macross said.

"Well seeing as I haven't seen her either, we'll both give her the once over but I trust Amazon's judgement." I said "But first you haven't seen a DS round here have you? Only I'm supposed to be meeting one here, she's my new partner and someone I'm supposed to know. But there's only you and me in the office? "

Someone then coughed as they entered the office and which caused Carrick Macross and me to turn and see who was coughing.

"Alright Jesty, what you' doing here?" I said before doing the introductions. "PC Carrick Macross, meet Special Inspector Jesty Dollamore."

"It's Detective Sgt Dollamore" Jesty corrected. "I'm your new partner in crime. My application to become a part time regular came through last week, with CID being my first option, when I knew that you'd applied"

"Gordon Bennett! This is a surprise" I said, as Jesty smilingly manoeuvred towards the desk, where she flung her arms around my neck and pounced with all the kissing force that she could muster.

'What is it about this office, first its Jubilee acting like Countess Dracula? Now it's Jesty acting like Roger Rabbit's girlfriend? All I need now is for Frenchy to join the force and I'll have to put a red light up outside the office door!' I mused

PC Macross then coughed to remind us that he was still in the room and to which Jesty apologised and said. "Oh sorry...it's just that Frisco and I are more than just good friends ...in fact were getting married at Christmas?"

Jesty's surprise announcement told me that something was amiss and which she confirmed when she whispered. "I've got a lot to tell you?"

"Congratulations. It looks like you two will have a fun time especially on the honeymoon?" PC Macross said.

"And if Bootsy's as half as frisky and just as good looking to boot, your luck will be in Carrick mate." I replied, while still intrigued about Jesty's revelation.

"And speaking of which" Jesty said. "I've just had a quick con flab with the DCI and he has told about the surveillance job on Bootsy Swanscat that Frisco has proposed."

"Can I also point out" I interrupted. "That the Saraband are, also very much interested in Bootsy, but they're not in the frame."

"While the target is one of our own, a delta bobby, called Leon Bradbeer and a candidate for the Wolverhampton Prowler. It's believed that he has designs on Bootsy and likes to cruise the beat and target the better class of rag trade brass, like the three toms already found murdered."

"Bradbeer" PC Macross said. "But he's the one who told me about Bootsy Swanscat and Amazon."

"Bradbeer doesn't drink at the Monkey House does he?" I asked.

"Why yes that's where I met him" PC Macross said "I think he's in a card school but the ones he plays with seem like funny guys and I don't mean funny ha, ha. The thing is that they haven't been round of late, they come and go at odd times and I don't know whether I should say this but word has it that Bradbeer's got debts …gambling debts and he's dragging his feet in paying them."

"Get the DCI now!" I said to Jesty as she picked up

the telephone.

PC Macross's story had opened up a real can of worms and while he studied the mug shot albums with Jesty. DCI Netherbourne and I studied the new evidence and concluded that Lusty Jewson was killed for at least two reasons. So that Jubilee could infiltrate the gang and take her place as Reno's sidekick and leave a warning to Bradbeer about welching on his gambling debts.

"Well I've just got word from a reliable snout, that Reno Dunster is cherry picking the robberies, but not taking part himself, just a share of the profits." DCI Netherbourne said. "And two that Lusty Jewson was having an affair with a copper that Dunster found out about and didn't like."

"And I bet that copper was Bradbeer? That's why he was at the station on the morning that Lusty's body was found. To try and find out what we knew, as he knew it was warning and now he's probably gone off the rails!" I said.

Then as I had just finished speaking Jesty came back in to the office with PC Macross and a list of names for DCI Netherbourne to peruse. "Ralph 'Thumper' Brompton released in March after doing three years ago for GBH at Stafford, Courtney Wooton a wheels-man from Birmingham, good at his job and likes to drive a French Sickle Pero four seat roadster as it can spin on a penny. Only one conviction, six years ago, he got six months in the Green over a stolen motor. Brett Sampford fraudster and burglar just done eighteen months at the Dana"

"They sound like a real factory of fun?" Jesty said.

"Oh believe me they are and now we know the gang responsible for Vegas's murder and the robbery beforehand" DCI Netherbourne said "Right get those details faxed to the North of England and London and let's get that knacker bag Bradbeer!"

It was decided not to arrest Bradbeer straight away, as playing cards with crooks and then getting in to debt with them was a disciplinary matter. But not one to warrant a murder charge and so the surveillance went ahead, with Jesty collating the dates of when Bradbeer would be off duty and preferably seen cruising in the area, as for the observation stints they would be co-ordinated between Carrick, Jesty and me as to when and where we would be required.

I also had some time on my hands, after the meeting and so before I went to work, Carrick and I decided to visit the former Clarence Hotel in Chapel Ash that was now the newly refurbished 'Pencil Skirt' and meet this sweet sounding Bootsy Swanscat to see if she was really worth all the attention she was about to receive. When we arrived at the Pencil Skirt, Frenchy looked fearful and something that I noticed but pretended not to all the same, as I asked to see Bootsy Swanscat in the back office where Carrick and I could not get over how much Bootsy and dressed in a pink midi skirt outfit was like 'Baby Spice' as she sat and quietly listened to what I said about Operation Abigail.

"Now we're going to make damn sure that nothing happens to you. Carrick here will be your mentor and main contact throughout the whole operation, just to make sure your safe. Now if you unsure about anything now's the time to speak up Frenchy and Domino and who you've asked to be here will vouch for Jesty and me and I'll vouch for Carrick...so have you any questions?"

Bootsy shook her head and looked at Frenchy who smiled, while Domino whispered in her ear after which Bootsy took Carrick's hand and led him to a corner in the Madison Lounge and where Carrick later told me she opened up over a drink.

"I'm not normally this shy...only I remember you from school?"

"School...which school...which one?" Carrick asked surprisingly.

"Cannon Bishop's' I was three years below you, Abigail Beecher. My father was the vicar at Holy St Joseph's at Bishop's End, Dudley...can I ask though, you do like me, don't you?"

"I remember your dad, but you were a coy, little schoolgirl with a pony tail, but that was five, six years ago, now look at you...a real teen angel." Carrick said

Bootsy then grabbed Carrick's hand and said. "C'mon we can't talk here, too many ears wigging. I take it you've got a car outside. So pick a pub and let's go for a meal then you can take me home for romance and cigars."

"Whose home...yours or mine?" Carrick laughed.

"Let me think about that one...how about one with a double bed in?" Bootsy said, as she hurried out of the Pencil Skirt and in to the fresh air where she started to laugh, before letting Carrick lead her to his car.

CHAPTER 9

THE GAME OF LOVE

Narrated by Frisco Kane

I was grateful to Domino and Frenchy for their help with regards to Bootsy Swanscat, but I was puzzled by Frenchy's reaction when she saw me and why she had asked about Jesty, when they were supposed to be a couple? I decided to ring Jesty on her mobile and ask her to meet me at the Econo Lodge at midnight, while not being too sure as to what to expect, when she arrived. I then went to work and where as the bells of St Barts at Penn chimed midnight, I looked up into the night sky, as a sharp frost started to take hold with an icy grip and Jesty's car pulled on to the motel car park.

"Hello trouble...my, it's cold tonight." Jesty said with a smile when she saw me waiting for her by the open lodge door.

I smiled and gave her a wink, as I was just as pleased to see Jesty who gently kissed me, as I said. "Go on inside, I've put the heating on in the lounge and we can talk better there."

Then after making ourselves comfortable with some hot coffee, Jesty spat with all the venom of a Cobra "I take it you've spoken to Frenchy, so what has the lying, cheating little madam had to say for herself?"

"Nothing, except ask how you are? But you should hear yourself, talk about sex in the city, your starting to sound like one punchy little broad, so tell me what's Frenchy done to get you so all worked up?" I asked.

"So she didn't tell you then how I caught her in bed, with that Norma Jean one...the one you arranged to help Frenchy refine her American accent, only it was

'Oral French' they were studying, when I walked in the room." Jesty snapped

"Blimey! Frenchy and Norma Jean, I didn't think Norma Jean was that way inclined?" I said surprisingly.

"And ever since when I've been staying at the section house." Jesty said.

"Well from now on you're staying at my house and I won't take no for an answer." I said in a direct manner while Jesty in a softer tone, related a story that captivated my vivid imagination.

At first it seemed that everything was great, Frenchy would take Jesty out to dinner and sometimes, Frenchy would ask Domino to join them. Frenchy and Jesty would play footsie with each other under the restaurant table and mouth the words 'I love you' as they looked at each other across the restaurant table. Frenchy also took Jesty dancing at one of the swanky lesbian bars, like 'Girls in Blue' where the all female staff wore American style police shirts and caps with their bikinis. While at the 'Palace Lounge' the home of Rudy Jonkys swing time, Frenchy gave an embarrassed Jesty her first kiss on a dance floor, until Jesty saw other girls kissing their girlfriends, so it did not seem that bad after all. Jesty also got used to Frenchy getting frisky when they went clubbing, like at the 'Hoochie Coochie' and styled on a glitzy lesbian bar in the American police series *'Killer Instinct.'* This club had an exclusive door policy that each potential guest, send by mobile camera, a picture of themselves to the club and if their face fit, their entry was then confirmed by text and the door staff. Hoochie Coochies was also where Frenchy introduced Jesty to two colourful punks in yellow front and red back mini skirt kilts.

"Bathsheba Menadalove and Darna Gold…they run the East End Club and that's probably why they got in...genial club managerial hospitality. It's not a bad sort of place the East End Club and part of the old Royal Hospital redevelopment.

Bathsheba's the one with the pink and blue Mohican and who institutes a female preference door policy while Darna's the boss and the one with the mop of black hair...and cute with it." I interrupt.

"Behave." Jesty said and gave me a playful slap on my arm.

"Okay, okay...but can I ask about this marriage thing, it's a bit sudden isn't it? I mean don't I get a say in the matter and what about Frenchy or is that all off?"

"I was just getting to that." Jesty said, as she then continued her story.

It was not long after that night out at the Hoochie Coochie, that Jesty came back early to the flat and let herself in, with a spare key that Frenchy had given her. Jesty then went straight to the bedroom and shouted 'Hello Love' as she opened the door. But before Frenchy could reply, Jesty had walked in to the room and found Frenchy and Norma Jean engaged in a passionate embrace, as they lay together in bed. Frenchy did try and gabble an excuse when she saw the look on Jesty's face, as she pointed at Norma Jean and told her to stay. Jesty then locked the bedroom door and kept the key on her, before grabbing Frenchy by her hair and dragging her screaming out of bed. Norma Jean looked petrified as Jesty barked 'Come here you bitch!' and slapped Frenchy hard around the face and who bitterly cried for Jesty to stop. Jesty though, was having none of it and said "I'll make you whine you sorry bitch...Frisco joked you were happy slapper and now I know he was right. So tell me brass what exactly has been going on here?"

Frenchy sobbed, as she told Jesty about how she asked Norma Jean if she would like to hear some music, as they practised the American vocabulary. Then as Frenchy was putting on the music, she felt Norma Jean lean close to her face and as Frenchy turned to look at Norma Jean, she felt her gently kiss her. This ignited a flame of frenzied passion, as Frenchy and Norma Jean engaged in a highly charged kissing spree that ended between the sheets and a madly passionate, labour of love.

"As for Norma Jean" Jesty said "I also dragged her out of bed and paddled her rump with a hairbrush, before pulling her hair in to a shank and giving it a crop. After which Norma Jean and Frenchy cried like mad, as I grabbed everything of mine, I had left at Frenchy's and stuffed it in to a carrier. I then stormed out of the flat, locked the bedroom door behind me and threw the flat and bedroom door keys down the nearest drain."

After hearing what Jesty had just said I initially went silent before saying "You're one fiery son of a bitch, I'd hate to cross you in a hurry. You and Frenchy may have fallen out, but she's certainly rubbed off on you and more than you think. She's certainly put some steel in to your fire and which needs tempering, so I think I'd better marry you and double quick."

Jesty then gently kissed me and whispered 'Thank you and I'll make you a good wife…I promise.

"Well just remember it's your big day…so you just tell me when and where you want me and I'll be there. But I'll still talk to Frenchy and Norma Jean though, you calling Frenchy a brass and giving her a slap will wound her pride, but she'll get over it. As for Norma Jean, you cutting her hair is a real act of woman scorned but the paddle with the hairbrush won't hurt her." I said.

"Do you know the one thing, I really miss about Frenchy?" Jesty said. "That's the sensual kissing sessions in the front seat of the car after a late night out. I can't remember the number of times I've lost my skirt somewhere in the car.

"Listen love…anything Frenchy did to make you happy I can reciprocate… all we need is a Lovers Lane and you can lose your skirt as often as you like. Now I'm going to put you to bed, it's late and I want to catnap while I think things over. So you can use the spare room tonight, then tomorrow morning when we go home, you can ascend your new throne as the mistress of the house." I replied.

Jesty smiled and whispered "Thank you" as she gave me a kiss for being so understanding, while I mused 'femme fatale certainly has a high price to pay.' My love life had once again been turned upside down, with Frenchy making me feel like a liar after I had promised Jesty that she would look after her. Frenchy and Norma Jean's moment of passion had also settled an outstanding quandary, as their spontaneous lust had knocked themselves out of the frame in my love life and which only left Jubilee Christian. But she had seemingly turned native and there-fore bowled herself out of the frame with regards towards a long-term relationship. I though still wanted to be friends with all my girlfriends while promising not to make the same mistake as Frenchy, with any illicit sparks being discreetly snuffed out at the first flame of passion. As for Norma Jean I guessed that she would come' bouncing back in to my life, full of the joys of spring and just as though nothing had happened.

CHAPTER 10

SUNDAY GIRL

Narrated by Frisco Kane

Breakfast time on Thursday morning and following the trial and tribulation of the wee small hours, the words of the song that was playing on the radio *'There may be trouble ahead?'* Seemed to literally come alive in the form of Norma Jean as she knocked on the front door, as Jesty and I drove up to Wheatville Terrace

"Hello trouble, how are you?" Norman Jean called out when she saw me. "I'm still here!" Jesty snapped, as she got out of the car.

Norma Jean then backed away from the front door, as I stopped the spat by nodding to Jesty to go inside and make herself at home. At which Jesty walked up the driveway and icily ignored a fearful Norma Jean, before entering the house and closing the front door behind her. Norma Jean then ran down the driveway towards me, but instead of welcoming her with open arms, I grabbed her arm and walked her, across the road to the West Park and snidely said. "I want to talk to you, young lady but first why are you wearing a baseball cap...someone cut your hair?"

"You know then?" Norma Jean said softly with a slight hint of tears.

"I know everything, down to the last detail and while you're at it you can forget about any ideas you may have had about you and me!" I snapped

"But...But" Norma Jean sobbed.

"But what" I snapped.

"But nothing" Norma Jean quietly said. "Only you promised."

"Promised what? It was you who broke any promise!" I snapped.

We walked back in silence to Norma Jean's flat at Vauxhall Rise, where she opened the door and I ushered her inside and followed her into the kitchen and said. "Right young lady, first things first, put the kettle on and while you're making the coffee...and seeing that you've had time to think about things, perhaps you can tell me why?"

"Spontaneous Combustion" Norma Jean said, as she started to make two hot coffees. "I'd never really fancied another woman before, but Frenchy just looked so delicious close up and smelled so great. I just had to kiss her, to see what she tasted like...to see what it was like to affectionately kiss another female...another woman?"

"What'd you think she was...a bloody cream cake?" I snapped.

"No...but" Norma Jean replied.

"But what...come on spit it out" I snapped.

"What happened with Frenchy was a spur of the moment thing" Norma Jean said. "But I still want to marry you, even if it means sharing you, you know bigamy. I'm broadminded enough. Now drink your coffee and come to bed."

The effect of working nights then suddenly hit me and I couldn't keep my eyes open, after which I stirred for just a few seconds and found myself staring at Norma Jean, wearing just a bathrobe. But as she went to speak I went back to sleep, as I lay on her settee, where I slept on for another hour or so and when I did wearily awaken, I heard Norma Jean's voice, but I did not fully register what she said.

"Hello Mickey Blue Eyes. I've been sitting here, stroking your head and thinking girly thoughts about our wedding day."

When I looked at my watch and saw the time saying a quarter to twelve, I knew that Jesty would be wondering what had happened to me, while Norma Jean who had manacled me in pink fluffy handcuffs, now gave me a French kiss.

"My you were tired, you know you fell asleep on me" Norma Jean said "Oh, and don't worry about the handcuffs, I just wanted to make sure you didn't escape …not before that is, you've screwed me all the way to heaven."

I began to realise that as amorous a stalker as Norma Jean was, she was also sexually psychotic, but in order to escape I needed to play along. I made out that we could be reconciled, but first I needed the bathroom which I could not use properly, as I was still in the handcuffs. Norma Jean agreed to remove them, if I promised to behave. I gave a wry smile and nodded in agreement to her demand, but which I had no intention of keeping and no sooner had Norma Jean removed the handcuffs, than I pulled her onto my lap and handcuffed her. Then just to show that there was no hard feelings I gave Norma Jean a French kiss, with my hands straying under her bathrobe. Norma Jean then put her handcuffed arms around my neck to keep me close, as I eased myself off the sofa and carried her to her bedroom. And where I unhooked her arms from around my neck and lay her on her bed then left the key where she could reach it at a stretch, before making good my escape.

I prayed that Norma Jean would forgive me for making a swift exit and she would get proper help for her psychotic fancies, as I quickly walked home, checking my watch, it said almost half past twelve and when I returned home, Jesty flung her arms around my neck and kissed me senseless

"I thought she'd kidnapped you?" Jesty said.

"Well here's the ransom note." I replied and gave Jesty a big kiss. "But to be honest, I fell asleep on her sofa and when I awoke Norma Jean had me in some pink fluffy handcuffs. You know she even proposed bigamy, as she became all amorous, as a way of getting me to marry her."

"The little minx" Jesty snapped "The handcuffs are the ones that Frenchy used on me, before I discovered that she liked being handcuffed by a policewoman in uniform and which gave me an edge."

Then as I hung my coat up and raced upstairs to the bathroom, Jesty shouted. "And while you're up there have a shower. I don't won't that cow's stench on you in my bed and chuck your clothes down…they'll need a good wash as well!"

I felt better for the shower, after which I put on my bathrobe and followed the smell of the brunch that was cooking. But it was when I entered the living room that I noticed Jesty's initial change, the picture of the bare hooker in an open white trench coat and using the phone booth on the red wall had been replaced by one of a pouting and colourful female punk rocker and a guardsman in a bearskin and who were standing in adjoining royal black and gold sentry boxes.

"It reminds me of Amazon and the DCI." I laughingly quipped.

"I was thinking about giving the other picture to Bootsy as a present." Jesty said. "I think she'll love it…I hope you don't mind?"

"No that's fine by me, I thought it looked better in the bathroom anyway, but please don't get rid of that Bachelorette Pad picture…as I quite like it and it reminds me that this is now, as much your home as it is mine." I pleaded.

Although life was now starting afresh for Jesty and me,

unbeknown to us at the time, life was about to be cut short for Norma Jean.

"I knew you couldn't resist me, you sexy beast." Norma Jean shouted after freeing herself from the handcuffs and answering a knock on the door

But when Norma Jean opened the front door, she was confronted by a goth looking female with long black hair and who smiled and said "Hello Norma Jean"

"Jubilee, Jubilee Christian I'm sorry but I thought you were someone else?" Norma Jean said in a startled tone.

"You thought I was Frisco Kane?" Jubilee said with an air of wickedness as she entered the flat and locked the front door. "It's alright I saw him dash off, but he didn't see me...I made sure of that. I thought though I'd drop by, seeing as I was in the area and say hello...and you are quite right darling, I am a sexy beast and I've always wanted to taste your fruit?"

Jubilee Christian with a wicked fire in her eyes then licked her lips as she then ushered Norma Jean in to her bedroom and pushed her on to the double bed and subdued her struggles by using the pink handcuffs to manacle her arms to the bed rail. Jubilee then took off her coat and pulled open Norma Jean's bathrobe and mused "Oh how sweet...schoolgirl sensible Rose Ann lingerie...whose teacher's pet then?"

Jubilee then left wheal marks on Norma Jean's neck and torso and just like a love bite from a vampire, before pulling a long church altar candle from a poacher's pocket inside her coat and giving a terrified Norma Jean a wicked look as she said 'Now let's see how much of a celestial virgin you really are?'

"You wicked, bitch!" Norma Jean spat.

"If you only knew the truth" Jubilee softly said.

Jubilee then slid the candle between Norma Jean's

legs and which caused Norma Jean to arch her back in pain, as Jubilee then tightly used a long silk scarf to strangle Norma Jean until her airway constricted and she seemed to breathe her last.

Jubilee then decided to make herself at home and rummaged through Norma Jean's wardrobe until she discovered her bottom drawer and mused 'Brand new Dr Syn lingerie for her wedding day, a blue garter and stockings and a photo of Frisco.'

Jubilee then sat on the bed and laughed. "Look at all this lovely stuff and in my size too oh but you can't can you... seeing as you're dead!"

Jubilee then played with Norma Jean's nipples and tongued kissed her to see what it was like to smooch a corpse, or so she thought, as Norma Jean flickered her eyes and then gave a faint and final gasp, before giving up the ghost.

Jubilee then put her clothes in the washer on a quick wash and ran a scented, bubble bath for a long hot soak. After which and wear nothing but bath towels she went in search of food, as she put her clean clothes in the tumble drier and a ready meal in the microwave to cook.

Jubilee then opened a bottle of white wine that she partially drank with her ready meal, before finishing off the wine, as she tried on the Dr Syn lingerie, plus the blue garter and the stockings and then paraded in front of a mirror and mused. "You beautiful bitch! If Frisco Kane could see me now he'd swear I was the real Jubilee Christian, even Norma Jean thought I was Jubilee Christian never mind that fool Dunster who *still* thinks I am the real Jubilee Christian!"

Jubilee then washed up, dressed in her clean clothes and new lingerie and emptied all the household rubbish and her old underwear in to a bin bag. That she planned to dump well away from the flat, as she made a final search off for anything of value or that took her fancy. Jubilee then gave Norma Jean's lukewarm corpse, one last kiss and left on her body a photograph postcard of two colourful male punk rockers, each of whom gesticulated with a single finger, the scrawled white message across the picture. 'Greetings from London'

CHAPTER 11

LOVE HURTS

Narrated by Jesty Dollamore

Friday morning and life as normal for Frisco and me, apart from a special visit to the Pencil Skirt, where Frenchy tries to kiss me in a fit of zealous enjoyment, but I was having none of it and turned my head away.

"Listen I haven't come looking for a fight or to kiss and make up. I've come instead to ask for a favour...and if not for me, then for Frisco?" I said as Frenchy showed me in to the back office.

"Ask away but you should know Frisco was here earlier?" Frenchy said.

"Was he...and what exactly did he have to say?" I asked.

"Well not a lot really, he just made it crystal clear I was in the dog house, especially when he called me a cheap brass which hurt, even off Frisco. So what is this favour you want doing then?" Frenchy said.

"I want to hire the Madison Lounge, Tuesday the twenty-first of December ...you see Frisco's agreed to marry me" Then to rub salt in to the wounds I said "My divorce will be through by then and Frisco's given me a freehand, as mistress of his house."

Frenchy checked the diary and scribbled in pencil was 'Jesty's Birthday' for December 21st, which I saw made her gulp as she said. "That's' no problem, in fact you can use this place free of charge and I'll throw in a hot buffet, seeing as it'll be December. But If you prefer to keep it a strictly business arrangement...then please make a donation to charity in lieu of payment?"

"Oh thank you for your generosity." I said with a

hint of sarcasm, as I stood up and shook Frenchy's hand and said. "Till December the twenty-first then"

"You know we can still be friends, if only for Frisco's sake?" Frenchy said.

"Remember that night at the Hoochie Coochie Club when I sang Dance with me sexy to that Etta James song *Dance with me Henry*'?"

"Oh I remember alright, but before you ask for a second chance I'll answer your question for you...not a cat in hells!" I softly exclaimed, as I stepped forward as though to kiss her, but then stepped back.

Frenchy then flopped back in the office chair and burst in to tears as I, with an air of superiority, walked out of the office. Frenchy had blown it, she had had it all and thrown it all away, she knew that she had no one else to blame but herself.

After leaving the Pencil Skirt, I drove over to Golf Four where with DCI Netherbourne, I discussed 'Operation Abigail'

"So as it stands Bradbeer finishes his course today and tomorrow is on a late turn from eleven to be on hand for the Wolves match then on Sunday he's off. After which it's three late turns followed by two days off and then three early turns...so he's got plenty of scope to strike!" I said

"Well what I'll do is have Carrick watch Bradbeer when Bradbeer's off duty and have Amazon baby sit Bootsy...then if Bradbeer does decide to go cruising, we can put Operation Abigail in to action and which leads me to another thing." DCI Netherbourne said "There's been some disquiet about Frisco being constantly on the rosta for weekday, first reserve detective constable. I know he works nights and he needs to sleep but if you and him, say can work a weekend graveyard shift."

"Message received." I said. "But now for some more important news...I'm well, getting remarried. Twenty-first of December at the Pencil Skirt to Frisco, I've asked the police padre, Father Bejazus of Holy Cross, Codsall to do the honours."

"Ah Bejazus, Bejazus...you mean the Reverend Shamus O Malley!" DCI Netherbourne said in a comical Irish accent. "I take it then you'll be having a Vicar and Tarts theme for your wedding. Seeing as you having it, at the Pencil Skirt with an ex Irish Catholic priest who jumped ship to get married and who has been...three times now...to conduct the service."

"Well I was thinking more along the lines of a Guys n Dolls theme, but then again though...perhaps we could mix the two themes?" I replied

DCI Netherbourne laughed "I'm glad that Frisco's making an honest woman of someone...sorry I mean you at long last."

"Oh don't apologise I know all about Frisco's girlfriends, I just can't believe it's been two years since I began divorce proceedings against my husband when he ran off with that policeman to West Brom." I said.

"Nasty business that" DCI Netherbourne said "I agree with Frisco, two birds romantically inclined and preferably good looking...say no more. But listen I'll get off my soapbox. So tell me about your relationship with French Angel, do I take it's all off then...even though your getting married at her and Domino's gaff?"

"How the hell do you know about Frenchy?" I asked surprisingly.

"I have spies everywhere...and you were seen smooching at an all girl bar." DCI Netherbourne said with a smirk. "Don't think you're the only female copper to fancy another woman in this nick...or this division even."

"Anyway it doesn't matter that's all finished now." I said. "But listen, this Saturday, you and Amazon are invited to join Frisco and me at the East End Club. It's an all girl bar run by a couple of female punk rockers."

"I know Bathsheba Mendalove and Darna Gold...they're a couple of my spies." DCI Netherbourne joked. "But listen you might as well know the truth, as it's bound to come out sooner or later...Darna's my daughter. The result of an illicit dalliance over twenty years ago, during a Hogmanay gathering of the clan, you see Darna's mum's my cousin!"

"Was it them who told you about me and Frenchy?" I asked amazed.

"That's telling...but no it wasn't them." DCI Netherbourne replied

It was now getting on for 1.p.m. and as DCI Netherbourne amended Carrick Macross's duty roster, so that he could keep observation on Bradbeer, I arrived back at Wheatville Terrace to find Frisco sound asleep in bed and so I climbed in beside him and snuggled up close and began to dream about our big day. It was around six oclock when Frisco properly awoke and finally staggered downstairs, with a yawn and where I was cooking dinner. Then as we sat down to eat and watch the news, Frisco told me about smoking the peace pipe with Amazon, as he told her the gist of the story about Frenchy, Norma Jean and me, as he felt it was only fair that Amazon should know the truth.

"It's only a pity you're off the market as I wouldn't mind one last taste of honey?" Amazon said.

"I think you'd better buzz off before the Queen Bee gets back, as I do not fancy being on the end of her sting if she caught us that's unless you want your hair cutting?" Frisco laughingly replied.

"Message received and understood." Amazon said. "But I will have words with Madam Frenchy…I never thought though that Jesty could be so vicious?

"Well Jesty can be a feisty little minx when she wants to be, but you'll have to contact the mistress of Wheatville to find out about the wedding plans, she'll probably want the Pencil Skirt…just to rub salt in to Frenchy's wounds?" Frisco said

"Well it might be a triple wedding yet the way things are going?" Amazon said. "You know Bootsy has proposed to that PC Carrick Macross you teamed her up with and the DCI has asked me to marry him…in Scotland of all places?"

"I know Jesty wants a Christmas wedding, but freezing to death at Gretna Green at the end of December I don't think is exactly what she had in mind?" Frisco laughed, as he gave Amazon a friendly kiss and showed her to the door. Frisco then went in to the kitchen to make sure that everything was switched off, but as he did so with a yawn, he swore he thought he heard Norma Jean's voice saying 'Hello Trouble.' Frisco then looked in the living room and where he had to blink as he thought he saw the ghostly figure of Norma Jean in an Angelic Blue negligee, lying on the settee and kicking her legs in the air.

"Blimey I must be more tired than I think?" Frisco said to himself when he took a second glance, only to find that the figure had disappeared, while the aroma of the perfume 'Euphoria' now lingered in the room.

"Jubilee, Jubilee Christian" Frisco shouted as he recognised the perfume's aroma and which faded as quickly as it came and which puzzled Frisco who then climbed the wooden hill to Bedfordshire.

Norma Jean's ghost and Jubilee Christian's perfume, I put down to tiredness playing tricks in

Frisco's mind, while having no reason to doubt about him laughing off Amazon's offer, as I updated Frisco on the new schedule for Operation Abigail and that DCI Netherbourne had rostered us' to work the weekend graveyard shift. I had though managed to wangle it so that we only worked alternative weekends from 7.p.m. to 7.a.m. while being on daytime first reserve every Tuesday to Thursday. It was then that I told Frisco about visiting the Pencil Skirt and about booking Father Bejazus to do the marriage service.

"I suppose calling Frenchy a cheap brass was a bit naughty but then again it won't hurt her, while I bet she must have loved you for wanting to get hitched at the Pencil Skirt. But I like your idea for a Vicars and Tarts/Guys and Dolls wedding. I wonder what the DCI will come as...the Pope or Al Capone?" Frisco said.

"Probably Don De Netherbourne...head of the Scottish Mafia" I laughed.

"Which branch Celtic or Rangers?" Frisco laughed. "But if that's going to be the case can I come as Convict Ninety Nine... with a ball and chain?"

"Behave I'm not that bad!" I teased and gave Frisco a gentle swipe and said. "I suppose you know that Darna Gold's his daughter?"

"What the DCI?" Frisco said. "Blimey he's a dark horse isn't he?"

"That's what I thought? But with regards to Frenchy...what I didn't tell you was that as I left her office I heard her crying...just like a whipped bitch!" I said.

"Ouch, that's savage!" Frisco remarked. "Even I felt the sting of that one!"

CHAPTER 12

CHAPEL OF LOVE

Narrated by Frisco Kane

I'd expected Friday night to pass as peaceably as Thursday's, except that I'd not gauged on the late arrival of 'Love & Napalm' that was an all girl band and who announced their arrival with the shrill cry of 'Shop' as they rang the brass bell on the hotel counter. The sound of which bought me from out of the back, only to discover that the person making all the noise was Darna Gold and to whom I said. "What you doing here... Bathsheba chucked you out has she?"

"No fear...but I didn't know you worked here?" Darna laughed.

"There's a lot you don't know about me, now what can I do for you?" I said.

I then shook a hand that stretched across the counter and voice said. "Love and Napalm, three rooms booked for two nights. I'm Jemma with a 'J' the lead singer and this here's Foxy, Grace, Kelly and Dawn."

"Pleased to meet you" I said as I eyed up a motley, gum chewing, pouting and fag dragging crew of adolescent female gothic rockers.

Jemma with a 'J' and who had a gold lip ring, a silver tongue stud and who wore a long black mock leather coat with knee length black and silver Doc Martens. Attempted to marshal the girls as she grabbed their room keys and the band trooped off to bed in a rather bedraggled fashion, as I gently grabbed Darna's arm and said. "Listen, now that we've got rid of Charlie's Angels, don't rush off...stop and have a coffee, as I've got a favour I to want to ask?"

I then led Darna in to the moonlight lit coffee shop and handed her a large Latte and a Mars Bar. "There you are, one London commuter breakfast!"

"Gee thanks...you sure know how to spoil a girl." Darna teased.

"More to the point how's tricks and what's with the band? You haven't given up club management have you?" I joked

"You must be joking." Darna said. "No the band's part of the re-launch... they literally closed the East End Club earlier this evening and tonight they are set to play open The Blackboard Jungle. You see we've decided to give the club a more catchy title!"

"Oh the Saraband will love that? They'll think your being racist which of course you are? Then they'll come down the station to make a complaint and which we'll file under scribble, doodle and bin!" I laughed.

"So what's this favour then... something naughty is it?" Darna asked

"Behave...No! What it is, is that four of us are planning to come down to the club tonight...Saturday. But I want to make sure we can get in, as Bathsheba will be on the door and I know she doesn't like me that much." I replied.

"Oh don't worry about her" Darna said. "Anyway you'll be my guests for the re-launch and you can see Love and Napalm in action. They're like a comic version of the Pogues. Now do you mind me being cheeky and sitting on your lap?"

"You know close up you remind me of that punk girl the one from the film *Jubilee*?" I said as Darna sat on my lap and put her arms around my neck.

"Most folk say I look like that Delilah Dingle." Darna laughed.

"Well my name's Simpson not Samson!" I joked.

Darna then gave me a saucy kiss and whispered as

she fished a box of fruit flavoured frenchies out of her pocket "While the cats away the mice will play?"

"So you don't fully bat for the other side then?" I said

"And I suppose you're going to tell me you're spoken for?" Darna laughed.

"Does the name Jesty Dollamore ring any bells? You met her at the Hoochie Coochie Club...she was Frenchy's girlfriend." I said.

"Oh I remember her...nice legs I fancied her myself." Darna said "But what Jesty don't know won't hurt her...just so long as we're careful."

"Sorry not tonight Josephine" I said as I put the unopened packet of French fancies back in her pocket. "A bit of discreet, pre marital slap and tickle is one thing ...as for the other, let's just say that's one line that I'm not prepared to cross."

"And just when I think I've struck lucky" Darna laughed. "Did I tell you that I was born under a wandering star and conceived or so I'm told in the back of an Austin A Four, it wasn't until I'd left school that my mum told me the truth about my real dad...but that was five years ago, when I was seventeen."

"You mean about him being a Scottish bobby in England. I bet that come as a shock and surprise?" I said.

"It was. You see my mum married an Irish publican, so my given surname is Clancy. Gold's only a punk surname, but I didn't know you knew?" Darna said

It was then that I told Darna that DCI Netherbourne was my boss at Golf Four and since moving in with Amazon, he had asked her to marry him in Scotland and something that made Darna laugh. "It might be fun having a high class hooker as a step mum?'

Darna then had to settle for a taxi back home, instead of her original plan of catching the first bus back to Wolverhampton, as she gave me one last smooch and said. "And that's to be going on with."

Then after Darna had gone I made sure that everything was peaceful, before having a hot shower and raiding a pack of clean clothes that I kept on standby. As I then used the motel's laundry to fast wash and tumble-dry the clothes that I'd come to work in, so there'd be no tell tale signs of anything untoward having happened.

Jesty then arrived to pick me up at just, after seven on the Saturday morning and when I had a very strange experience, the song *Chelsea Dagger* suddenly began to play in my head. I then realised, how much I loved Jesty, as she walked towards the motel after parking the car on the forecourt, so in spontaneous and appreciative affection, I gave her a great big kiss and proposed. "Let's get married today?"

Jesty was stunned and surprised and after a brief moment of reflection, said. "Come on give, you got a guilty conscience about something?   So what is it…come on spill the beans?"

I felt bemused, just as though I'd been found out, but all the same, I decided to try and bluff it out. "Jesty you're beautiful when you're angry, but can't I say an affectionate good morning to my best girl. Are you that paranoid that you don't trust me?   Because frankly my dear…I don't give a damn!"

"Listen I'm sorry, of course I trust you" Jesty replied. "I   trust   you   more   than   I   ever   did Frenchy…never mind my first husband."

"Do I take it, that's a yes then?" I said.

"Only if your' buying breakfast?" Jesty answered.

"And what did your last slave die of?" I asked.

"Boredom" Jesty replied.

Saturday breakfast at the Dairy Queen was then

interrupted by a mobile call from Father Bejazus. The police padre having been ordained as a Catholic priest had lapsed in to the Anglican faith, but he still believed in some principles of the Church of Rome. Like saying mass in Latin at Easter and hearing confessional in a box that he had especially installed in his small church that had replaced the original place of worship after the great fire of St Nicholas and after the original church hall had held a special screening of the Billy Connelly film *'The Man Who Sued God!'*

It was the confessional though that had caused Father Bejazus to phone Jesty and make us hurriedly finish breakfast and drive over to see him at the Holy Cross Church in Codsall. However no sooner had I got in to Jesty's car than I fell asleep and where Jesty left me, as she heeded the padre's urgent call.

"Ah it's good to see you, bejazus and how is the lovely bride now and the groom...full of nerves now is he, I expect at the prospect bejazus of marrying such a fine lady as yourself' now bejazus?" Father Bejazus said as he handed Jesty a cup of tea as she sat in the warm confines of his church vestry.

"Oh he's outside right at this moment...fast asleep in the car." Jesty said. "You see he works nights at the Econo Lodge...so I don't want to wake him."

"Ah bejzus the poor man" Father Bejazus said. "Donkey tired he must be?"

"So tell me." Jesty said. "What is the big cause for concern?"

"Well do you know a young woman at all who goes by the name of Jubilee Christian?" Father Bejazus asked.

"Go on...I'm listening?" Jesty said as she leaned forward with interest.

Father Bejazus then explained that a young woman with long blonde hair, dressed in black like a vampire and wickedly doused in a strong scent had come to see him, just after evensong, the night before. She had enquired about booking the church for a special marriage on Christmas Day, to which Father Bejazus explained that it would require a special licence, as not many churches, if any would conduct a marriage on such a holy day. But he would all the same, take the name of the bride and groom Jubilee Christian and Saffron Frisco Kane. Father Bejazus then realising something was amiss, told this young woman who called herself Jubilee Christian and who had a presence about her, just as though Hob was on the prowl and which made Father Bejazus bless the church with holy water and Latin scripture, once she had gone. Once she had obtained a special licence, he would be happy to conduct the service. Father Bejazus then opened the church for early morning prayers, when the buzzer went for the confessional. He swore it was the same young woman who called herself Jubilee Christian, but this time she had long black hair and was asking for absolution before she entered in to an impending holy day marriage, for the rape and murder of a female nurse and the murder of a prostitute.

"That's when bejazus and not bound by the sanctity of the confessional …I thought I should call you bejazus." Father Bejazus said before kissing the sign of purity, a silver crucifix on a silver chain.

Jesty did not know what to make of Father Bejazus's statement, except that it warranted further investigation, as the woman who claimed to be Jubilee Christian did match her general description, while the murdered prostitute was probably Lusty Jewson and who Jubilee Christian was already in the frame as a suspect. However the confession to the murder and rape of a nurse could well be Norma Jean and if it was her it could well be a blessing in disguise, if it meant getting the little minx out of her and Frisco life and if she was dead, well she was not exactly going anywhere except the morgue and only, as and when her body was discovered?'

Jesty then walked outside and rang Amazon, but the answer machine was on and so she left a message for the DCI before ringing his mobile and leaving another message. Jesty also rang the local hospital where Norma Jean worked and was told that Norma Jean was on a three-day rest period and was not on duty until Monday. Then when Jesty went to wake me, she found I was not in the car and so looking around she found me talking to two gravediggers. But what Jesty did not realise was that after awaking from a restful catnap, I had eavesdropped on the end of her and Father Bejazus's conversation, before making myself scarce when Jesty started to walk out the church.

Jesty told me the gist of what Father Bejazus had said, but I knew she was not telling me the whole story. I though decided to play along and gave Jesty a kiss and told her to go and freshen up, if she still wanted us to get married, while I had a quiet word with Father Bejazus and did a little horse dealing.

Father Bejazus for the princely sum of £100 and which meant I had to make a quick dash to a local cash point, duly agreed if somewhat rascally to marry Jesty and me today at Holy Cross with a blessing service and the wedding vows being taken again at Christmas. While the entry in the parish records would record today's marriage, 15th October, 2006 and with a side entry about the renewal of vows unless something untoward happened between now and Christmas

Jesty meanwhile, as she looked in the church toilet mirror and refreshed her makeup and perfume, saw this unexpected dress rehearsal as the chance to scupper Jubilee Christian's phoney marriage plans. And any ideas Frenchy might have about making any objections at the gala wedding on December twenty-first. Jesty also realised, she had let her hair grow, to such an extent that she was starting to look like Farrah Fawcet Majors. While her denim jacket and jeans, 'Fisherman's Pearl', roll neck jumper and ankle length, tan cowboy boots were not exactly what she had planned to wear to walk down the aisle.

'And I'm going to have to watch my weight' Jesty thought, as she patted her stomach after feeling that her jeans were getting a bit too tight. Then as she gave her hair one last quick flick of the comb, Jesty thought she saw, reflected in the mirror, the ghostly figure of Norma Jean in an angelic blue negligee, but when she turned around there was no one there. Jesty then got a whiff of Euphoria as she slung her brown leather handbag over her shoulder. Then as she went to leave the toilet, Jesty suddenly felt sick and quickly dived in to the cubicle, where she proceeded to throw up. It was only after wiping her mouth, following a drink of water and redoing her lipstick that she realised that it was the third time this week she had been sick and so a trip to the chemist would not go amiss. Jesty eventually joined me the vestry, with a mug of tea that had a drop of whiskey in it to keep out the cold, as I chatted to Father Bejazus.

"And here comes the blushing bride." I said, as Jesty walked in to the vestry. "Where you been…I thought you'd done a runner…so are you fit?"

Jesty smiled and gently laughed. "It's the bride's prerogative to be late?"

"Ah now bejazus do you the condemned, sorry I mean the bridegroom, have you any last requests?" Father Bejazus said with a mischievous smile.

"Do you know, *the March to the Scaffold*?" I joked.

"Will you behave or I'll put you on a collar and

leash!" Jesty laughed before we walked to the altar and where Jesty and said I do, while Father Bejazus and after several bejazus's and the gravediggers witnessed the ceremony. Father Bejazus then reminded us that this particular ceremony was like an Insurance cover note with the full policy, God willing, being enacted at our Christmas wedding in December.

Jesty then threw her first wedding ring across the churchyard as we left the church and I said. "Now how do you fancy a celebratory drink at the Madison, as I want to see the look on Frenchy's face when she sees the wedding ring and you tell her what's happened…or do you want to go and visit Norma Jean?"

"You know don't you?" Jesty said as she fingered the surprise wedding ring that while on route to the cash point I had bought her from a local antique shop and a ring that she would now treasure, after thinking at the last minute that we would have to use her first wedding ring.

"Yes Father Bejazus did tell me about the nurse and like you I guessed it was Norma Jean. But if she's dead then she's not going anywhere and if she's not then like Jubilee Christian you've put paid to her marriage plans. So when do you want to visit Norma Jean's flat?" I asked.

"Tomorrow's early enough I think." Jesty said as she gave me a kiss.

CHAPTER 13

DAUGHTER OF DARKNESS

Narrated by Frisco Kane

Jesty was driving towards Chapel Ash when DCI Netherbourne returned her call and so I brought him up to date about someone matching Jubilee Christian and asking Father Bejazus for absolution after admitting to committing rape and murder, as she was getting married on Christmas Day and which I said was another story in itself. I then changed the subject slightly to stop the DCI from asking any awkward questions and queried the whereabouts of Reno Dunster, if Jubilee Christian was in Wolverhampton on a solo killing spree? Could Dunster have got himself, put on remand under an assumed name? A trick he had done before, to draw off the heat, with his gang lying low considering the last reported bingo hall robberies where the six jobs up north? This I thought would give the DCI plenty to think about while he asked for Bootsy Swanscat to join the party at the Blackboard Jungle as he had had a tip off that Bradbeer would be cruising that night. I meanwhile privately prayed that the alleged murdered nurse, was not Norma Jean because she was really too nice a girl, deep down to warrant the menace of a rogue Jubilee Christian.

Jesty walked just ahead of me in to the Madison Bar and just as the song of *'Every little thing she does is magic'* was playing on the jukebox and so out of pure devilment I sang along to words with my donkey serenade making Jesty blush, until she saw Frenchy singing along to the same song and which made Jesty quietly snarl 'In your dreams…bitch!'

I ordered a celebratory drink of Brandy and Babycham for Jesty, Frenchy and Bootsy who helped behind the bar, as well being the Pencil Skirt receptionist. Jesty deliberately played with her wedding ring in front of Frenchy who said how nice the ring was, as Jesty broke the news about our getting married that morning, to which Frenchy, dropped a bottle of brandy that smashed on the bar floor and cried 'Sorry', as she fled the bar in a flood of tears. Domino came over to see what all the commotion was about and opened a bottle of Bucks Fizz in congratulations.

Jesty then had to run to the ladies toilet and when she came back to the bar, she whispered to Domino that was the fifth time this week and the second time that morning that she had been bad. Domino winked and whispered "Congratulations...I won't say anything" as she gave her a Tomato Juice to steady her stomach.

Then just as Jesty and I were walking out the door of the Madison Bar, the jukebox suddenly began to play *'Knockin' on heaven's door'* and which made Jesty and me both turn to each other and say 'Norma Jean?'

Jesty and I had intended to go home and go to bed for the afternoon, but we felt we couldn't really leave things any longer and so Jesty drove to Vauxhall Rise. And where as I banged on the flat door, an old woman came out of a neighbouring first floor flat and asked if the nice nurse was alright? Because she had not seen or heard her since Thursday morning, only a strange woman in black and who had the mark of Old Nick about her. I then booted the door lock until it gave way and once inside the flat, Jesty and I were greeted by the scent of Euphoria as we found Norma Jean's naked body.

"This is the work of Jubilee Christian." I said as DCI

Netherbourne held an impromptu team meeting amidst a sea of blue flashing lights outside Vauxhall Rise and uniformed personnel attracted an audience, while the forensic team conducted a thorough search of the flat.

"The postcard 'greetings from London' and the candle between the legs are all the hallmarks of Jubilee Christian." I said. "It's her way of recreating a sacrificial style murder!"

DCI Netherbourne had a WPC take a statement from the aged neighbour, so as to place Jubilee Christian at the murder scene, while Jesty and I paid another visit to Father Bejazus who looked surprised to see us so soon, until he learned about the fate of Norma Jean. Father Bejazus then asked us to join him in prayer for Norma Jean's soul and during which Jesty reflected that although they'd quarrelled, Norma Jean didn't deserve such a death. Then after taking Father Bejazus's statement, Jesty switched off her phone and steadily drove wherever the road twisted and turned, until it led us to a secluded nook. Jesty on this her somewhat impromptu wedding day then parked up the car and switched on a small radio with *'Lover's Concerto'* by the Toys serenading our brief honeymoon of sorts. The romantic tryst then ended at just before 3.30.p.m. when my mobile phone rang and the DCI informed me that Jubilee Christian had just committed another murder, but this time it was at the Pencil Skirt. The timing of which coincided exactly with Reno Dunster and his gang robbing the Dale Bingo Hall at Willenhall near Walsall.

When Jesty and I drove up to the Pencil Skirt, it was almost 4.p.m. and the centre of Chapel Ash was awash with a sea of blue flashing lights. But as we began to walk in to the Madison Bar, we had to stand to one side as an Ambulance crew carried out a blanket covered body on a stretcher as an arm in the sleeve of a black suit suddenly dropped from under the blanket. Jesty and I saw the rings on a hand and recognised them as being Frenchy's, this sent a cold pain searing through our stomachs, as we entered the Madison Bar and found DCI Netherbourne trying to interview a visibly shaken Bootsy who was holding a double rum that the DCI had given her to steady her nerves. As for Domino, she was numbed by the experience and just sat in silence in a corner of the lounge bar.

DCI Netherbourne had asked Amazon to take charge of the bar and organise the Pencil Skirt's girls, before relating to Jesty and me that Jubilee Christian in her usual black garb and carrying a silver crash helmet, had marched in to the bar and pulled out an automatic pistol and demanded all the available cash on the premises. Frenchy though came from behind the bar, all guns blazing and began to berate Jubilee, who then put the pistol in Frenchy's mouth and softly told her to play nice. Jubilee then made everyone lie on the floor in front of the bar except for Frenchy who she erotically frisked, as she emptied the tills. Jubilee then grabbed Frenchy by her hair and put a small and shiny bladed knife to her throat, before giving her a French kiss and cutting her throat. Jubilee then grabbed the money and fled out of the bar, as Bootsy scrambled to her feet and pushed the panic alarm to the Police and Domino dialled 999 and cried murder.

For the life of me I couldn't understand the reason behind Jubilee Christian's actions, one minute she is asking for absolution, so as to cleanse her soul for a Xmas Day wedding. Only to commit another foul sin of sexual murder as well as armed robbery a few hours later. I did though notice that Jubilee had committed her crimes at places where I had a personal interest and shortly after I had visited the places, just as though she was watching my every movement.

The Pencil Skirt was closed until further notice, with Frenchy's murder closing a colourful and intimate chapter in mine and Jesty's lives, while alerting me to the fact that Jesty was probably now in danger, Jubilee had assaulted two of the main people in my love life, just as though she was ticking off a list. Although Jesty had quarrelled with Frenchy, she still affectionately remembered their time together, as a couple, while I would never forget our playful spats or her amorous kindness after Vegas's murder. The Dale bingo hall robbery was on Walsall's patch and they would coordinate any investigation with Wolverhampton CID. The problem now was what to do with Bootsy and Domino as they were much too traumatised to be left alone, but Bootsy was still needed for tonight as bait to catch Bradbeer. It was Amazon though who took charge of Bootsy and Domino and promised to have them at the Blackboard Jungle by seven that night, while I told Domino not to worry about Frenchy's funeral arrangements, to which Domino surprised me with a kiss. Jesty then drove us back to Wheatville Terrace and where after a hot shower and a change of clothes, I suggested that we use Jubilee's Mini Cooper as bait to flush her out of her hiding place.

Jesty was unsure at first, but she agreed to try anything once while finding that driving a Mini Cooper was somewhat different, as she normally drove a Golf. I rummaged through the Mini Cooper's glove box, just to make sure that I hadn't missed anything on my initial search. I also brought along Jubilee's CD of the Honeycomb's and played selective tracks, while remembering the broken Latin 'Anno Domino Spritus Santu Sai Nom Dom Nee Patrious...Dominus Vobiscom Et Cum Spiritu Tui' That I had recited when Jubilee and I first met and which I now felt I needed to remember.

However before we went to the Blackboard Jungle, Jesty stopped off at Golf Four, so that we could book on and book out a couple of Police radios. Then as we did a radio check, we caught some traffic that Reno and his gang had struck again at the bingo hall in Ashmore Park and all in the space of two hours after the Dale robbery. Golf One' would handle that robbery, it was on their patch and liaison with Walsall and DCI Netherbourne. The murders and robberies now covered all three Golf divisions, with the only divisions that overlapped being Golf Three and Golf Four that took in the city centre and back up for Golf Sierra the central police station, anything outside that patch would only involve Golf Four, if it was connected with Vice. The first big trouble of the night though began when Jesty and I arrived at The Blackboard Jungle and where Bathsheba Mendalove snorted when she saw me and said that I was not welcome. But when I told her I was on the guest list, she pointed out that that also meant 'At the management's discretion.'

Bathsheba's bloody-minded refusal of my entry turned in to a verbal standoff and which caused customers to begin asking the bar staff about the commotion at the door. Darna realised that Bathsheba might be playing up on the door, as Jesty had walked into the club without me, so Darna jumped from behind the bar and grabbed Jesty to follow her. They were just in time to see me grab Bathsheba by her nose to ear chain across her face, with the force of the pull breaking the chain and making her squeal with pain. Jesty then intervened and ushered me away, as Darna give Bathsheba a subtle warning that her bloody-minded beef could cost the club its licence, while I felt angry about losing my temper, as I did not want to spoil Jesty's night out.

Darna though could not apologise enough for Bathsheba's behaviour and gave her condolences at hearing about Frenchy's murder. Darna also included a special round of drinks on the house, when I told her that Jesty and I had got married that morning.

The interior of the club was like a red brick Wild West saloon crossed with a high school sports hall and where a neon sign said 'The Blackboard Jungle' and as I stood at the bar, I noticed a silver crash helmet peeking out from under a bar towel. When I asked about the helmet, Darna told me it had been left it behind the bar for safe keeping while the owner was inside the club and last seen entering the ladies toilet. But when I asked if the helmet's owner was a hot, gothic female, Darna got jumpy and pleaded with me not to cause any trouble, while I began to sense a pair of eyes burning in to the back of my head and when I turned my head, I had to gulp before saying in a loud voice for everyone to hear "Well talk of the Devil and his daughter appears!"

The loudness of my voice caused DCI Netherbourne and Jesty to look to see what was happening, before jumping up from their chairs, only for me to put up my hand to tell them to keep back as Jubilee Christian and I squared up to each other.

"That's me darling the harlot in black...the whore from hell! And speaking of which is she your bitch?" Jubilee sneered as she pointed to Jesty and who saw me slap Jubilee hard across the face.

The slap caused her lip to bleed and Jubilee to reel back, before licking the blood on her lips and snarl. "You've done it haven't you, you've married the bitch!"

"And you're just as venomous as ever, even the Euphoria perfume you wear has turned to poison and yes we got married this morning...just to scupper your plans." I said as I pulled over my head, a silver cross and chain that hung around my neck and which caused Jubilee to snarl and bare what looked like vampire fangs.

'Anno Domino Spritus Santu Sai Nom Dom Nee Patrious…Dominus Vobis-com Et Cum Spiritu Tui' I recited over and over again as I walked in to the shadow of death of Jubilee's arms and pressed the silver cross in to her forehead. At which point the club was unexpectedly plunged in to darkness, when the lights suddenly went out and which caused screams of terror and fear and Darna to grab a torch and scramble to find the fuse box. The club's main power switch had tripped for some unknown reason and when the lights came back on, Jesty saw that I was precariously holding Jubilee Christian who had collapsed in a dead faint while I and just as precariously, removed a set of vampire fangs that spanned her mouth, as the club's jukebox suddenly began to play *'Spooky'* by the Classics IV.

CHAPTER 14

EYE OF THE TIGER

Narrated by Frisco Kane

'Light's Camera, Action!' Darna said as she stepped down off the club's stage, while trying to make light of what had just happened in order to capitalise on events as part of the club's official re-launch. "Well sorry about that folks, but that's the Blackboard Jungle for you...fun, thrills and all the horror of a theatre of blood floorshow, complete with an impromptu blackout that was as much a surprise to the management as it was to you. Now coming up we have that all girl goth band Love and Napalm, but first it's the grand house master Captain Skippy spinning the grooves and grooving the wax with his Avery Tronix laser show and to kick off the show it's Space and *Magic Fly!*"

The music seemed to settle the clubbers mood, as DCI Netherbourne, Jesty and me stepped outside for some fresh air and as we did so Bathsheba sarcastically asked me 'Are you leaving now then?'

And to which I mischievously stuck up a single finger and gave Bathsheba the bird, after which the DCI, Jesty and I searched for Jubilee's motorbike, as we already had her silver crash helmet. When we found the black Japanese roadster, the pannier box contained a replica automatic pistol, a switchblade with congealed blood on the blade and a long blonde wig. But no indications of where Jubilee had been living though rumours abounded that she may have shacked up with other single females and so nobody really knew just how many more bodies there may be. Jesty meanwhile radioed for a van to came and retrieve the motorbike and ask how Jubilee was liking, languishing in the cells at Golf Four, while DCI Netherbourne smoked his pipe and discussed the spontaneous events

"Call me an old sceptic but that collar was too easy for my liking...just as though Jubilee was playing a game with us?" DCI Netherbourne said.

"Perhaps she wanted to be taken?" Jesty replied. "And which has put paid to her plan to marry Frisco...either way she's locked up tight now."

"Jubilee thinks she's a genuine vampire... a blood lust swinging psychotic! All I had to do was play along and recite broken Latin in order to fight fire with fire." I said with a smug smile.

"While you two pair of dark horses get married in secret... So tell me how is Father Bjazus?" DCI Netherbourne laughingly said.

"Well you can ask him yourself, when we reaffirm out vows in December." Jesty said with a smile. "As I still want my Christmas wedding"

"But I think were forgetting one thing this fancy Christmas wedding has so far been murder and despite any ups and downs, neither Frenchy or Norma Jean deserved to die the way they did...so here's to absent friends." I said.

My words caused a quiet pause for reflection, after which DCI Netherbourne checked his watch it was almost 8.30.p.m. as he said. "Amazon should be here soon with Bootsy, but whether Domino will come as well I don't know I'm just glad they were not here when Jubilee Christian kicked off."

"And so say all of us." I said "But just out of curiosity, what are you and Amazon coming to the wedding as Al Capone and Mae West, Bonnie and Clyde ... John Dillinger and Machine Gun Kelly?"

"How about the Godfather and Gypsy Rose Lee" Jesty teased.

And to which DCI Netherbourne laughed as he

sucked on his pipe and said "Behave...I was thinking more along the lines of the Pope and Modesty Blaize?'

The three of us where then joined by Darna who had come outside to escape the madding crowd and as the four of us raked over the local gossip as we joked, DCI Netherbourne asked, why a lot of so called gays tended to bat for both sides?

Jesty admitted that she did not like the word gay as it sounded so cheap and nasty, while DCI Netherbourne blamed the tabloid press for being able to vulgarise the most inoffensive word, if they tried hard enough. But it was Darna who said that she had found that attractive females were attracted to other women, out of safety and security. They still wanted children, but they also wanted to be loved in a very personal way and the caress of another female could be very affectionate.

"Well you've just answered another question for me?" DCI Netherbourne said. "Why it is that most of the good looking females tend or claim to be gay?"

"Well I'm glad to have been of some help." Darna said.

When Amazon and Bootsy finally arrived, it was getting on for 9.p.m. with Amazon telling the DCI that Bootsy was still feeling rather shaky after her sanguine experience, but she wanted to reciprocate her acceptance by the clique of W/ton's foxy high-class hookers and maverick police, after initially feeling like an outsider looking in and due to the fact that she was not involved in the immediate equation of things.

"It's all bloody happening tonight!" I mused as I glanced at Darna and then quickly explained a rough idea to her and Jesty and who thought that the DCI would not go for it, but what the heck, time was against us. DCI Netherbourne did not get time to argue, as Jesty enlisted Amazon and Bootsy to help search through Darna's wardrobe and make Darna look like a hooker from the top end of the rag trade with everything hinging on Bradbeer coming out to play. DCI Netherbourne phoned Carrick to check on Bradbeer's whereabouts and learned that since he arrived home in Parkfields at just after eight, Bradbeer had not moved. The Uniform Golf carrier meanwhile had arrived to pick up the motorbike, after I had made a chase up radio call and asked the DCI what he wanted to do about Jubilee's Mini Cooper?

"Keep it under wraps for the time being...as I have an idea about using for a Christmas present." DCI Netherbourne said as he then asked for my advice on what to do about the running of the Pencil Skirt. Frenchy's murder had caused a problem as Domino's delicate condition meant that she could not manage on her own, while Bootsy was too inexperienced to take over Frenchy's role. DCI Netherbourne had thought about putting Amazon's name on the licence, as she had the qualifications and experience of running licensed girls and she could help train Bootsy up to take over when Domino was on maternity leave.

I must admit the idea did have merit, as it would give DCI Netherbourne and Amazon a more respectable long-term relationship, rather than being just a top rank detective, whose girlfriend was a high-class hooker, playing out the pretence of a swanky lifestyle. No matter how cautious one was, there was always the big risk of catching something nasty with DCI Netherbourne thanking me for being honest. As he then asked if I was going to enter the karaoke talent show, only to laugh when I said that right now I just fancied a drink and to which DCI Netherbourne told me to hang on till the band was on stage. Then we could enjoy that interrupted courtesy drink off Darna, while not forgetting that it was the custom for the bride and groom to have a slow dance on their if somewhat impromptu wedding night.

That drink and slow dance though would have to wait a little bit longer for just as Jesty was about to rejoin DCI Netherbourne and me and Amazon applied the finishing touches to Darna, Jesty received a patch through on her radio from me that Leon Bradbeer was heading for the beat. The time was now nine forty-five with the DCI taking Darna to one side and telling her that it was a dangerous job and that she could bow out if she wished. Darna though shook her head she did not want to be seen as a quitter at this late stage, while I radioed for a car to chauffeur the DCI and to act as uniform back up. But as Darna made her way to the Swan Gardens pub and where she was to wait under observation for Bradbeer to make his move, Carrick radioed to say that Bootsy was on the plot and to which DCI Netherbourne radioed back to keep a look out for a second pigeon after deciding to run with both girls, as to openly pull one at this late stage, could alert Bradbeer. Then as Amazon waited at the club, Jesty and I raced across the ring road and along Duke Street towards the junction with Walsall Street and where Golf Four stood just across from the Swan Gardens pub. But just as we reached the junction, Carrick radioed that one of the Saraband was now leaning against his car that still had the keys in the ignition as he sweet-talked Bootsy. I recognised the lean and snazzy dressed brother as Winston Alphonso Leroy Errol Smith aka Little Winston and who luckily had no bodyguard.

I then whispered an idea to Jesty at which we dashed across the road and I happy slapped Little Winston, as Jesty jumped in to the driver's seat and we stole his car. Carrick meanwhile mischievously filmed everything on his mobile phone, including Little Winston as he shouted 'What the fuck?' and punched the air with a fist at being thumped and robbed.

Carrick then radioed to Golf Four that a member of the Saraband was about to report an assault and theft, but the report was to be misfiled as it could contravene an ongoing operation. Bootsy meanwhile had backed against the front of the pub, before sidling in to the shadows and where Darna stood after she recognised Little Winston, but she did not want him to see her. Then once the coast was clear, after Little Winston had angrily marched across to Golf Four to make a complaint, Darna and Bootsy emerged from the shadows and just as Bradbeer drove by, stopped and backed his car up. Carrick felt he was the only cop with a ringside seat as Bradbeer took the bait. Jesty and I meanwhile had doubled back on ourselves and were using Little Winston's car to tail Bradbeer with DCI Netherbourne and Carrick bringing up the rear, at a discreet distance and just like the seventh cavalry.

"I can't believe what we just done?" Jesty said. "I mean we've broken every rule in the book...assault and vehicle theft and now were following a bent cop in a stolen motor?"

"No let's get it right...what you cant believe is how generous Little Winston was to allow us to use his motor in pursuit of a felon...now lets see what we have in here?" I then rummaged through the glove box and found three large rolls of notes. "Well, well, well what we got here, with your permission DS Kane I'm confiscating all this lovely money that I haven't had time yet to count, but I do believe that Little Winston on behalf of the Saraband wishes to donate to the victims of crime fund." I said with a wicked gleam in my eye.

"Permission granted. It'll pay towards Norma Jean and Frenchy's funeral expenses...so is there anything else of interest?" Jesty said with a smirk.

I also found Little Winston's little black tally book that recorded the names of his girls and what he expected, as his pimps fee, plus a list of unlicensed brothels that were also paying him immoral earnings. Jesty though pointed out, this was in principle a stolen motor, so the obtaining of such evidence may be suspect in court. Unless the notebook was handed in at the station by person or persons unknown, so any coincidental Police raids would be as a result of information received.

"There is another way though? I suppose we could always, leak it out that Winston had volunteered the information, that would stuff up his street credibility no end and even more after tonight's little caper?" I said with a mischievous smirk.

"What and have him shot dead on the Monkey House car park by the rest of the Saraband...I don't think so!" Jesty exclaimed. "Let's just leave it at acting upon information received and concentrate on Bradbeer."

Jesty and I pursued Bradbeer over Newbridge lights and towards the Rock at Tettenhall with the last sighting of Bradbeer's car being his taillights' as he drove in to the darkness of the rural Wergs Road and where Bradbeer switched off his car lights and disappeared in to the night. When Jesty reached the junction with Shop Lane, she stopped the car and look all around before turning the car in to the pitch black of Shop Lane, where she pulled on to a narrow dirt track and parked up in the dark. I then radioed in that we had lost sight of our quarry as Jesty switched off the car's engine and lights and so as to concentrate on any unusual sounds or sudden movements. Then as Jesty leaned forward and across the steering wheel, I couldn't resist putting my arm around her and giving her a smoochy kiss.

"Do you normally get this passionate with girls down dark country lanes?" Jesty teased, as she sat back and lolled her head on my shoulder and gently kissed my neck.

"Only with those who I've just married this morning" I joked, as I struggled to free my trapped arm. "Or perhaps you'd prefer that I'd brought some dolly bird up here?"

"Behave." Jesty teased and gave me a gentle slap on the arm. "But you know earlier on, when you called me DS Kane. It felt so funny, as does sitting here in the darkness and the silence with you, because for some strange reason and don't ask me why...I keep thinking of that American TV show *Moonlighting*"

"What me Bruce Willis, you Stephanie what's her name...that'd be fun?" I laughed. "But whenever someone calls me DC Kane, I keep thinking of the BBC TV series *The Paradise Club*. You know with Leslie Grantham and which reminds me I've been meaning to ask...your name is it Cornish American or something?"

Jesty then went silent and squeezed my hand, before saying. "Listen I've got a confession to make. Jesty Dollarmore isn't my real name it belonged to my great grandmother who came from Redruth in Cornwall. All I've done is adopt the name and change the spelling of Dollomore to the American style of Dollarmore."

Jesty confessed that her father was care of her majesty, while she and being an only child was named after her deceased mother with her real name being Jessica Valerie Ann Cornwallis Cox. This aroused my curiosity and I was anxious to know more, while remembering that Jesty had not put her father's name on the marriage certificate. But in order to discover the truth, I deduced would require some discreet detective work. I then whispered that regardless of whether she was Jesty or Jessica I would readily marry her again and for which she gave me a very passionate kiss.

I then looked at the time and realised that some fifteen minutes had passed since we had last seen Bradbeer's car, while the dark and narrow Shop Lane led all the way to Codsall. Bradbeer could be anywhere in the wilds of the Shropshire and Staffordshire, like the ghostly shell of White Ladies Priory.

But just as Jesty was thinking of driving back to the Blackboard Jungle, the figure of what appeared to be a semi-naked young girl and clutching a jacket around her shoulders came running and screaming out of the woods. It was Darna and when Jesty and I caught her, all Darna kept crying were the words "He's killed her!"

Jesty then took charge of Darna as I radioed in for assistance before haring off in to the woods. The only thing was, I had no torch and was going by moonlight and the senses of touch and sound to guide my wild pursuit, like foxes barking and the sound of badgers and other assorted wild life rustling around in the undergrowth but no sign of anything human. That was until I kicked something that felt unusual and when I bent down to feel what I'd kicked I found it was a body. I then fumbled in the darkness to determine whether it was animal or human or even if it was alive or dead, with my questions being answered when I heard a groan and the whisper of an English word. I then did my best to drag the body in to the nearest pool of moon light, only to swallow hard when I discovered that it was a naked, bruised and near dead Bootsy Swanscat. Then after another hard swallow I radioed for an ambulance and picked up Bootsy's body and stumbled my way out of the woods, until I saw DCI

Netherbourne waiting with Jesty, Carrick and a sea of blue flashing lights and uniformed officers. Darna was already on route to hospital in the ambulance, when the paramedics from another ambulance took Bootsy's body off me, but it was too late, she had died in my arms and all the ambulance crew could do was cover her body in a blanket.

"If I catch him...I'll kill him" Carrick swore

"Then you'd best get in line, because that bastards coming in dead or alive, now spread out and find him!" DCI Netherbourne growled.

DCI Netherbourne knew that a search of the woods in the dark was hopeless and would have to be conducted tomorrow morning at first light, while Shop Lane was closed except for emergency traffic and all dog walkers and pedestrians stopped from entering the area. Bradbeer though would be long gone. A manhunt began of every known haunt to be associated with Bradbeer and his home was raided, to take care of his dog, before a car that matched the description of Bradbeer's, was spotted on the Monkey House car park. Jesty had gone to hospital to be with Darna, so Carrick and I went inside the pub and where Bradbeer sat nervously smoking and drinking a pint in an empty lounge.

Carrick and I told the landlord to lock down the back bars, while we stopped anyone from entering the lounge. We then said hello to Bradbeer and dished out a bruising retribution before dragging him out of the pub in handcuffs, while he looked like a panda after allegedly resisting arrest.

DCI Netherbourne meanwhile had accepted the notebook and the rolls of notes with the same generosity that Winston had unknowingly donated them. As for Little Winston's car that would be mysteriously dumped and torched somewhere on the outskirts of Wolverhampton, so as to give the appearance of joy riders.

The time was now 11.30.p.m. and it had been a long and eventful impromptu wedding day for Jesty that she would not readily forget, as we joined the small after hour's party at the club for a large drink. While DCI Netherbourne stated that Darna although unharmed was badly shaken, while we could stand down, before saying to Carrick and me. "Two murderers bagged in one night, has done wonders for the clear up rate…while I trust there was no witnesses?"

"No there were no witnesses…we made damn sure of that." Carrick said as I softly sang 'Two lovely black eyes…oh what a surprise!'

The club closed at midnight, after which Bathsheba was packed off home, while 'Love and Napalm' that looked like a band of dead beats, stayed behind for a drink and encored a few special numbers to make Frenchy and Bootsy and Norma Jean's wake as lively as possible with: *Big Willy Broke Jail Tonight*, *Mustapha* and *'The Old Bazaar in Cairo*. These were old Clinton Ford songs before a Judge Dread medley of *'Come Outside, Will I What, Je T'aime* and *Big Six* and *Fairytale of New York* that I sang as a duet with Jemma with a 'J'.

Then came the karaoke with Jesty singing *'I only want to be with you'* while I softly serenaded her as we danced to Carrick's rendition of *'Wives and Lovers.'* DCI Netherbourne and Amazon then surprised everyone by singing a duet that of *'Hit the road Jack'*, before Jesty rounded off the wake by narrating a ghostly law and order love story.

CHAPTER 15

The Dangerous Days of Latigo Smith

Just when you thought it was safe to go back to crime, there came the state paid bounty hunters. Latigo Smith had a boyish charm and a mum's apple pie smile just like Michael J Fox. But it was Latigo's official bounty hunters shield and firm belief in law and order from a '44' Magnum when it came to bringing in prisoners dead or alive and which made him a cross between Axle Foley and Dirty Harry. Latigo's partner was a foxy lady named Sutton o Hara and who had the style and character of V.I Warkowski P.I crossed with Christine Cagney and together Latigo and Sutton where like a real life version of the TV cops *'Dempsy and Makepeace.'* A prime example of their oddball law and order was at a drive in movie and when Latigo sang "Shimmy, shimmy co, co pop, shimmy, shimmy pop" as he and Sutton sat in his Ford Capri.

The film though was not too hot and so Latigo turned on the radio and used a ballpoint pen as a microphone to serenade Sutton with the song that was playing. Don't throw your love away, no, no, no don't throw your love away…for you might need it some day…' Latigo then leaned across and gently stole a kiss from Sutton that made her blush and close her eyes as his hands began to wander. That was until the sound of gunfire following a botched, armed robbery at the cinema box office, set Latigo off in hot pursuit and dent the metalwork of the surrounding parked cars, as he bounced from bonnet to roof. While irate drivers shouted and shook their fists in anger as Latigo sang "Ooh Scooby Dooby and a Go Cat Go!" Before firing two shots in the air, but the teenage robber kept on running and so Latigo took deadly aim as he sang out "Bop a Lena, Bop a Lena... wont you be my gal?" and brought the youth crashing to the ground with a bullet wound to leg.

Latigo then took Sutton for a terrace supper to make up for the interrupted evening at a whitewashed coffee bar called 'The Rickshaw', where caricature busts of Bogey and Bacall sat both sides of the red lettered name just like *Casablanca*.

A sign inside the milkshake, coloured walls of the coffee bar, said welcome to the Aroma, while a bust of Al Capone said no smoking, and a bust of Charlie Chaplin pointed to the toilets. Then to add to the madness Latigo serenaded Sutton across the table "Venus...oh Venus..." before jumping up on to the table and bursting in to a chorus of *'Blue Jean Bop!'*

Such incidents though helped Latigo colourfully embellish the romantic trysts that he had written up in a little black book that he called his 'Dangerous Days'. One such tryst was with Corrina who was a farmer's daughter come Beverly Hillbilly tomboy with rosy cheeks, deep blue eyes and a sultry smile, just like Eli May Clampett. Latigo and Corrina first met just like the Hollies song *'Bus Stop'* and where they shared a passionate kiss, before catching the bus to Sunnybrook Farm for a romp in the barn and a roll in the hay. Latigo and Corrina then took a ride on her Lambretta, deep in to a bushy cornfield and where she used her fishtail parka as a ground sheet, with Latigo reciprocating her smoozy passion with equal pleasure. Then when Latigo and Corrina emerged from the corn circle that marked their tryst, they were pushing the scooter, while covered in straw and strawberry flavoured lipstick'.

However crime busting was Latigo and Sutton's

main job, like the time they spied a transit van being revved up outside a provincial bank and so they decided to take a closer look. This though made the driver rev up the engine even harder as three figures in camouflage jackets and ski masks then raced out of the bank Then upon seeing Latigo and Sutton snooping about the van, the ski-masked robbers fired a sawn off shotgun in the air, only for Sutton to shoot at the van's tyres and which made the robbers return fire. One robber then jumped out from the front of the van, only to find Latigo pointing a '44 Magnum in his face and cry 'Oh my Soul' as he shot him stone dead. Sutton meanwhile had fired two shots through the back of the van's windows, with one bullet hitting the driver who slumped forward, causing the horn to blare. Then one of the robbers clambered over the van's seats and burst through the backdoors and this revealed another dead robber in the back of the van, and who had been killed by one of the two bullets Sutton had just fired. The last robber though kept on running despite Latigo shouting 'Freeze or I'll fire' and so Latigo squeezed the trigger and watched the last robber fall. Then when Latigo removed the last robber's ski mask he felt sick when he found that the last robber was that of a young woman as he did not relish shooting females, however in the line of duty he always made sure that the criminal fraternity lost out...

The story however does not end there and when he went to bed that night Latigo was haunted by a dream in which he was dressed like 'the fastest gun alive' in black drape suit with a brocade waistcoat while sharing a kiss with Sutton, who was like the Teddygirl from *Absolute Beginners* with a red velvet bow in her hair and wearing a sky blue drape jacket. As they stood under an orange street lamp in the early hours of the morning, while the stars paraded across the heavens to

'Just like Eddie' by Heinz.   The dream then changed slightly with Latigo and Sutton still sharing a kiss, but while standing on a grave in a churchyard on top of a flat grassy knoll. And where Latigo and Sutton faded in to the mist, as the sound of music played from beneath the grave... *Boys Cry* by Eden Kane.

CHAPTER 16

FLOWERS IN THE RAIN

Narrated by Frisco Kane

The afterhours lock in at the Blackboard Jungle drew to a close when we all fell asleep during the early hours of Sunday morning and after a karaoke encore that saw DCI Netherbourne singing *Little old wine drinker* Me, Carrick and me singing *Viva Suspenders* and the band singing *The Irish Rover*. Bathsheba was then taken aback when she found the normally empty and darkened club, early on the Sunday morning, still occupied by sleepy bodies that lay under and on top of the tables and in chairs, until they were aroused, with coughs and splutters and cries of 'Pwgh' at being drenched in the face by Bathsheba who had decided to say good morning with a soda siphon. Bathsheba was then held her down by two of the rudely awoken band girls while a third band girl spurted the soda siphon inside Bathsheba's jeans. This made her cry with indignation at having soaking wet knickers from the watery assault before she was bundled in to a backroom and the door locked, as everyone else wearily recovered with coffee laced with 'Sailor Jerry' spiced rum, as a hair of the dog and cleaned the place up as best as they could, to one final blast from the jukebox. That saw Carrick and me use two pool cues as air guitars and dance and dance around the floor to a variety of rock n roll music. After which a note was left for the bar staff to let Bathsheba out of her kennel, as everyone went their separate ways, with DCI Netherbourne and Amazon visiting Darna in hospital while Jesty and me steadily drove home in the mini.

When the DCI and Amazon told Darna about the

wake and what happened to Bathsheba after she awoke everyone with a soda siphon. Darna laughed until she ached with the pain from Bradbeer's rough handling, before getting dressed after being discharged. Darna did not feel up to running the club straight away and so she took up Amazon's gracious offer to recuperate at her flat and where she could set about designing promotion T. shirts for the Blackboard Jungle. The T. shirt logo was taken from a fun sticker that had been stuck to the wall of the ladies toilet and showed a brunette in a mauve bikini as she relaxed on a giant yellow banana. That emitted small love hearts like shooting stars, above which would be the club's name of 'The Blackboard Jungle.'

DCI Netherbourne meanwhile had arranged to meet Carrick at the Golf Four on the afternoon and where he was informed that Reno's gang had struck again, only this time at Northfield in Birmingham at 10.oclock on the Saturday night.

'Three robberies in one day, what's Dunster going for…record breakers?' DCI Netherbourne said as he prepared to interview and formally charge Leon Brad beer and Jubilee Christian, but for which there was no rush, as this was Sunday and the Magistrates court was not sitting until the next day.

Bradbeer's interview was an expected formality and who in the presence of a solicitor made a full and tearful admission in writing to the murder and rape of three prostitutes and the murder and rape of and the attempted rape of two acting police civilians. Jubilee Christian though was not remorseful and despite admitting to the murders of Lusty Jewson, Norma Jean and French Angel, with Jubilee saying that she had turned native after enjoying rough sex with Reno Dunster and the thrill of doing a blag, while swearing that she would escape from her 'Custodial Chains'.

I attend the remand hearings at Wolverhampton magistrates for Leon Brad beer and Jubilee Christian that were rapid affairs to confirm their identities, pending a crown court hearing sometime in November for sentencing reports and as both parties had pleaded guilty, there would be no need for a jury, with the female I purported to be Jubilee Christian surprised to see me when I visited her in the cells at Red Lion Street. But she wouldn't look me at when I entered her cell and just sat on her cell bunk with her head bowed as I asked. "How are they treating you?' To which she quietly replied "If you only knew the truth!"

I threw her a packet of cigarettes to either smoke or trade, before leaving her alone to contemplate her fate at the new women's prison of HMP Blazebank on the outskirts of the village of Wombourne. As for Leon Bradbeer he was sitting with a sorrowful expression on his face and staring at a blank wall as I looked through the cell door peephole and said. "Don't worry you'll soon be on Rule 43...then you can spend all the time you like staring at blank walls in solitary confinement...unless that is, you do everyone a favour?"

The last two weeks of October were subtle compared to that wild weekend, with the Chief Constable awarding me a meritorious commendation that I dedicated to all those who'd helped capture Leon Bradbeer and Jubilee Christian. Meanwhile Jesty continued to have bouts of sickness that she managed to hide and excuse from me, while Domino had realised that her own condition meant she was unable to run the Pencil Skirt alone. And so she snatched up DCI Netherbourne's offer to buy out Frenchy's share of the business with Little Winston's money. Amazon now became the new managerial partner of the Pencil Skirt, while Frenchy it seemed was from the south coast, but no family came forward to claim her body and so the Reverend Beecher and not wanting to seem unchristian, agreed to the double internment of Bootsy and Frenchy ashes at the windswept, Victorian church of Holy St Joseph's at Bishopsend, Dudley on October 25th 2006. Domino used part of her windfall to pay for a New Orleans style Jazz band to play *When the saints go marching in* as they walked in front of the hearse through Chapel Ash and then again at the church on Corngreaves Road with the Reverend Beecher thanking everyone for being a friend to Abigail as he called Bootsy by her real name. This unwittingly reminded me to ask Jesty about the ghostly love story that she had read out at the Blackboard Jungle and to which Jesty revealed that it was one of several short stories that she had written for magazines and made a small profit from.

The bulk of her income came from the interest from an inheritance that her mother had received from Jesty's father who had been a proficient cracksman, until he got caught and for which he was now serving a long stretch. Jesty revelation also came with a pleading stare not to reveal what she had said and to which I agreed by putting a finger to my lips. "Silence is golden and everyone has a skeleton hidden in their cupboard and for your sake if no other, this one's going to stay hidden" I said.

The double funeral took place at 11.a.m. on the morning and which meant I had to cut and run, as there was still Norma Jean's funeral at 1.p.m. at Bushbury Crematorium. I knew that Jesty would not attend Norma Jean's funeral and I had expected to go alone, but DCI Netherbourne and Carrick came along for moral support and as a Policing PR exercise. Norma Jean had never mentioned her family and so it was a surprise that the mourners were a motley crew of well known local faces.

"What's this open day at Winson Green?" DCI Netherbourne said.

"Now I know why she said she came from Birmingham and not Bushbury ...she was probably the only good apple in the whole rotten barrel?" I mused.

The DCI and I quietly pointed out to Carrick an array of criminal talent from shoplifters and fraudsters to car thieves and burglars. This though was not the only surprise at the funeral, with the song *'Flowers in the Rain'* being played and which matched Norma Jean's mom's biscuit brown coat with large violet flowers and her dad's flower power shirt of sky blue with large brightly coloured flowers that made Carrick muse. "The last time I saw something like that, it was the curtains and table cloth in my granny's kitchen?"

The three funerals had drawn a line under a chunk of my life then at the end of the service, after paying our respects to Norma Jean's parents while ignoring the mixed bag of cousins. Carrick, the DCI and I made our escape in to the arms of three smart looking females in triangular hemmed scarlet overcoats, who had been sitting at the back of the chapel. Sue, Jacky and Terri were from Walsall and the only branch of the family that Norma Jean stayed in contact, as all four females regarded the rest of the family as trouble, while Sue, Jacky and Terri had an idea that Carrick, DCI Netherbourne and I were Old Bill.

The three females also did not need persuading twice to join the three of us for a wake, meal and drink at a modern country pub called 'The Romping Donkey' in nearby rural Coven. It was far enough away to ensure discreet privacy, with this impromptu blind date eventually turning in to a frisky affair where all the normal inhibitions were dropped, as the alcohol flowed and the girls giggled as hands set to wandering. The girls then decided to continue to trust, we three officers of the law and accept an invitation to continue the private party at Carrick's flat, as this would allow him to have a drink.

The flat was over Penn Village shops with the local off licence supplying the liquor to fuel the high jinx that saw Carrick and Jacky retire to his bedroom and the DCI and Sue make good use of the sofa. While Terri and I took a walk to a local playing fields and where under the evening sky we climbed on the jungle gym, sang and laughed and had an impromptu kick about with an old football that we found, before retiring to a kiddies play hut on top of the slide for some romantic pleasure. Terri though found it a bit of a squeeze before we went back to Carrick's flat and where a couple of duvets under the dining table did make things more comfortable. The only light in the darkened lounge, apart from the glow of a cigarette, came from the moon that shone through the curtained window, with the DCI, Carrick and me pooling our loose change to buy some protection from a machine in the gents in the pub. I saw the passionate wake, as being my belated Stag night and which saw Carrick swap telephone numbers with Jacky when the party finally broke up the next morning and the girls caught the two buses back to Walsall.

Although Terri didn't mind seeing me again, Jacky wanted to reciprocate her lustful pleasure with Carrick with a view to cajoling him in to a relationship, while Sue their mum had only been interested in a one-night stand. However back on the home front, Jesty was not so discerning and having sovereignty of the house meant being matriarchal, as I soon discovered when I found a pillow and duvet on the sofa and a cold and congealed dinner in the oven. This made me feel somewhat apologetic at not telephoning to say that I would not be back that night, while the rights and wrongs of what had taken place was another matter for my conscience. But it was when I rang the Econo to apologise for not being at work last night that the guilt stakes rose. I was told that Jesty had stood in for me after saying that I was unavoidably detained on police business and which made me feel rather awkward as it showed that she cared enough to cover for me with a white lie.

I therefore decided to try and make amends by warming up and eating the dinner and tidying up the house, before going shopping to buy a peace offering for Jesty to say sorry and thank you. But when I returned like a Greek bearing gifts that included a large Teddybear, a big basket of fruit and chocolates, a big card that said 'Sorry' and a big bouquet of flowers. Jesty was still not home and so I placed the gifts on our bed and put the flowers in a vase of water, she was deliberately staying away, to teach me a lesson about playing fast and loose with our marriage. While I got bored watching the clock and waiting for Jesty to return for what I expected was an inevitable row and went to work three hours early. Although she could not stay mad at me, Jesty decided to string things out, by not calling me at work during the night or picking me up the next morning. I decided though to play it cool and when I walked in the house at around 8.15.a.m. I went straight in to the kitchen to make a drink while hearing the sound of Jesty's footsteps galloping down the stairs. But before she could speak, I thrust a mug of coffee in her hands and gave her a kiss to say sorry and good morning. Silence then reigned until I apologised. "Listen I just want to say I'm sorry and thanks for standing in for me. I just hope you liked the peace offerings."

"Okay apology accepted." Jesty said with a mischievous smile. "I just hope you like the framed *Emmanual* film poster that Domino gave me to hang over our bed, after helping to clean out Frenchy's room at the flat. Then when I came home, the house still looked just the same as it was when I'd left it, until it hit me that the bedding had been put away, the dinner in the oven had gone and the washing up was done. That's when I found the peace offerings and which made me smile, as it showed that you'd made an effort to say sorry. The only thing missing was you, as you had already gone to work, so I put the *Emmanual* poster on the sofa, it was my way of saying thank you for being so apologetically sweet."

"Well I must admit that the *Emmanual* film poster is rather fetching" I said with a cheeky smile.

"So you fancy me in a lace basque and stockings?" Jesty asked.

"Well...it's an interesting idea?" I replied "You running a brothel?"

"Frisco Kane...will you behave." Jesty said, as she pulled me towards her for a smouldering kiss and whispered. "This one girl's more than enough tart for you ...never mind a licensed maximum of six."

CHAPTER 17

WHO LET THE DOGS OUT

Narrated by Frisco Kane

Monday 15th November 2006, DCI Netherbourne and his Golf Four Irregulars' as we were called had been busy processing the outcome of a series of raids on illegal brothels and other shady activities that came, as a result of entries in Little Winston's black book, while Leon Bradbeer and Jubilee Christian were set to appear at Crown Court for sentencing.

Wolverhampton Crown Court opened at 8.a.m. but by 8.45.a.m. the security where struggling to screen the mass of press, court officials and public that included a large party of vixens. These foxy ladies of the night regaled at being all done up like a dog's dinner, though for some it was more a case of mutton dressed as lamb. Yet despite their grades of finery, they all had one thing in common that was to see Leon Bradbeer and Jubilee Christian given capital sentences for their guilty pleas to wilful murder and robbery.

Carrick, DCI Netherbourne and I arrived at court at 9.55.a.m. and by passed the busy brown marble foyer by using the side door that led to the inner sanctum of courthouse. Jesty, Darna and Domino had already arrived by the backdoor and were sitting in the comfort of a witness room in a secure corridor, while the sentencing was to take place in Court Six on the second floor gallery that was like being up in the god's with the melodramatic atmosphere of a Victorian theatre, while looking down in to a Romanesque public baths.

The court also played supposedly, smooth music to calm worried attendees, but the music could be mischievous like *I Fought the Law* and *'There aint no good Chain Gang'* through to Elvis's *Jailhouse Rock* and *'99yrs'* by Guy Mitchell

I spoke briefly to some of the girls as they waited to grab a seat in the public gallery as the sound of Johnny Cash and *'I Walk the Line'* echoed along the landing and the courts digital monitors said. 'Leon Bradbeer – Court Six – 9.30.a.m.' and 'Jubilee Christian – Court Six –10.a.m. The judge was to be Mr Justice Morris Mimms, an affable old hack who was nicknamed 'The Bloodhound' as he sniffed as he spoke, while looking like a bulldog chewing a wasp, as he squinted behind the monocle in his lazy eye. The courtroom opened at 9.15.a.m. to a flood of press and public and by 9.25.a.m. all the seats were taken. I took my place in court and toyed with a black handkerchief with this gallows humour making Bradbeer finger his shirt collar, as he knew it signified the death penalty. But when the judge took his place on the bench, I quickly stuffed the handkerchief back in my pocket.

The court usher read out the charges of four counts of rape and murder and one count of attempted rape and murder and to which Bradbeer pleaded 'Guilty.' Then before sentence was passed, Bradbeer cried out 'I'm Sorry.'

"Leon Bradbeer 'sniff sniff' you were a Police officer 'sniff' a most trusted position 'sniff' and one that you abused 'sniff'. Your tally of murderous rape 'sniff' makes you a reprehensible criminal 'sniff' just like Hitler crossed with Moriarty and Jack the 'sniff' Ripper 'sniff'. While your blubbering 'sniff' just like a baby 'sniff' leaves this court resigned to only one legal course of action 'sniff sniff' for such a miserable reprobate like you 'sniff'...the shadow of the noose 'sniff.'

Leon Bradbeer, tears streaming down his face was led away by the dock officer and back to the cells, while out on the landing, the sound of Johnny Cash and *'The Burning Ring of Fire'* rang like a celebratory moment of triumph.

Carrick meanwhile had nipped to the witness room to tell Jesty, Domino and Darna of Judge Mimms sentence of the gallows rope. 'The death penalty had been returned after a three line whip parliamentary vote, with the rope and a lethal injection being the only two types of execution allowed in Great Britain.'

Jubilee Christian was up next, but not before a short recess to compose the court and during which I lounged by the gallery balcony and as I did so, I seemed to recognise a face. It was the eyes that first got me thinking and then I saw the facial Cheshire cat grin from within a bushy beard. It was at this point that I suddenly jerked my body straight and yelled out loud 'Dunster' and who in turn yelled 'Fuck Off' while the three men he was with then scattered as they were chased by Police officers led by DCI Netherbourne.

I chased Dunster down the stairway and knocked anybody out of the way that posed a threat then upon reaching the first floor balcony Dunster paused. There was only a tall, ornamental lamppost of three globe balls to break his fall if he jumped from the balcony on to the marble floor that would also break his legs. Then with only seconds to spare before I caught up with him, Dunster charged along the balcony and knocked two Police constables down the last flight of stairs. Before he laughingly shouted 'Behave' as he lashed out with his fists and feet in a martial arts street fighting style at the frontline security. Dunster then raced out side and round the path that led to the ring road underpass and where I lost him as Dunster ran towards the city's ramshackle red light area.

Meanwhile back inside the courthouse it was like the Keystone Cops with Dunster's gang of Brett Sampford, Courtney Wootton and Ralph Brompton racing here and there. Sampford dashed along the gallery to the fire escape door that he shoulder charged, but as the door pushed open Sampford stumbled and fell down the stairway with two Police officers on his trail. Sampford now limping just about managed to stay one step ahead of the law. That was until he lost his balance on the last flight of stairs and went sprawling, while hitting his head against the outer fire exit door and where he lay, as the heavy breathing constables snapped on the cuffs.

Ralph Brompton was a bit more daring and leapt on to the tall, ornamental tree that grew in the middle of the courthouse. Brompton although cut and stung by the tree branches, still managed to scramble down the tree on to the foyer floor. It was here that he raced to the door that led to the cells, only to find a secured second door. Brompton growled at the approaching security and Police as he emerged from the dead end and grabbed a woman usher and then with one arm around her neck he backed his way in to the lift that he took to the top floor. Brompton then ran in to Courtney Wooton who had fled in to the court's robing room by mistake, where a barrister Mr Vikram Singh Brooknight chased Wootton back on to the landing. Courtney Wootton then took hold of the female usher who screamed and who was given a happy slap by Wootton to keep her quiet, before being made to buzz open the door to the secure corridor. That led to the second lift and back downstairs to the courthouse's secure car park. While the barrister Mr Brooknight squared up to Brompton with the result being an ensuing fight of toss and tumble Judo verses the rough and tumble of street fighting that sprawled back out on to the second floor gallery to the sound of Johnny Cash and '*A Boy named Sue.*'

The sound of screaming alerted the witness service who came to see what was happening, while Jesty after seeing the woman usher being pushed in to the lift radioed for assistance. Wootton then made his way to the secure car park and where the usher managed to break free, as the Police who now surrounded the court house, let two Police dogs loose to collar Brompton as he and the barrister slugged it out. While Courtney Wootton, having hot-wired a car, now sat dazed in the driving seat after crashing in to the compound gates.

Meanwhile as Dunster's gang was being arrested, Jubilee Christian escaped from custody after physically subduing the dock officer and using the dock chairs to scramble over a perspex screen in to the main well of the courtroom. A tall, and muscular Court Usher who had locked the courtroom doors when the hue and cry was sounded, told Jubilee not to be silly. But what no one knew was that Jubilee Christian had taken Korean martial arts lessons from Dunster, when she had joined his gang and had proved to be a pretty good pupil.

Jubilee launched a drop kick to the Usher's abdomen and threw a punch to his Adam's apple in quick succession, before a swift kick to his Solar Plexus that caused him to crumple and gasp. Jubilee then rifled the Usher's pockets for the courtroom keys and stripped him of his gown that she used to cloak herself, before unlocking and then relocking the doors behind her, as two women clerks cowered behind their desks. Jubilee then made her way to the lift and descended to the foyer and where amidst the all the mayhem and the sound of Ronnie Barker and '*Going Straight*', Jubilee quickly and quietly slipped out in to the street and the fresh air of freedom.

The courtroom drama soon became news headlines, while Dunster and Jubilee Christian where the subject of fresh bench warrants as fugitives of justice. DCI Netherbourne meanwhile, invited Carrick and me to join him for a drink at The Runcible Spoon that was originally a rock café that stood just over the road from the Crown Court. DCI Netherbourne knew the landlord and who for a drink let the three of us use the small function room for a private party. This escapade also saw the three of us serve themselves with top up halves of beer direct from the pumps while we chatted and played pool. The only thing that we all regretted was that the crown court antics had not taken place on a Friday that was normally a dead day and when the court cafeteria and affectionately known as 'Rat up a Drainpipe' would usually show a movie like *'Porridge'* with Ronnie Barker, Michael Caine's *'The Italian Job'* or episodes of *'Rumpole of the Bailey'*.

Meanwhile as Jesty questioned Sampford, Brompton and Wooton back at the station about their part in several armed robberies, the liquid brunch took its toll on the three of us, who retired to our respective homes to sleep things off. I though, during my snooze on the sofa had a strange dream in which I entered a shadowy, gaslight courtroom that was more like a broody, Victorian study with an aroma of camphor oil and the warm glow of an opulent and copious Dickension coal fire. Then at the far side of the small room, sat a gauntly looking and sharp-nosed judge with a pleasing smile and who wore a long ribbed wig and full red robes. While to the judge's right hand side there was a darkened alcove of brown varnished wood with a thick brown gallows rope and trap door. And above the polished dark oak, hooded judge's bench there was a scrolled notice 'The Case is Altered''

CHAPTER 18

MOULDY OLD DOUGH

Narrated by Frisco Kane

The inscription 'The Case is 'Altered' was a benchmark in more ways than one, starting with the Econo hotel's general manager Bab's offering me a balance between part time policing and not having to continuously snatch bouts of sleep. A new trainee assistant manager was needed to help run the Econo since its purchase of the adjacent field in order to house a small number of chalets, while ensuring the pleasant greenery would be retained. Babs also surprised me with a passionate kiss when I arrived at work on the night after the daydream, after which she switched on the 'No Vacancies' sign and gave me a second kiss before taking my hand as she led the way to the spare backroom. Babs then undressed down to her white uniform blouse before pushing me on the bed and saying "I've been, wanting to do this for a long time…but I've never had the nerve before."

I then realised that Bab's had grown from being like Tamazin Outhwaite in *Hotel Babylon* to being like Patsy Kensit in *'21'* a gorgeous good time girl with a sense of style, as we engaged in a sexual romp of playtime and pleasure. While she teasingly called me a 'Naughty Boy' after learning my secret about using the hotel laundry to fast wash and then tumble dry my clothes, before having a shower and changing in to the spare clothes I kept at the hotel for keeping 'Once in a blue moon selective, discretion, discreet. While I made it clear that Jesty and I came first in our relationship and we were both like Judge Dread…strictly for the birds! Babs knew about the rules of engagement in

130

Jesty and my relationship and so she took a deep breath before dropping a bombshell. "I've left my husband...for another woman!"

This was a real bolt from the blue, as I never took Bab's for a pendulum... able to swing both ways. But I was even more gobsmacked when Babs revealed that the other woman was Jesty. Femme fatale had struck again like an arrow from Cupid's bow, during a girlie chat when Jesty stood in for me on my impromptu stag night. Babs revealed that one moment she and Jesty were talking and the next they were unwittingly holding hands and sharing a kiss. After which Jesty took Babs in hand and introduced her to the tender touch of a soft and gentle feminine caress and since when they had been dating each other and visiting girls clubs like the Hoochie Coochie and the Sugar Plum unto the early hours.

"No wonder she seemed to look so tired of late!" I mused.

Jesty arrived early to pick me up and after I gave her a good morning kiss, I made an excuse to go out back and watched as Babs and Jesty shared a passionate embrace. I then deliberately walked in on them and grabbed Jesty by her hand as I walked her to the darkened coffee shop and said "C'mon Sugar Plum...I think we need to talk!"

"Babs has told you everything then?" Jesty said sheepishly

"She sang sweeter than a nightingale...but I've got no qualms about Babs being your girlfriend, even though it's somewhat of an unexpected surprise. But it's got to be strictly Gerry Anderson...no strings attached, Babs leaving her husband is of her own volition!" I said as I then gave Jesty a gentle kiss.

"Thank you" Jesty whispered as we returned to the foyer and where I told a thrilled Babs. "It looks like you've got a new assistant manager and the extra cash will come in handy, as will the more reasonable hours…if only for Jesty's sake!"

This surprise was only the start of things to come, with the next being a chance encounter with Reno Dunster at Wolverhampton's Railway Station that had been had been remodelled on the railway stations of Carlisle and Edinburgh and the frontage of the Scottish Parliament. The frontage also housed a copy of Liverpool's ornate, black 'Stebles Fountain, while behind the station's smoked glass lay '221b' an Edwardian style bar that was bedecked with Sherlock Holmes memorabilia.

It was one night, shortly after the crown court drama that I decided to enjoy a quiet pint at the 221b, the station was busy and I was in mid swig when I spotted Reno Dunster lurking amidst the throng in the foyer. I immediately dashed towards a fire exit that led directly to the foyer and knocked over a table and chair as I gave chase, while Dunster saw me charging at him and instinctively he barged past the ticket barrier staff and raced up the Georgian stone balustrade stairs and across the emerald and parchment rustic foot bridge. I was right on Dunster's tail as he raced downstairs and along platform 2, then up a white tiled stairs to a covered bridge. Dunster then raced downstairs to platform 4 and jumped off the platform and on to a gravel pathway that ran alongside the railway track. The pursuit then continued through rubbish and weeds while the turbulence from high-speed trains buffeted us, until we reached a distant viaduct in Lock Street.

Dunster then dived in to the cold and murky water of the Shropshire Union Canal to shake off my pursuit of him with a search of the canal area by Police and dogs revealing nothing, Dunster had gone, while November had seen things move so fast, first there was the crown court drama, then Jesty and Bab's and now a chase around the railway station.

The penultimate result of this game came a few nights later when Carrick and I went for a drink at the Monkey House pub that had a special showing of the film *'Easy Rider'*. Carrick and I were in the pub lounge, watching the film, when the door creaked and I turned and exchanged a fleeting glance with Dunster who bolted as fast as he came. But as Dunster ran in to the darkness of the pub car park a shot rang out, but when Carrick and I ran in to the car park, there was no sign of Reno Dunster, only the sound of a motor vehicle driving away at high speed. There was no point in putting out a Police alert, as there was no description of the vehicle that had just sped away, all we could do was report a missed opportunity to close the case and go back to watching the film over a drink. As for who fired the shot, I had a sneaking suspicion, but hunches were not proof with the next piece of the puzzle coming at breakfast the next morning. DCI Netherbourne summoned Jesty, Carrick and me to the Monkey House pub and where the landlord had been awoken by the sound of a vehicle exploding after it had been set on fire on the car park. The fire brigade had managed to douse the fire, but it was when they opened the boot that they discovered the body of Reno Dunster who had not only been shot in the head. But was well baked by the heat of the fire, with the smell making Jesty throw up something chronic

"So Dunster's luck has finally run out... he has cheated the hangman and in the same way as his girlfriend, but I would love to know who his deadly accomplice was?" DCI Netherbourne said as he chomped on his pipe.

"Try the female of the species and I don't mean

Bathsheba Mendalove... just think about the way Norma Jean died?" I said.

"You mean Jubilee Christian?" DCI Netherbourne said with disbelief.

"Well if that's the case...then why the hell couldn't she have killed him off earlier and saved us all the trouble of a bloody manhunt?" Carrick snapped.

"Because like Tommy Edwards said...it's all in the game" I replied.

"Jubilee Christian is like a fox in the hen house, she won't stop killing until she's caught and killed herself...and there's nobody here but us chickens!" Jesty managed to add to the conversation.

"Well who's the Rooster that's going to be killed last?" Carrick asked.

"Cock a Doodle Do!" I said with a wry smile.

"Over my dead body..!" Jesty quietly mused to herself

CHAPTER 19

SHOTGUN WEDDNG

Narrated by Frisco Kane

December 21st 2006 was our themed wedding day with Jesty screaming "Get Out" when I knocked on the bedroom door.

It was approximately 8.a.m. as I made my way over to the Pencil Skirt where I had arranged to meet Carrick for breakfast coffee and said. "I was only going to enter the bedroom to wish her luck and she literally ripped my head off...so I left her and Bab's too it."

"Well you know it's supposed to be bad luck to see the bride in her wedding dress, before getting hitched." Carrick replied.

"You mean all that Mother-inlaw's Tongue. I do, he does, they will?" I said. "Well I can't see what the problem is, I mean were already bloody married, this is just the costume party."

I then looked at my watch and mused mischievously "Here how do you fancy, you and me, dressed as we are, like something out of *LA Confidential.* Disappearing off to Liverpool or London?"

"Jesty d' bloody kill you!" Carrick laughed.

"She'd probably marry the vicar?" I laughed.

"What the Reverend Bejazus...now that'd be a laugh?" Carrick said.

"Mind you its still a bit strange...Jesty having a girlfriend" I said.

"Well whatever keeps the little lady happy!" Carrick said.

"And how are things in Walsall?" I asked.

"Oh I've got enough on my plate...with Norma

Jean's cousin" Carrick said.

"So its cake all round and eat it." I said, as the jukebox played Billy Idol and *White Wedding*.

I looked at my watch again, it said 8.40.a.m. The wedding was not until midday, so we had to think about what to do to relieve the boredom. I got Carrick to drive us to Wolverhampton Central, where we jumped on a train that was heading north as I said. "How do you fancy breakfast at Teddy Edwards, then we can play pool over a pint and a couple of cobs."

"What Stafford...but he don't open till midday?" Carrick said.

"He'll open for us...don't forget were the Feds!" I said in a mock American accent and flashing my police badge, before telling Carrick about Reno Dunster's funeral "It was a funny affair, there was only one song, *Forever and Ever* by Silk. But the mourners didn't include any family not even a tom and those who did go, were like me...only there to make sure, the bastard was firmly planted!"

A gawky looking lad, who clearly wasn't all there and who had the name Keith on a badge, on his jacket then marched down the carriage aisle, stood at the end and constantly talked in to a 'brick' of a mobile phone. Keith was so loud that it caused the train passengers to complain, so Carrick and I walked up to Keith and snatched the phone off him. Keith tried to grab the phone back, but I hooked an arm around his neck, as Carrick said "It's not even bloody real...it's a rubber dummy!"

"Right say goodbye to your phone." I said, as Carrick threw it between the train and the tracks and helped me manhandled Keith off the train when it stopped at Penkridge, while he cried "But I'm going to Crewe!"

The train passengers cheered and which made us realise that we must look the business in Fedora hats and heavy topcoats while wearing shoulder holsters with replica 45's and carrying replica Thompson machine guns in a carpetbag.

Then when we reached Stafford we got a taxi to Teddy Edwards that was a refurbished pub, painted red, cream and black and stood on the edge of the town's square. Carrick and me stood imposingly on the pub doorstep with the 'Chicago Pianos' in our hands and which caused a stir amongst some of the local citizens, as I rang the bell and shouted 'Open up it's the Feds!'

The publican was Big John, a part time Police officer who was happy to open up, as he knew me from serving in Wolverhampton, moreover when I slapped a £20 note on the bar and said "Four crusty cobs with onions, two pints of lager and lime and a pint for yourself"

Big John laughed, as he said cheers while Carrick explained the reason for the gangster look, to which Big John gave us a cigar a piece, as he pulled the pints and ordered the cobs.   Carrick and I removed our jackets and settled down to play pool with me dancing the 'Duck Walk' around the pool table, while using a pool cue as an air guitar to a jukebox rock n roll of Chuck Berry.   Yet, no sooner had we begun to play than the door knocked again and in walked two female detectives in trench coats. Big John introduced them as two of Stafford's finest and our opposite numbers. DI Blan McJones was a curvaceous blonde like the sexy DS Sandra Pullman in *'New Tricks'* while DS Fiona Netherseal was like the female detective from *'Taggart'*

"Good morning gentlemen were looking for two American style gangsters with Tommy Guns' and judging by what's on the counter...I take it your

Machine Gun Kelly and your Al Capone?" Blan McJones said

"Gee Carrick I told you this was a swell joint, they even provide dames and broads without having to ask." I said in mock American, as I chomped on a cigar.

"Listen sister how about you and me do a deal, you drop the heat and shoot the breeze, as we all play pool." Carrick said in the same mock accent. "And we'll buy you a drink and something to eat, with the loser at pool paying a forfeit?"

"Well that leaves a lot of things to the imagination?" Blan said as she and Fiona looked at each other with raised eyebrows, before slipping off their coats and taking a sip from our pints, as they chalked up a couple of cues and said "Now let's see if you can handle some real women…sugar?"

It was to be the best of three games, during which the girls shared our cobs and drinks, as both sides jokingly taunted and sang 'So you think you're a hot cop?' And parodied verses to the Shania Twain song *'That don't impress me much!'* The first two matches were drawn one a piece, but before the tiebreaker, Big John took a photo of Carrick and me in shirtsleeves and loose ties and lounging against the bar with the Fedora's slouched and the Tommy Guns held on the hip. While the girls stood between us, with my arm around Blan's waist and Carrick's arm around Fiona's waist. The girls then gently kissed us, with Blan scribbling down her details on a scrap of paper and saying "Here keep this safe. But don't get any ideas about trying to get in to my knickers…well not just yet anyway?"

"Don't worry I won't, were only here to kill time and escape all the fuss… before we go back to Wolves where I'm getting married at twelve oclock." I said.

Blan raised her eyebrows in surprise and said. "If

you were my husband, I'd have you chained to a kennel. But all the same give us a bell...just don't leave it too long."

"I won't...there's still the forfeit to pay yet?" I said as I played a shot.

"And I think we both have the same idea?" Blan smilingly said.

"I think we all have the same idea?" I replied, as Carrick and Fiona got fresh while we purposefully let the girls win the match.

I then looked at the time it was nearly 11.a.m. with Carrick getting a phone call from Babs that Jesty was running half an hour late.

"There's a train back to Wolves at five past twelve, so there's still time for a leisurely forfeit!" Blan said as we all retired to the pub's beer garden to engage in frisky bout of French kissing.

The time though seemed to fly and so Carrick and I had to jump a taxi and race up and over Stafford station, bridge to catch the Wolverhampton train that was on platform four. We just managed to catch the train in time, before catching our breath and discussing the brief encounter at Teddy Edwards.

"Well it's been a fun morning?" Carrick said while brushing himself down.

"Well you know what they say about what's sauce for the goose and all that." I said while hoping that I didn't noticeably smell of perfume "And if Jesty can have a discreet girlfriend then why not...you know. So what about yourself"

"Well Norma Jean's cousin in Walsall and Fiona's in Stafford" Carrick said "And never the twain shall meet!" Carrick and I say together.

"Does that mean your now off the market?" Carrick asked.

"I suppose it does, but I never really saw myself as

being on the market I just took advantage of the romantic opportunities that arose. I mean, I've got a wife in Wolves, a girlfriend in Stafford...and then there's Babs?" I replied.

"And what is she...a bit on the side?" Carrick said cheekily and to which I laughed and said "Here...fancy a transfer to the Stafford Constabulary?"

"You naughty old policeman" Carrick replied with a cheeky grin.

When the train arrived in Wolverhampton it was almost 12.30.p.m. and so we jumped a black cab to the Pencil Skirt and arrived just as the clock struck 12.40. p.m. Yet before we could apologise for being late, I was told that Jesty was still running late and to which I said. "She'd be late for her own funeral, if you let her?"

Then after another quick wash and brush up, Carrick and I joined the wedding party guests who were dressed like something from *'Mullholland Falls'* including DCI Netherbourne in a beige pinstripe double-breasted suit and Fedora hat. Amazon was all in powder blue with a pillbox hat and helped out at the bar as over a drink Carrick and I related to DCI Netherbourne what we had been up too.

"You're a right pair...aren't you? You'll have to introduce me to *Cagney and Lacy!*" DCI Netherbourne chuckled. "But then again you could be working with them soon?"

Carrick and I looked puzzled as DCI Netherbourne explained. "I take it you haven't heard then...Golf Four is going *Heartbeat*, you know uniform only. It seems that CID is considered too maverick and so I've transferred over to Stafford CID as its new DCI...so how do you fancy a transfer to pastures new?"

Jesty then finally walked in to the Madison bar in a long red silk dress with a hood, she was a vision of loveliness who smiled to me as she patted her stomach and whispered "Yes...I'm expecting!"

Yet no sooner had Jesty broken the news about her forthcoming event, than the ceremony was gate-crashed by Jubilee Christian and waving a revolver.

"I wondered when you were going to come out of the woodwork... now give me the gun or I'm going to slap you hard!" I snapped.

"Always the masterful one" Jubilee Christian said, as I grappled with her to get the gun, with Carrick and DCI Netherbourne's help.

Things though did not go that easy and I had the gun barrel pointed at my face during the struggle, for which I feared for my life if the trigger was pulled. I did though manage to push the gun barrel away and down towards the middle of the scrum. That was when the revolver went off with DCI Netherbourne staggering in pain and clutching his hand, as blood oozed through his fingers. Carrick caught another bullet with a flesh wound to his thigh, while I screamed as a bullet went in to my foot. We three detectives then fell away, as Jubilee Christian uneasily waved the revolver about and said. "This is the gun I did Reno Dunster with...me Jubilee Christian, the only one, to bring that bastard down and with one of his own guns."

Jubilee Christian then laughed as she pulled the trigger, but her laughter was to turn to screams, as the gun exploded and shards of gun metal pierced her hands and face. As I agonising in pain then watched in horror as two mystery shots were fired in rapid succession, with the first bullet killing Jubilee Christian outright, just as though it was a *coup de grace* to the head. While the other bullet made Jesty reel with a sting to her back as a dark stain spread across her red silk wedding dress.

CHAPTER 20

ICE, ICE BABY

Narrated by Frisco Kane

Chapel Ash was once again a sea of blue flashing lights, with the first Police officers on the scene rendering emergency first aid and calling for paramedics and ambulances. The sirens and lights of which wailed 'Blue and Twos' as they ferried a wounded Carrick, DCI Netherbourne and myself across the city with a Police escort. Then when the news broke of the bloody shooting incident, the local media interrupted programmes with news flashes that a Police officer had been killed and three more wounded by two females, one of whom had been killed at the scene. Wolverhampton Police had circulated a brief description of the second female who had been seen fleeing the pub after the shooting.

The shooting incident had deliriously traumatised me, but this did not stop my brain from recognising the description of the second killer and in my delirium

I garbled a message at a constable who was guarding me.

"The enemy of my enemy is my friend. The description its Bathsheba Mendalove ...she's the second killer...The Blackboard Jungle!"

A flying squad of armed Police descended on the Blackboard Jungle, but all they found was Darna Gold who was gobsmacked at the news of the shooting, as every local Police force sent their condolences, from Birmingham to Stafford. And where at Teddy Edwards, the manager Big John, DI Blan McJones and DS Fiona Netherseal heard the media break the news and name

Carrick and me, as two of the Police casualties, as the jukebox played *'Don't Marry Her Me.'*

My enforced stay in hospital lasted four days with the shock causing me to sweat profusely and gabble deliriously as I kept visualising Jesty being murdered. While on a daily basis Babs, Domino and Amazon visited Carrick and me and held our hands in comfort as they sat between our adjoining beds.

It was Christmas Morning when I came round from my delirium and after hearing that Carrick had been discharged the day before, I discharged myself, as I didn't want to be stuck in hospital on my own. But back in the eerie emptiness of Wheatville Terrace I was haunted by the ghost of Jesty's love, then on Boxing Day I had a Christmas drink with the Reverend Bejazus and opened with the words

"Bless me father for I have sinned... I just wish I had known that Jesty was expecting beforehand, then I'd not bothered with Blan or Babs. I mean I didn't mind Jesty having a girlfriend but it was bloody Jubilee Christian, she just couldn't leave it alone could she. Even though she was attractive in her own way, even when she turned renegade but then look what happened. Now I'm haunted by the song *'Ghost in my house'* except that ghosts don't catch crooks. But I'll always think of Jesty every time I look at the picture 'Bachelorette Pad' and the sexy punk female and guards man in the sentry boxes."

"Ah bejazus there my boy...you unburden your soul now...you and Carrick bejazus are going to look a right pair of walking wounded, sure enough bejazus, at Jesty's funeral. And see if you can catch up with Bathsheba Mendalove bejazus... and when you do bejazus...you'll have to hold each other up as you belt her with your crutches?" The Reverend Bejazuz said and which made me give a wry smile, as he opened two more bottles of beer and raised a toast.

"Well now bejazus…you'll have another drink with me I'm thinking… bejazus she was a lovely woman was Jesty and in child as well, that's a crying shame. Murder though is a mortal sin and her killer will be damned, surely enough when they come to face the Lord. But for now bejazus here's a toast…to absent friends and new tomorrows."

January 2nd 2007. The West Chapel at Bushbury Crematorium was packed with Police uniforms and dark suits, as close friends and colleagues paid their last respects to Jesty. While the song *'Miss Grace'* was played to start the service that was conducted by the Reverend Bejazus. Then after the traditional hymn *'The' day thou gavest Lord has ended'* had been sung, I said a few tearful words. "I asked for Jesty be laid to rest in her scarlet wedding dress…so that she would be like beauty personified."

Then as the curtain closed over the coffin that was covered in red roses, Gerry and the Pacemakers sang *'Don't let the sun catch you crying'* and a pigeon on the chapel roof cooed to the words. I smiled, I knew it was a sign from Jesty, but when a pigeon dropped a message of peace on Fiona Netherseal's coat, I took it to be a warning from Jesty that something was amiss. Bab's had not attended Jesty's funeral and something that would require further investigation.

Carrick meanwhile told me that he was supposed to be spending Christmas in Walsall with Jacky, but she had demanded that he should pack the job in and do something less dangerous. But, as he said the danger of being shot came with the territory and to which she made it clear, it was either her or the job? And so he raided the bank balance, jumped a taxi, which cost an arm and a leg on Christmas Day and telephoned Fiona once he got back home.

"Ah well your still young mate and you were a copper when you met Norma Jean's cousin, so it should have gone without saying. But I suppose it was too much to hope for Bathsheba to make an appearance, word has it that she's joined the punk underground scene in London and is touring Europe with 'Fruit Salad Mary' who described themselves as hardcore lesbian punk bitches." I said.

Meanwhile I gave Fiona the psychedelic Mini Cooper as a present as she thought it was a cool car while I put the house up for sale. Bab's and I had tried to get things together but it'd not really worked out between us, although I had found her attractive that vital spark was missing. Bab's had also found a 'Girl in Blue' admirer after making her acquaintance at the Hoochie Coochie and who gave Babs a shoulder to cry when she realised that Jesty was truly dead.

"Well how do you want to play this?" Bab's asked as she stood in her flat while wearing nothing but a baggy jumper, as the girl cop took off her trench coat.

"I want you...darling!" The girl cop said as she popped a chocolate square in to Babs mouth and then gave her a sensual kiss. But the sweet began to swirl Bab's mind and she realised that she was about to be date raped and so she spat out the chocolate square, but role played the effects of the drug, as the girl cop stripped down to her lingerie and fulfilled her lustful desire. Then as she took the belt from her trench coat, Babs turned the tables and in desperation, left the girl cop with a shallow breath and weal marks from the ligature. Babs then unsaddled herself from the girl cop's semi naked body and quickly got dressed, before picking up the girl cop's warrant card that was lying on the floor and which said 'Detective Sgt Fiona Netherseal, Staffordshire CID'.

Babs realised that attending Jesty's funeral could lead her to being arrested for the attempted murder of a Police officer and so she knew she had to disappear. Fiona meanwhile and once she regained her senses was thinking about how to hide or explain away any ligature marks on her neck, as she prepared to resume her role as Carrick's girlfriend at Jesty's wake that was being held in the Madison Lounge of the Pencil Skirt.

"You don't let the grass grow...do you?" Darna said with reference to Blan and Fiona who were guests of Carrick and me as we ordered a round of drinks.

"If you must know they're going to be our new governors. You see like your dad, we're also transferring full time to the City of Stafford Constabulary." Carrick said, before hobbling back to the table with a tray of drinks.

"You know you could have come to me for moral support...but do me a big favour, please be careful' that Fiona can be trouble, she's like poison and they don't call her the Viper for nothing. Oh I've seen her around at the best clubs, she had a strange attraction for Babs. Then after Jesty died, Fiona turned on the charm while it's strange Bab's hasn't come to pay her respects?" Darna said as she squeezed my hand for luck, before melting away in to the crowd of mourners, while I hobbled back to the table and where my appearance was marked by Fiona who joked "Been chatting up the barmaid?"

I just smiled, Darna's words began to make me suddenly visualise Fiona in a rather different light, as Carrick raised his glass and said "Well cheers and happy new' year everyone...here's' to new tricks!"

"And a Copper's Lot..!" I mused

CHAPTER 21

WATCHING THE DETECTIVES

Narrated by Frisco Kane

New Year 2007, saw my resignation from the Econo and Carrick and I upgraded to regular detectives 2nd class or Bad and Super Bad and transferred to Whiskey Victor aka South Staffs or 'Straw Suckers' Constabulary, Vice and Unusual Crime Squad and which covered Stafford and the WV postcode. And where the 'Wolverhampton Sniper' who was a sharp shooter who thought they were Death Wish and armed with a telescopic rifle while signing themselves the 'Ghost of Lee Harvey Oswald'. Had turned Queen Square into a fluorescent shooting gallery, where at night the primary targets were old lags and associates of the late Reno Dunster, who hit the slabs with a thud after a shot to the head. And to this day 'The Ghost of LHO' has never been caught, despite a sudden ceasefire in their activities.

There was also another distinctive winter chill that was the discovery of Babs empty and dishevelled flat, after she failed to turn up for work at the Econo Lodge or answer her phone. This only pushed me to sell Wheatville Terrace as the place had too many ghosts, ghosts of the heart and lost loves, like Jesty, Babs, Frenchy and Norma Jean. So as from today Valentine's Day 2007, Carrick and I have moved to the city of Stafford and where as we stepped off the train on platform 5 and climbed the steep stairs to the footbridge, Carrick said. "Stafford station never changes does it it's just like something out of that cop show *Life on Mars*...a retro station for retro cops...just like us?"

"More like snake eyes." I said as I spotted DS Fiona Netherseal.

She was standing with her arms folded and talking to D.I Blan McJones as they waited like two impatient wags for our train to arrive. Then after a welcoming hug, Blan and Fiona showed Carrick and me our new digs at the Royal Victoria Park that was a broad 1960's office block that had been converted in to five floors of flats that stood on the corner of Station Road and Railway Street.

"And just next door is Charlie Golf Two Four, your new police station" Blan said pointing to a tired looking, red brick building.

"Out the depths of despair...dig a bigger hole!" I mused.

"It says Stafford Institute...what for...the Insane?" Carrick quipped.

"What did you expect the St George's Brass Band? We're on the frontline here mate, shot and shell on every corner or is that Cannock" I said.

"No that's Stoke on Trent. This is Stafford...no man's land!" Carrick replied.

"And there are some spare offices on the footbridge of the train station...you can see them if you look up from Railway Street." Blan said.

"That's for us" I whispered to Carrick "Clandestine obscurity!"

DCI Netherbourne was our governor at the regional vice HQ in Stafford with all three of us having recovered enough from our gunshot injuries to return to work. Fiona and Blan meanwhile had specially prepared our new digs by hanging the 'Call Girl' picture I gave Carrick in memory of Bootsy over his bed. While in my lounge the 'Bachelorette Pad' picture took pride of place with Blan hanging the 'Punk and Guardsman' picture over my bed. Then as Blan took off her coat to make coffee, I unzipped her dress, undid her bra strap and made her purr "I think you forget that I'm your Inspector."

"Well you're off duty now!" I replied as I spun Blan around, pulled her dress and bra down over her shoulders and gave her a kiss.

My passionate assail on what had been up to now Fortress Blan, saw me lying in bed with my arm around an equally naked Blan and although she may not have been as game as Jesty with respect to girlfriends. Blan was a solid woman and the sort of partner I was looking for, as I gave her a kiss on the forehead and a gentle hug to say thank you. I then left Blan asleep while I got washed and dressed, before standing on the flat's balcony, where I contemplated my next move. Bathsheba had still not surfaced, while remembering Darna's warning about Fiona, who I felt there was more too than meets the eye. As for Jubilee her funeral was to be a cordial affair with only Carrick, the DCI and me as the mourners, the song of *'Colour Slide'* by the Honeycombs was my choice as was an aromatic bouquet of red roses and white lilies. While on the morning I had received notice that Jesty's parental trust fund had been bequeathed to the police betterment fund or Carrick, DCI Netherbourne and me.

It was DCI Netherbourne who had broken the news about a uniform patrol finding Babs flat empty, but with signs of a struggle, sexual activity and a partially chewed and saliva covered square of chocolate by the sofa that the pathologist was able to discover, contained traces of a date rape drug. This particular aspect of Babs disappearance stayed in my mind, as I sensed Blan standing behind me, in a cotton kimono, as she put her arms around me and kissed my neck, before resting her head on my shoulder.

"Come back to bed love...I haven't finished with you yet...you know."

Blan said before spinning me round and giving me a passionate kiss.

"On one condition" I managed to reply.

"And what's that?" Blan asked inquisitively.

"How well do you know Fiona Netherseal?" I said

"Well enough why do you ask?" Blan replied like an alert watchdog.

"Just curious" I said as I pulled open Blan's kimono and kissed her

"Well you know what they say about curiosity and the cat. Only we had the rat squad sniffing about, not so long ago and believe me it got messy?" Blan replied, as she pulled away from me.

"What with regard to Fiona?" I asked as though scenting a Fox.

"No it wasn't her...it was a couple of rookies who got caught with their hand in the cookie jar. Anyway don't worry about it it's just me being paranoid. Listen if you don't mind, I don't fancy bed, I'll just make us some coffee and something to eat." Blan said

I then pulled Blan towards me and gave her another kiss and ran my hands inside her kimono and patted her buttocks. "But listen, love can I ask with regard to our little conversation, I would appreciate it if you...you know."

"Don't worry, it'll stay just between us but I'm curios about why you want to know about Fiona?" Blan said and to which I just smiled as she said. "Now what do you fancy across the sofa...me...or beans on toast?"

DCI Netherbourne and I then met for a chat on the Monday morning of my first day on duty as a fulltime Detective Constable while exploring the CID offices on Stafford railway station footbridge.

"I see they've got a couple of bunk beds in the back room...oh and Amazon says thanks for the Emannual picture, she's got it over the bed." DCI Netherbourne said as he tapped his pipe.

"And while we're at it can I have a word, but off the record so to speak?" I said and revealed what Darna had said about Fiona Netherseal and Babs.

"Just as long as you're sure, it's not a case of putting two and two together to make five, though I've no reason to doubt Darna's word. Just be careful though, the personal files are in the desk drawer in my office. I just hope you find what you're looking for by the time I get back, after which it's back to business. There's a body down the morgue and from the initial reports, it's not as straightforward as it seems ...Carrick will fill you in." DCI Netherbourne replied.

I made good use of my head start and behind the locked door of the DCI's office, I not only perused Fiona's file and noted her personal details, but also Blan's file and made some notes about her personal background, just out of curiosity. Then after making a note to do some digging at Stafford archives, the Peter Gabriel song *Salisbury Hill* suddenly began to play in my mind. I returned the files to the drawer and ensured that no one saw me, leave the DCI's office. I could not though get the song *'Salisbury Hill'* out of my head, especially the words 'She's so popular' then once outside Charlie Golf Two Four, I realised that I didn't know where the Police Mortuary was. But I was lucky enough to spy a panda car cruising in to town and so I flagged it down and sweet-talked the tall and slender WPC in to giving me a lift to the morgue.

"Are you one of the new CID boys at Charlie Golf Two Four or Dusty Bin, as they call it?" The WPC said all smiles, as though trying to over impress.

"And how is Charlie Golf One aka Stafford

Central...not as forlorn as Dusty Bin I bet? But at least it keeps the top brass away and lets us get on with the job... like *New Tricks*" I laugh. "Anyway my name's Frisco...DC Frisco Kane."

"Well I'm WPC Diane Parker or Dixie to my mates."

"Can I ask...your haircut one hundred? Are you an ex Hersham Boy ...you know Ska Skirt?" I said.

Dixie laughed "Don't tell me, you're a Mocker? Only a Mocker would call me Ska Skirt or a Hersham Boy."

I smiled as Dixie then said. "Well, street blade it's good to meet you, you and me will have to do a T. Rex sometime. You know *I Love to Boogie*?"

I smiled cheekily and said. "That's a date. It might be fun, you and me on the dance floor, interacting to the Judge...and the Leader of course!"

Then after being dropped off at Stafford General, I pushed open the morgue doors to a familiar voice. "And what time do you call this?" Blan said.

"Sorry I'm late, only I had a meeting with the DCI and a bit of business after that...but I'm here now that's the main thing, so who's Kent Reeks then?" I replied, as I looked at the body, the clothes and a photograph of the deceased taken at the scene, while Blan looked at me as though I was talking gibberish.

"Was there any photos found on the body? Preferably showing the deceased in the company of a couple, dolly birds and two fancy dans?" I asked a perplexed Blan who handed me a couple of photographs.

"Just as I thought...some one's having us on?" I said.

CHAPTER 22

PARALLEL LINES

Narrated by Frisco Kane

"Call yourself a copper...you don't know much about local police history do you?" I teased Blan who was still puzzled at what I was going on about, as I related the story of Kent Reeks.

"Tuesday 20th January 1914. Kent Reeks a twenty four year old Australian was found shot dead in a narrow trench by a large mineshaft in Ettingshall Road Wolverhampton. He'd been shot twice in the forehead and once in the left eye and was identified by a letter on him from an Aunt in Manchester, who told Staffordshire Police that Kent Reeks was a wealthy traveller. He was last seen in Liverpool on Monday 19th January, in the company of two women and two mysterious and fancy dressed gentlemen. The only thing missing was a large amount of American Dollars but other than that he wasn't robbed, as he was still wearing a gold fob watch on a silver chain and had nine pound odd in notes and loose change on him. And that my dear Inspector was ninety three years ago, with his murder remaining unsolved."

"Well his murderer will be well and truly dead by now!" Blan exclaimed.

"While Reeks ghost is said to haunt Wolverhampton's Princess Square" I said.

"What are you trying to say? That we hold a séance?" Blan asked.

"What and have you go all hot, wet and steamy?" I said cheekily.

"Behave!" Blan snapped while trying not to blush.

"Okay, Okay. But our victim has been made to look like Kent Reeks, the same blue serge suit, naval style topcoat, bowler hat etc, all made to look very fancy and expensive. I take it our modern day victim has a name?" I asked with a wry smile.

"Lazarus Crispin would you believe?" Blan replied. "He was a twenty eight year old undertaker and embalmer from Manchester, according to a business card in his wallet. He had thirty pounds in his wallet and forty-two pence in pocket and a fob watch on a chain that had stopped at ten to three. I've already been in touch with Manchester with regard to any family for Crispin, who was found by a man walking his dog earlier this morning, under the canal bridge by the Doxey Arms on the corner of Doxey Road and Castle Street."

"The pictures were taken in Blackpool. I recognise the club in the back of the snapshot. It's the Black Pearl. It has as a sign of a native South Seas Island female, wearing a garland and a pink fushia in her hair and kneeling in a Clam shell. It's a very expensive and gentlemen's only lap dancing, cabaret club." I said, as I cheekily looked at Blan, who hit me with her shoulder bag.

"I love it when you're angry" I teased. "But more to the point, has a toxicology report been done on the victim?"

"Toxicology report to do what? Determine if it was lead poisoning? He was shot, there's a bloody great bullet hole in the middle of his forehead!" Blan shouted.

"And a faint whiff of Almonds, if I'm not mistaken" I said.

"You mean Cyanide?" Blan said leaning close to the corpse. "But I can't smell, hold on I've just caught a very faint whiff of something. You may be right...but why poison the corpse and shoot him?"

"Belt and braces, do a Neville Cream then finish off with a Blind Beggar" I said. "Now do you fancy a drink, the Doxey Arms should be open by now...and if it's not it soon will be."

"But I've got Fiona and Carrick doing house calls...let's wait and see what they turn up first and in the meantime you can join them?" Blan said.

"Well a second sweep of the broom won't hurt." I said.

"Now I've got a couple of jobs I've got to do...but first I'll give Blackpool a bell and ask them to check out the Black Pearl?" Blan said.

It's always dicey to leave me to my own devices, as I never stick to the game plan and so after arranging for Carrick to cover for me and meet him later. I made my way to Stafford archives and where after having a quiet word with the archivist,

I was able to go trawl the English and Welsh birth, marriage and death records from July 1837 through to December 2005 that were on microfiche and the Internet.

My police credentials also let me stay over when the archives closed for dinner, as I examined a sheet of paper that held Jubilee Christian's personal details: born 12th May 1979, parents Frank and Terri Christian nee Porter with Jubilee's father's date of birth being 10th September 1951. I found Frank Christian's birth in the July/Sept quarter of 1951 with the mother's maiden name being Grocutt and Frank being born in Walsall. Fiona Netherseal born 28th April 1972, parents John and Mary Netherseal nee Christian, I now began to see a possible connection and so I looked up the January/March quarter of 1949 for the birth of Mary Christian who according to Fiona was born on the 22nd

January. I could not believe it, when I read that Mary Christian was born in Walsall with her mother's maiden name being Grocutt and exactly the same details as Frank Christian. I also decided to check out Jubilee's birth for the period April/ June 1979 and found a stunning surprise. Jubilee Christian had a twin sister Charmaine Christian, so I began to wonder if they were identical twins. While their first cousin, if not kissing cousin was DS Fiona Netherseal and now all I had to find was Jubilee's grandparent's marriage and think about my next move. But first I checked the deaths for Charmaine Christian from 1979 to 2005 and found no trace, so I took it that she was still alive, up to then end of 2005. I also did not find any deaths for a Frank and Terri Christian that would fit their birth dates and this left me with a choice of which name to check Christian or Grocutt, when it came to trawling the marriage records. Either way they were not overly common names and so I went with Christian, starting with Jan/Mar 1949 and then Oct/Dec 1948 and so on, until I finally found what I was looking for in April/June 1946 when a Frank Christian married a Jean Grocutt in Walsall.

I was more than happy at this finding, but I needed confirmation that Frank and Jean were the parents of Frank and Mary and for which I would the need the help of DCI Netherbourne, who I phoned to ask for a meet and who told me that Blan was in the office.

I then made my way through the backstreets and across Victoria Park to avoid being, readily seen before arriving at DCI Netherbourne's office and where Blan was still present when I entered the room. I was hesitant at first about speaking in front of Blan and so I showed the DCI what I had found.

"So you see I need you to get the okay for Walsall to confirm the details." I said and to which Blan looked puzzled at what was going on.

"I thought I told you to team up with Carrick and Fiona?" Blan asked me.

"Detective Frisco here is working on a dual investigation and is the only person, other than myself that is party to the information you are about to hear. So we are putting you on trust." DCI Netherbourne calmly said.

"Fiona Netherseal and Jubilee Christian are cousins. Jubilee is also a twin with her sister being Charmaine Christian and who was still alive until 2005 with Fiona's mum and Jubilee's dad being brother and sister." I said.

"You're investigating Fiona...why?" Blan said to me as the DCI was already on the telephone to Walsall Register Office.

"Accessory to murder if not murder itself" I sharply replied.

"Murder...but I don't understand?" Blan said while shifting her look between DCI Netherbourne and myself.

"Right, Walsall register office is expecting you at three oclock this afternoon ...so don't be late, DI McJones will drive you there." DCI Netherbourne said after hanging up the telephone receiver.

"The problem now is that our Jubilee Christian was cremated and so we can't do an exhumation order to check the body, not that would help much if they're identical twins...but why weren't her parents at her funeral?" I said.

"More to the point, it means that Jubilee Christian could well be alive and be wrongly accused of robbery and murder." DCI Netherbourne replied.

"Jubilee could also be dead...but we've not yet found her body." I said.

"Well, as of now we don't know who exactly died at

your wedding...Jubilee or Charmaine?" DCI
Netherbourne replied.

But I still don't understand?" Blan said loudly

"Listen I will explain everything, once we're in the
car" I replied

CHAPTER 23

THE HEAT IS ON

Narrated by Frisco Kane

"It's just after two oclock now and Walsall is about forty five minutes drive... so we've got about fifteen minutes to play with." I said looking at my watch.

"So what exactly is this game that you and DCI Netherbourne are playing?" Blan demanded, as she began to drive to Walsall.

"Call it Cluedo." I said as though not initially giving anything away

"Cluedo...listen I've just about had enough of this Sherlock Holmes, cloak and dagger nonsense so will you please tell me what the hell is going on or you can walk to bloody Walsall." Blan shouted as she banged her hands on the steering wheel in frustration.

"Okay, Okay, just calm down. What I'm about to tell you is slightly offbeat in terms of relationships, after which you'll hopefully understand things better." I said as I explained as best as I could about my relationship with Jesty and our connection with French Angel, Norma Jean, Babs and about Jubilee Christian.

Blan thought this tri-sexual set of affairs was bizarre, as she was not interested in having an affair with another woman, but she realised that Jesty and I must have been in love, to go along with such a marriage.

"So where exactly does Fiona fit in?" Blan asked.

"According to a very reliable source and only known to the DCI and myself... Fiona is a player on the girlie scene and who was attracted to Bab's who disappeared before Jesty's funeral...and Fiona is Jubilee

Christian's cousin." I replied.

"But you only met Fiona on the morning of your wedding, so how could she be involved. Though after you left she did disappear for a short while?" Blan said.

"Probably to phone the fake Jubilee who I'm beginning to think was Charmaine Christian, who had already set up a real jack in the box dyke. Bathsheba Mendalove who hates me with a passion, but don't ask me why. To act as the patsy in Jesty's murder." I replied.

"I take it this very reliable source is female and a player, to have such intimate knowledge. Is this source connected to Bathsheba Mendalove?" Blan said without realising that her curiosity was overstepping the mark.

I suddenly stared hard at Blan and growled. "That's a bridge too far."

"Excuse me, but I am the Detective Inspector around here!" Blan shouted.

"Not on this job darling! You're playing second fiddle to me and the DCI, as more than just your life may depend on it?" I snapped back.

My broadside chilled Blan, she had got herself caught up in something that could easily bury her, while I apologised for snapping and said I would make it up to her, once this off the record trip was safely out of the way. Then at Walsall register office, Blan and I saw that the parental details on Frank and Mary Christian's births matched the marital details of Frank Christian and Jean Grocutt. I also asked if they could check for any deaths for a Charmaine, Frank or Terri Christian in Walsall since January 2006 to date, but nothing surfaced, as I copied down the details in an unofficial notebook.

"Governor its Frisco, it checks. Jubilee and Fiona are first cousins and Blan just told me that on the day

Jesty was murdered, Fiona disappeared after she ran in to me and Carrick." I said as I telephoned the DCI. "Listen do you mind if I contact, you know, yes Blan's been warned. Okay I'll speak to you later."

"Do I get to meet...you know?" Blan said as I ended my phone call to the DCI.

"Well as luck would have it, no. But they've requested a meet for later tonight when you're safely tucked up, out of harm's way." I said jocularly

"Don't be so bloody patronising!" Blan retorted.

"Listen I've already lost one love of my life!" I snapped.

"Frisco Kane what are you saying?" Blan said while sounding surprised.

"Long term engagement, with no strings attached." I said brusquely

"Okay. But I want this mess cleaned up, before you put a ring on my finger." Blan said with a blushing smile.

"I wouldn't have it any other way!" I said in a brusque fashion. "Complete hush, hush... now let's go and have a drink at the Doxey Arms."

"Not before you give me a French kiss." Blan said, as I saucily caressed her.

Then as Blan geared herself up, to being called DI Kane, the tune the 'Runaway Rocking Horse began playing in my mind, during the long drive back to Stafford and where Blan parked the car at the flat. We then walked to the Doxey Arms, as it gave me the chance to check out the scene where Crispen's body was found, an unkempt grassy area by a murky river and a dirty grey concrete bridge. The underneath stank of piss and damp, as for the area, right on a main road with run of the mill terraced backstreet houses and a pub.

"Right this is Castle Street and Doxey Road, just up

the street is a student pub, the Railway Castle. This here's the Doxey Arms and known to accommodate the odd tom. "Blan said, as she pushed open the pub door and was greeted by that smell of fag ash, stale beer and commercial bleach, to disinfect the pub.

I had already telephoned Carrick to meet me at the pub, so as soon as Blan and I walked through the door, Carrick joined me at the bar, while Blan joined Fiona at a pub table.

"Well you're a dark horse...where have you been all day?" Carrick asked.

"Don't ask. But listen do they do rooms here?" I asked

"I think so, I don't really know, but you won't get much out of the landlord, he's dry as a stone. Didn't see nothing, don't know nothing." Carrick said.

I smiled and threw my badge on the counter, as I called the landlord over and who was a small tubby guy with dark greasy hair. He wanted to know why I wanted to see his guest register, when he saw my badge. A customer then needed serving at the other end of the bar and so Carrick and I studied the book without interruption and noticed fragments of rubber on the last used page, just as though something had been erased. I then used a small stub of pencil that went with the book, to shade over the rubbed out area and came up with 'Lazarus Crispin, two nights with breakfast. No 3. Saturday and Sunday 10th and 11th February'

Carrick was already on step ahead and went behind the bar and took room key three off the rack with the landlord shouting that we needed a warrant. Carrick and I ran up the pub stairs, with the landlord racing after us and telling us to come down, though his cries were ignored, as Carrick opened the door to room three and where we found the personal effects of Lazarus Crispin.

The landlord huffing and puffing then entered the room and managed to shout that there was nothing here to concern us, as Blan and Fiona having heard the fuss then entered the room and just as Carrick pinned the landlord against a wall and said "Your nicked!"

"What the hell's going on?" Blan demanded.

"The personal effects of one Lazarus Crispin" I said. "Mr Know Nothing here has been holding all this stuff!"

"Okay let's get this lot bagged up and down the nick and him with it...and close this pub." Blan shouted, while pointing a finger at the landlord.

A quick inspection of the luggage found an invitation to a conference of funeral directors at the Prince of Wales Theatre, Cannock, Sunday 11th Feb and some fancy calling cards that advertised personal services around the country. It seemed that Crispin was a regular player while a leaflet entitled 'Cold Case Murder Mystery' had an advert for a web page, the Cold Case Theatrical Group that re-enacted cold case murders to see if the killer could be identified.

This Cold Case aspect Blan gave to Fiona to check out, just as though she was reading my mind, while Blan would check out the funeral conference. I then helped close the pub, gave the pub's barmaid, who moaned about losing her job, a hundred quid out of the till, as compensation. And serve up a round of free drinks from the bar, before exploring the rest of the pub and where I gave Blan a passionate surprise when we found ourselves alone in an empty bedroom.

Then back at Charlie Golf Two Four, Carrick and I were allowed to question the landlord, while Fiona searched the 'Cold Case' website

"In fact it was Frisco acting on a hunch with Carrick's help that led to the discovery of the luggage." Blan said with quiet admiration, as she helped the DCI search through Lazarus Crispin's luggage.

"Frisco's a good copper, don't underestimate him" DCI Netherbourne replied as he champed on the stem of his pipe.

Meanwhile in the interview room, the landlord was nervously sweating, as he drank water from a plastic cup and explained that the room had been booked over the phone by a man, for two nights. Then just before closing time on Saturday night, a man calling himself Lazarus Crispin booked in and stayed in his room until it was time for breakfast the next morning. Then a strange lady who was smartly dressed, with a fur stole and a Pillbox hat with a veil then came to the pub after breakfast. Lazarus Crispin it seemed was expecting her and they drove off together in a vintage open top car with two men in the back, also smartly dressed but very old fashioned and the last that the landlord saw of Lazarus Crispin.

The landlord did not want to get involved and was going to dump the clothes, as the room had been paid for up front. While in return, the landlord was given a caution with a warning that his pub licence was under review. Fiona meanwhile had come up with a P.O. Box for a Blackpool theatre group with a national membership, while also ringing Blackpool CID and asking them to check out the group and a list of members in the Midlands area. But in the meantime, I still had a date with Darna Gold and for which I invited Carrick to come along as well.

CHAPTER 24

THE NIGHT HAS A THOUSAND EYES

Narrated by Frisco Kane

Railway Street was a terrace of red engineering brick houses that faced the steel chain link fencing and tracks of Stafford railway station, Carrick and I found a warm welcome at the Stafford Arms. That was a black coaching inn with a white moulded Staffordshire Knot and below which are the red letters of 'Titanic' in reference to the original brewery that owned the pub. The pub's interior was a long black and cream bar with red barley twist pillars that arose from a black and white chequered floor. The only decoration was a large framed sketch of the crazy cartoon from the album cover *'Rock n Roll High School.'*

The pub's range of real ales like Soxdale Brindley, Spartan Fricker and Winkle Webster that were three 18th century, champion racehorses, give the place character, according to the barman who served Carrick and me with four bottles of *'Leffe'*, a sweet, golden, Belgium beer that was on the house.

The pub was having a quiet night, as Carrick and I played darts and the jukebox with the Monotones singing *'You can't sit down'* when in trundled a young woman and wearing just jeans and a cardigan over a tank top that exposed a large pregnant belly. The barman was just about to lock the doors, but looked at Carrick and me as the woman ordered a half a lager and blackcurrant and lit a cigarette and to which I shook my head and said. "Make that an orange juice, then get off home and get yourself dressed…you look disgusting."

Carrick then took the young woman by the arm and ushered her out the door, while she swore and yelled, as he bolted the doors and used the keys that the barman threw at him, to lock the doors, before throwing the keys back.

"Thanks for that lads." Darna said, as she came from behind the bar, her black hair now sporting petrol blue streaks and a ponytail.

"So this is your pub?" I asked enquiringly.

"And what's with the Chastity Dingle look?" Carrick added

Darna laughed as she poured herself a drink and said. "I've still got the Black Board Jungle, only this was going for a song and Stafford's hasn't got a beatnik pub. I'm keeping the old pub sign and I've started turning the coaching area in to a beer garden for music and dance…with a retractable glass top roof."

"What about the smoking ban?" Carrick asked.

"That's what the retractable glass roof is for and the big coaching doors…if you get my drift?" Darna said with a smirk.

"So what's this news that you think I might be interested in?" I asked

"Bathsheba's on her way back!" Darna said in a soft tone.

The sound of Bathsheba's name made me seethe and glare with rage and which made Darna nervous, as she poured Carrick and me another drink and said. "She's teamed up with a band, called Sexual Alchemy. They're booked to play the London underground club scene…and there's something else I think you should also know… Jubilee Christian has risen from the dead!"

"You what" I snapped.

"I've seen her. She's working at the Blueberry Spearmint at London Bridge, its run by the same management as the Mascara in Bank Passage and the

166

Eye Candy in Birmingham, but you'd best let Jubilee tell you the rest." Darna replied hesitantly.

"So I was right then that was Charmaine Christian." I said with a triumphant smile "Well London here we come, but first, you and me Carrick, will pay a visit to the Mascara, tonight and see if we can't gleam some information beforehand."

I apologised to Darna for being snappy, before Carrick and I walked in to town and saw the young woman talking to another female who I recognised as WPC Dixie Parker. Then as we passed the two females, standing on the bridge on Station Road, I asked Dixie for a cigarette and a light. Then when Dixie saw it was me, she smiled and as she gave me a light, I whispered "Are you up for a job...you know a caper?"

Dixie gently nodded as I whispered. "I'll call you tomorrow."

"You wouldn't go far wrong there." I said as I nodded towards WPC Parker as Carrick and I continued on our way.

"What that boot girl?" Carrick said.

"Dixie may look like a boot n braces, but she's a good copper underneath... mark my words." I replied tapping the side of my nose.

"What she's a copper?" Carrick laughed.

"Street blade recognises street blade." I said. "I met her earlier on and if I'm to go muckraking down the smoke, a bit of female bovver wouldn't go amiss"

"You naughty old policeman...what if Blan finds out?" Carrick asked.

"You know the rules...discretion is the better part of valour." I replied.

Then as we crossed over a road junction and in to a dark passage that separated the Crown Court from Stafford College, the sound of running feet coming up behind us, made Carrick and me disappear into the buildings large shadows. Then silently watching from within the shadows, Carrick and I see Dixie stop to catch her breath and look around for where we had got too. Then as we stepped out of the shadows I said. "Carrick meet WPC Diane Dixie Parker."

"Pleased to meet you" Carrick and Dixie said together as they shook hands.

"So what you lads up too?" Dixie said with a cute smile.

"Night Owls on the prowl...we thought we'd see what Stafford is like after dark. Like this Mascara night club?" Carrick said.

"It's closed on Mondays. But we can walk up to the square and down to where the girls hang out on the traffic island." Dixie said as she led the way.

There were very few souls about, while Carrick's and my eyes darted about, as we and Dixie walked down the dimly lit passage that led from the Bird in Hand pub, past the dark and looming St Mary's church, through the ghostly gateway and down the narrow passage towards Stafford High Street. The bright street lights made it a more comfortable atmosphere, while the sound of *'Ghost Town'* from The Bear pub that stood in the middle of the darkened rows of shops, broke the quiet of the night.

The three of us talked and sang the chorus to *'Lily the Pink'*, as we walked along the High Street towards the traffic island. Carrick and I began to get a lay and feel of the place, as we explored the Island's pathways and eyed up the Vixens.

"Hello Frisco, do you remember me...I just got out this morning." A girl said.

I stopped and took a hard look at the girl speaking and said. "Are you one of the Raby Street regulars? So what you doing operating in Stafford, escape from the clap clinic?"

"Cheeky sod, I ain't been in no, clap clinic. I've just done six weeks for non- payment of fines and now I need some money…if you know what I mean?" The girl said and who in the streetlight was podgy, with a freckled face and her hair scraped back in to a working class facelift.

"Viscous circle isn't it. Back on the batter instead of going clean and getting a job…it's hard I know but it's the only way forward!" Carrick said.

"I've tried for various jobs." The girl said.

"Then try harder, like the Kennel Club." I said, as the girl walked off, swearing.

"Ouch that hurt" Dixie said.

"Street trade is street trade…the world over." Carrick laughed

The three of us then made our way back along the high street, to the shadowy alley at the side of McDonalds. Carrick then went on ahead, as he was ready for his bed, while at the ghostly gateway, I grabbed Dixie and pulled her in to the darkness. Dixie and I kissed as I explained about the job. "It would mean spending a night or two down in London, to catch a female cop killer. I need someone who can blend in at an all girls club and handle herself…without raising too much suspicion."

"What you mean role play?" Dixie asked with some alarm.

"Don't worry…you'll be okay." I said only to be pushed away as I got frisky.

"Listen Alfie, oh I know all about your reputation. I've done my home work." Dixie said with a smile. "If we're going to get it together, even for a one night stand then I don't want, just a midnight knee trembler in the shadows of St Mary's. I want a hotel room when we go down to London…nothing fancy just discreet."

"You fancy yourself then do you?" I said.

"Where little boys like you are concerned...oh yes" Dixie said as she licked her lips with her tongue and engaged me in a saucy French kiss.

I thought I could see shadows, darting from behind gravestones in St Mary's Churchyard, just as though Dixie and I were being watched, as we walked towards the streetlights of Victoria Park. Dixie and I then shared a goodnight kiss, before she walked to her cramped digs in a small row of seaside, style cottages, on the corner of Railway Street and Castle Street. While I made my way to Victoria Park and where, as I entered my flat, I heard Blan shout. "And what time do you call this?"

"Oh don't start" I mused and looked at the clock and my watch and said "It's One oclock or there abouts and I'm going to bed. I need to see DCI Netherbourne in the morning, as I've got to go away for a day or two."

"Away? Where too" Blan demanded.

"Where all the away's go, down the smoke, where else." I wearily said, as I got undressed and climbed in to bed.

"When" Blan persisted, while locking up and turning out the lights

"Tomorrow, the weekend at the latest, it all depends." I wearily replied.

"Depends on what?" Blan said only to be greeted by a sleepy silence, I heard what she said, but I was too tired answer twenty questions.

CHAPTER 25

CHELSEA DAGGER

Narrated by Frisco Kane

Blan greeted me with a stony silence after I awoke, I was in the doghouse but this didn't bother me, as after a breakfast coffee I made my way to the station and an impromptu meeting with DCI Netherbourne.

"What it means is I need to go down to London, to try and nab Bathsheba. But most of all, bring Jubilee back in to the fold and officially amend the records, so that Jubilee no longer has a criminal record, now that we know that it was her sister Charmaine who so troublesomely, masqueraded as her and while I'm away, it would help if Fiona could be confined to barracks."

"That can be arranged...and get a list of tour dates and places for this band Sexual Alchemy. In the meantime I want you and Carrick to get acquainted with the local Saraband and their mopsies and check out Stafford's licensed foxholes." DCI Netherbourne said while sucking on his pipe as he reclined in his chair.

"There's one other thing. I get the impression that Darna also wants to go to London, as the key to accessing the clubs." I said in a quiet voice.

"Just be bloody careful...if she wants to go along then I want a chaperone!" DCI Netherbourne snapped as he sat up and pointed his pipe stem at me.

"I've the very person in mind and she's up for the job." I said a hushed tone.

"And who's this piece of hot fuzz?" DCI Netherbourne laughed.

"WPC Diane Parker from Charlie Golf One, she's not so much sapphires and sables as Blan…but she'd make a good replacement for Fiona." I said

DCI Netherbourne telephoned Stafford Central to arrange for WPC Parker's secondment for the London job, while I ran in to Carrick and asked him to meet me in an hour at The Slammer pub that stood, just opposite Stafford Gaol. The time was now 10.30.a.m. Dixie was on the day shift of 10.a.m. to 6.p.m. as I telephoned Darna and asked for a meet and find out the playing schedule for Sexual Alchemy. I then called up Dixie and asked her to make her way over to the Stafford Arms, where the coach house doors were opened to park her panda car, out of sight in the courtyard.

"I'm sorry for all the mystery." I said as I introduced Darna to Dixie. "But the capper is strictly OTT, as one of the targets is a close to home, female cop."

Darna then showed Dixie and me the Internet web page print off that showed that Sexual Alchemy was not due back in England until the start of April, with their first date being at the Catwalk Chemistry at Tower Bridge. That was the catchment date and preferably on the night so we could steal away in to the dark. Meanwhile as we chatted, Darna asked Dixie if she had ever been friendly with a girl before.

"No…Never. I'm not that way inclined." Dixie said hesitantly.

"Then we'll keep it simple like holding hands, but we may have to kiss and its best if we practice, as I'm not getting frisky in some train toilet...I take it we're going down by train?" Darna said as she embraced Dixie

"We'll travel to Brum and catch the Marylebone train from Moor Street." I said, as I saw the look of horror on Dixie's face, when Darna gave her a passionate French kiss. Then when Darna finally allowed Dixie to come up for air, she made a beeline for the ladies toilet, as though she was about to be sick.

"Don't worry." Darna smilingly laughed. "She'll be fine...most are sick the first time. I was...whether I could bed her though, is another matter."

"In your dreams" I laughed. "She's already on a promise. So you can forget any ideas about strip jack naked...I'm the dealer in that game."

"We could always make it a threesome?" Darna said stroking my hand.

"I don't think so. Your way too close to home, you can flirt as much as you like...I'll play the game. But that's about it." I replied with a wink and a smile.

Dixie then came out of the toilet and apologised for suddenly dashing away, to which Darna told her to think nothing of it. Then after checking that the coast was clear, I guided Dixie's panda car out of the courtyard and returned to Charlie Golf Two. I found Blan sitting at her desk, with my shadow in the doorway making her look up and sharply say. "I'm busy...I'll talk to you later."

I though, was not put off by her dismissive attitude and closed the door behind him and dropped the deadlock.

"I told you I'm busy...now unlock the door." Blan said in a brisk manner, as

I took the papers from her hands, leaned in to her face and gave her a big kiss. Blan pushed me away, only to have me whisper. "When you finish tonight and no later than six oclock, get on your glad rags, as I'm taking you dancing that's a promise. Now, as we're alone and behind closed doors ...I just want to say I'm sorry!"

Blan then flashed her big eyes and softly said.

"You're taking me dancing alright Tiger...but first I want my pound of flesh!"

The impromptu tryst made me late in meeting Carrick, so I flagged down a panda car and hitched a ride to The Slammer that had grey stone cladding that made it look like a funfair, ghost train castle and decorated in raving loony style tribute to Screaming Lord Sutch and the twangy guitar era. The licensee was a retired prison officer named Jockey, while the pub was where the licensed girls had a drink most afternoons, so while we waited for the girls, Jockey told Carrick and me about how things had changed in the prison service.

"I feel sorry for the cons now." Jockey laughed. "No more heated hand rails or colour TV's, since the new basic but humane ruling. Visitor partitions, tobacco tubs, guarded lights to stop the wing barons, hard labour and basic staple when in solitary and corporal punishment for causing disruption. Alcatraz style Cat A. gaols or the seven gates of hell like the titan on the Isle of Wight, a fortress prison built on the same lines as the real Alcatraz with each wing named like Ketchams Corner, Birdcage Walk and Newgate Alley. The D Blocks housing condemned prisoners, as they wait to take the walk of shame to the long drop!"

Jockey's then put some music on the jukebox...*Wild Wind* and *Johnny Remember Me* and *Jack the Ripper*. The girls then arrived, all smartly dressed with not too much war paint and a minder, a big and balding man in a tight suit and who according to Jockey was Billy Bull, the girls paid him a retainer to maintain security at Stafford's only three licensed brothels: The Mascara, Just for Chicks, a red and white pub on the corner of Eastgate Street and Can, Can 62, a small yellow and blue café bar in Martin Street.

"There you are ladies." Billy Bull said as he opened the pub door. "Perhaps the two gentlemen would like some company?"

Carrick and I had to smile at the last remark, as Carrick and I flashed our detective badges and replied. "We are the company!"

Billy Bull gulped and one girl asked if it was a raid and which made Carrick laugh and reassure them it was not. Carrick and I introduced our-selves as the new primary vice cops on the block, while the girls babbled a bunch of names like Trudy, Lolita and Kelly, as they shook hands. Billy Bull meanwhile stepped back as though to leave the party, but I called him back and over a drink, got him to explain his role with regard to the girls.

Carrick and I stated that we would not interfere with the licensed security arrangements, unless we had good cause. Then when Carrick went to the toilet, Billy Bull gave me an envelope asked if I would pass on to the lady cop in the trench coat, it was the Legal Fee for if the girls got in to trouble. I was immediately intrigued by this unexpected break and pressed Billy Bull who described the female cop as being tall and slender and who called herself Fiona. I was in two minds, as what to do next and so I rang DCI Netherbourne to attend The Slammer public house on Gaol Rd. I then told Billy Bull that I wanted him to meet another gentleman who would be very interested in what he had to say about the Legal Fee. Then when Carrick returned, I told him that DCI Netherbourne was on his way as he wanted to meet Billy Bull, but while we were waiting we should better acquainted with the girls.

DCI Netherbourne made an impressive entrance as he pushed the pub-doors open and stood with his trench coat undone and his pipe in his mouth and then seeing all the girls, he laughed "Are you pair running an unlicensed brothel?"

Carrick went to the bar, while I quickly told DCI Netherbourne that I had not said anything to him, but he should have a quiet word with Billy Bull. The DCI then thanked Carrick for the double malt, before moving to a table on the far side of the room. Billy Bull showed the DCI a notebook with fortnightly, dates and amounts with regard to the Legal Fee that included a free pass, to engage with a girl of her choice at any one of Stafford's three, licensed foxholes.

DCI Netherbourne mulled over telling Carrick, although he could be trusted, if Fiona got wind of him acting suspiciously around her, she might smell a rat. Then if Billy Bull told Fiona of this conversation, the game would be up, so until Monday morning, DCI Netherbourne ordered Billy to do himself a favour and take a sudden holiday. Billy asked his cousin Raymond Bull to take over the clubs security at short notice while DCI Netherbourne, like most of us had no real qualms about the free passes. It was the money aspect that wrangled, as it could readily lead to corruption, especially from the Saraband and the rag trade, while the temptation was great to tell Blan about Billy Bull and his monetary affair with Fiona. Carrick on the other hand was intimate with Fiona, so for him to keep the meeting with Billy Bull a secret would be even harder, so DCI Netherbourne decided to send him instead of Fiona to Charlie Foxtrot at Wombourne, this way all bases would be covered and Fiona could be kept on close restraint without realising it.

CHAPTER 26

JIVE BUNNY

Narrated by Frisco Kane

got back to the flat before Blan and was therefore able to relax and play *'True Grit'*, a CD of classic music from John Wayne movies and watch the John Wayne Western of *'Stagecoach'*. I also thought about the rumour that I had deliberately let slip to the licensed girls that Carrick and I where the shield part of a new tricks, strike force. I knew the rumour would filter back to the street, thus tempting Stafford's Saraband to come out to play and therefore allow names to be put to shadowy faces.

Blan arrived home later than she expected and so she took over the bathroom and bedroom and from which she emerged looking the business in a black midi dress with a fake leather and fur jacket. The Mascara did not open its doors until around 8.p.m. and it would be pretty warm inside, so we went for a drink at Teddy Edward's where we played pool and I explained to Big John that I was doing some begging your pardon, to which he laughed and said. "Welcome to the doghouse."

Then as Blan leaned over the pool table to play a shot, I could not resist the temptation and signalled to Big John to watch this, at which I patted Blan's backside and said. "All behind...like a cows tail!"

"Oi behave...you cheeky sod!" Blan rebuffed with a cheeky smile.

It was only a short walk from Big John's to The Mascara that was a carved stone building with arched windows and a glass doorway that led to a illuminated gold and silver foyer, with a chandelier that seemed to sparkle and shimmer. We passed through a smoked glass door, into a subtly light, mauve lounge with neon lights like a fish tank. The Mascara was holding a 'Retro' night and when Blan walked in to the lounge, the DJ played *'The Girl can't help it'*, to which I sang along too, as I danced and joked with Blan "They're playing your song!"

Blan and I danced to a comic pop and rock mix: *'Wake me up, before you go, go. Stars on 45, Baby Elephant Walk. A Kick up the 80's and Jive Bunny.'* Before we took a break at the bar where the wide screen television was screening the Madonna movie *'Desperately Seeking Susan'* as a single white female introduced herself' with a line from the film. "Hi I'm Trudy the manager of the Mascara…did you know that one in five prostitutes are lesbians!"

Trudy Godsend as she called herself was in her late twenties, slim build and wore a dark trouser suit with long, black hair that curled under. I remembered Trudy from The Slammer and prayed that she did not mention Billy Bull, with my prayers being answered in a strange way. Blan it seemed had attracted the lusty attention of the manager and another female who had short dark hair and a sharp nose on which sat a pair of penny round glasses and who stood across the room and raised her glass whenever Blan looked over.

"It looks like you've scored." I whispered with a laugh.

"What do you mean? Scored?" Blan asked

"Well this is chiefly a girl's only club that caters for posh toms and bisexuals and you have caught the eye of the Uma Therman style manager and the Sue Perkins look alike over there…and she is sexily stunning." I said, while sexily envisaging the girl who was giving Blan the eye, standing with her hands on her hips and wearing nothing but a shirt that showed off her slim figure, especially her long legs.

"Behave!" Blan rebuked me with a playful slap to my arm.

"Go on ask the one across the room for a dance, I bet you end up snogging her!" I said, knowing that I was pushing his luck with the dare.

"On your bike, sunshine, I'm not kissing another female. You'll have me in bed with her next." Blan said, as she kept eye contact with her admirer, who then put down her glass and walked over.

"Not on your first date, no, here look out she's coming over." I said.

"Would you like to dance?" Blan's admirer said.

"Of course she would." I replied with a smile and gave Blan a gentle push.

Blan danced with her admirer and gave a laughing me, a savage look. The music changed to *'Little Town Flirt'*, as I went to the bar, but on my return Blan was not on the dance, floor. Blan's admirer, Trixie had invited her to join her for a drink at her table that was situated just out of sight of the dance floor by a partition wall. But instead of sitting down and chatting, Trixie caught Blan off guard with a surprise kiss that Blan did not parry or make her feel sick. The amorous attraction instead just made Blan feel awkward and want to wipe her tongue and spit.

Trixie then surprised Blan even more when she said "Would your boyfriend like to join us? It's alright I do swing both ways."

"I'm sure he would." Blan said and stepped back on to the dance floor and beckoned to me to join her and when I walked towards, where she had disappeared around the partition wall, I found her and Trixie enjoying a kiss and to which I said surprisingly. "I never knew you had it in you?"

"She's all yours. I've got to go to the ladies." Blan said with a wink, as she disengaged herself from Trixie and walked off.

I then shared a kiss with Trixie and kept imaging her in just a shirt, as I took her outside, while knowing this would really wind Blan up, especially if she asked Trudy, the manager to spill the beans. Then as expected Blan grabbed her coat and stormed outside, to where I burst out laughing when she appeared, all guns blazing and giving me a venomous look. I told Trixie that it would best if she went back inside, before saying to Blan with a gentle laugh. "Ever been had?"

"You rat" Blan softly said with a smile, before throwing her arms around me for an amorous embrace.

A Police helmet then came, flying out of Bank Passage, as a Police Constable reeled under a reign of heavy blows from three youths, one of whom shouted. "Give that to your strike team!"

My ears pricked up and realised that Stafford's Saraband had sent a message. They would not fight themselves, but they would cause trouble, by using teenagers to do their dirty work. I immediately broke free from Blan's embrace and told her to call for assistance as I rushed over to where the assault was happening and yelled 'Police', as I grabbed one youth by his jacket collar and ordered the other two youths to stand still.

I then fumbled for my badge, while Blan who was on her mobile phone flashed her badge. The Mascara's two female bouncers helped restrain the collared youth, as Market Square became awash with blue flashing lights and sirens. One of the youths then scarpered while the other youth put his hands behind his head to be handcuffed. Uniform backup then arrested the two youths and an ambulance took the assaulted constable to hospital, as I joined the chase for the third youth, as this was the lad who had shouted the threat against the strike team. I phoned Carrick's mobile and asked him to quickly meet me by the aviary in Victoria Park, where the youth was last seen on the riverbank. I remembered that Big John had mentioned a police launch that was stored in a boat shed by the aviary, as Blan rang Big John who had a key to the boat shed and asked him to make his way to the park.

When we four, Police officers assembled in the park, Carrick and I were amazed to find that the Police launch turned out to be an RNLI style dinghy in orange with the words Staffs Police painted on the side. Then once the boat was in the water, Carrick and I climbed aboard and hastily donned lifejackets, as we pulled the ripcord on the motor and steered the boat as it bounced its way through the water and alarmed the wild birds that slept.

"Yahoo" I cried as we gave chase after the youth who had broken from his cover in the bushes and was running down the towpath, while Carrick did his best to steady the police radio, a searchlight and a torch and most of all, himself.

Meanwhile patrol crews, a dog handler and a Police helicopter with a search light joined the chase along the park's riverbank that was until the park and the River Sow divided at a weir. The youth hesitated with the decision to surrender or swim was made for him when he was caught by the swell of the boat, as it flipped when it hit the weir, with the youth, Carrick and me ending up in the water on the other side of the weir. Although it was dark and the water flowed fast, the boat had survived the water drop and was the right side up, as Carrick and I managed to cling on to the boat and struggle on board, soaking wet. The youth cried out for help, with the only light we had being the water logged police searchlight that flickered, as the Police radio and torch were at the bottom of the river. Carrick threw a rope that he found in the boat to where he saw the youth waving, as he bobbed about in the water. The youth grabbed the rope and was dragged in to the boat, as I managed to steer it towards the riverbank and where, as the three of us sat, sopping wet and shivering on the riverbank, I asked. "Anyone got a mobile phone?"

"I wouldn't mind a cup of tea and a fag." The youth said.

"I just wouldn't mind the tea...with a drop of scotch in it." Carrick replied.

"Well it's no good sitting here moaning, there should be a phone box around here, somewhere?" I said, as I hauled myself to my feet and gave Carrick and the youth a hand up.

Carrick kept hold of the youth while I made sure the boat was tied to a tree, after which Carrick handcuffed the youth, while saying. "Sorry about this...I'm just glad I managed to keep hold of these things."

We three wet and weary individuals made an interesting sight, as we trod the riverbank, squelching and dripping water at every footstep until we came across a couple of students who were having a smooch in a vandalised phone box. The light of which had been painted out, so I could not tell in the dark, if the students were a male and female courting couple or two long haired puffs, as one kept their face hidden while the other student let me use his mobile phone, once I had flashed my detective's badge. The three of us then waited by the telephone box, but not too close, as to disturb the tryst, before being picked up by a panda car with Carrick and I apologising to the Police driver for making a mess of the car, as it sped back to Charlie Golf One.

Then as the youth was being processed, Blan and Fiona embraced Carrick and me, while Big John said "Where's the boat?"

"Tied up on the riverbank somewhere...just make, sure that youth doesn't get bailed until I speak to him in the morning." I replied.

"Is there something I should know?" Blan said looking me in the eye.

"Let's just say Stafford Saraband have just declared war!" I replied.

CHAPTER 27

GOOD MORNING STARSHINE

Narrated by Frisco Kane

The river escapade left Carrick and me tired out, but not tired enough to stop us being wide-awake by six in the morning, when after a quick wash and brush up and a swig of fruit juice for breakfast. I left Blan fast asleep in bed and made my way downstairs to the car park where I found Carrick watching the sun come up.

"Are you wide awake as well? I asked and to which Carrick laughed as I then explained that I was on my way to Charlie Golf One for breakfast and interview the youth we apprehended last night.

Carrick looked puzzled, until I explained about the 'Strike Team' rumour and what I had heard the youth say when he punched the policeman. That was why I wanted first crack at the youth and asked Carrick to sit in on the interview, while our interview techniques where based on British Police training and US Police dramas like *NYPD Blue* and *Law & Order*.

"I want to talk about what I heard you say, when you assaulted the constable... give that to the strike team. So tell me who ordered the hit?" I said as I circled the nervous youth, while Carrick lolled in the corner of the old interview room that had no video camera, thus allowing me to jolt the youth's dumb silence with a sudden thump in the back.

"Hey you can't do that I know my rights! I want a lawyer. I want to evoke the fifth." The youth yowked

"Wrong answer kid, now shall we try again?" I said with a sharp slap.

"Listen kid, give yourself a break, unless you want

it spread that Johnny 'Elvis' Reggae sang sweeter than a gospel choir and have you seen with us, to show what good buddies we are." Carrick said while I nosed through the youth's wallet.

"I see you've a lot of cards from a place called the Backgammon Club, what is that an illicit gambling den? Don't tell me a brothel and you're the kid who breaks the girls in? How old are they thirteen, fourteen and you're what eighteen, nineteen? Or do you like older women with more experience like Lady Luck as it says on this card?" I prodded the youth.

"I know what let him take us to the Backgammon Club and he can introduce us to Lady Luck and show what good buddies we are?" Carrick added.

"But first let's get the doctor in here...just in case he's caught anything? We don't want any little viruses spreading around the prison population, have you been to the clap clinic lately? I hear they shove an umbrella up your scrotum and... well it's like being circumcised or was that castrated with a blunt knife?" I prodded the youth some more.

"Okay, okay you win...just let me keep my man hood intact!" The youth gulped and said

Then just as the youth was about to speak, the door burst open and in stormed DS Fiona Netherseal "What the hell is going on?" She shouted. "This is not your case, return him to his cell and I'll speak to you two later?"

Carrick and Fiona took the youth back to his cell as I slipped the two fancy looking business cards for the Backgammon and Lady Luck that had phone numbers on the back, in to my pocket. I then returned the wallet to the custody officer and asked him if the youth had made any phone calls since his arrest.

"No not that I can think of...though he was playing games on a mobile phone that he brought in with him."

The Custody Officer said.

'Or he text someone on a mobile that he'd deliberately hidden?' I replied

I remembered the youth looked relieved when he saw Fiona burst in to the room, while her sudden appearance made me wonder if Fiona was the person, the youth had texted. I though, had not made it a secret that I wanted to interview the youth, something I now realised was a tired mistake.

I then asked to see the youth's mobile phone and quickly jotted down on a scrap of paper the last numbers that had been texted, as Fiona and Carrick returned to the custody suite, just as I returned the mobile phone to the custody officer and slipped the scrap of paper in to my pocket. Fiona was pulling rank as our Detective Sgt and told Carrick and me to wait for her while she went to the ladies room after which she would escort us back to Charlie Golf Two, to explain our actions to DCI Netherbourne. I though, had no time for Fiona's games and once she was out of sight, Carrick and I hitched a lift in a panda, before explaining to DCI Netherbourne and before he could get his coat off, about the river ride, the interview and the false rumour, as the DCI chuckled about the rumour…as a sprat to catch a mackerel!

Then just as the meeting ended, Fiona marched in to the DCI's office and in a demanded that we should be reprimanded for conducting an illegal interview and ignoring her orders to be escorted back to base. DCI Netherbourne then raised an eyebrow, as he stole Fiona's thunder "For your information DS Netherseal, I granted DC Frisco's request to the interview the youth Johnny Elvis Reggae when he phoned me late last night. These two officers are not at liberty to disclose the reason for the interview and anything further, you will be told on a need to know basis."

Fiona was stunned by DCI Netherbourne's retort as Carrick and I then went off with DCI Netherbourne to the secondary offices at the railway station.

"Well you two have made a good start to your first week in Stafford. Not only have you uncovered a cold case re-enactment society that commits murder and we are still waiting on Blackpool to get back to us, on that one. But and this where I'm trusting, your honour Carrick, as what I am about to say may hit home hard. Frisco here has exposed DS Fiona Netherseal, as being a as a corrupt police officer and a suspect accomplice to the murder of Jesty Dollamore." DCI Netherbourne said after closing the office door and pulling up a chair.

I then showed the DCI the two business cards and the piece of paper that contained the last two numbers the youth had texted. DCI Netherbourne seemed to recognise one number and so he rang it, with the result being 'You have reached the voicemail for Fiona Netherseal, please leave a message after the tone.'

"So Fiona's playing three coins in the fountain" DCI Netherbourne said as he light his pipe, while his mobile phone suddenly rang and he asked Carrick to escort Darna up to the sparsely fitted police office at Stafford railway station.

"So this is where you hide, when you don't want to be seen?" Darna said as she looked around the room

"A real home from home…but what is so important to warrant this meeting you've requested and don't worry you can speak freely. Carrick's been fully briefed while we were waiting…even if he is sleeping with the enemy." DCI Netherbourne said, as I used the office kettle and made mugs of sweet black coffee, after gingerly smelling a bottle of milk.

"There's a change to the plans for London" Darna said. "Bathsheba will be in Birmingham with Sexual

Alchemy this Friday. It's an impromptu gig, they're flying in for a birthday bash at Eye Candy in Burlington Parade"

"What that tatty bar, stuffed full of ornate junk. Then again it's a perfect trap to catch a rat as its all downstairs with only one way out!" I said with a wry smile

"The same...only they held a charity clearance auction to get rid of all the junk and only needed a mini skip in the end...or so I'm told." Darna laughed.

"So the new game plan is this." DCI Netherbourne said while trying to get back to the point. "Frisco on Friday you will take WPC Parker and go to Brum and bring Bathsheba Mendalove back to Stafford."

"But I'd still like to speak to Jubilee Christian. So I'd like to go down to London tomorrow to the Blueberry Spearmint and take WPC Parker with me as back up." I said with an air of curiosity.

"Okay...but be careful and Carrick I want you to shadow chaperone Fiona. I don't want her getting wind of anything." DCI Netherbourne said with a sly grin.

"In the meantime what do you know about the Backgammon Club and Lady Luck?" I asked Darna

"The Backgammon Club" Darna laughed. "It's a computer game that allows you to run your own brothel, while Lady Luck is the madam who manages the girls. The aim of the game is to keep one step ahead of the law, the pimps and the jokers in the pack until you become the King Pin of Vice'"

"I'll kill that bloody kid!" I snorted as DCI Netherbourne made a phone call on his mobile to Charlie Golf One, before relating their answer.

"The youth put his hands up to the assault and was about to be ferried to the Magistrates with his two mates for a bail hearing but I've ordered him to be held for further questioning at Charlie Golf One and not allowed to use a telephone. Now all that coffee's gone through me, so I'll meet you two out front once you've cleaned up that is?"

Then after DCI Netherbourne had left the office, I briefly told Darna and Carrick about what happened at the Mascara and to which Darna laughed and said. "So you've met Trixie and Trudy. Trixie's a schoolteacher would you believe but Trudy is strictly for the ladies though I can set you up with Trixie if you wish?"

I gave that offer a miss, while Carrick kept his feelings mute about what he had learned about Fiona, as he and I left the train station ahead of Darna and joined DCI Netherbourne for a walk to Charlie Golf One

"Now sunshine, no more games with the Lady Luck and Backgammon cards. That's unless you'd like a dose of Stafford Law! So who ordered the hit against my strike team?" DCI Netherbourne snapped as he punched the youth in the back, as he sat in the old interview room, while Carrick and I rechecked the youth's wallet, just in case we had overlooked something at the first interview.

"What's Stafford Law?" The youth said nervously.

"Originally it was a sound beating with a stout staff!" I remarked as I banged the tabletop with my extendable baton.

"While you like to leave a paper trail like these fake business cards that you use to jot numbers and names on. Like Toffee and a Wolverhampton phone number written on one card and tucked away in your wallet?" Carrick said with a wry smile.

"I don't know what you're on about?" The youth cried while eyeing the baton, I kept gently hitting into the palm of my hand. "I dunno what you mean?" The youth then cried as I once again banged the baton on

189

the table.

"Toffee is the nickname for Ronald, Reginald Smith aka Everton Winston Smith, the white cousin of Little Winston one of Wolverhampton's main Saraband." DCI Netherbourne replied.

"And being a Snow Coal or for the uneducated, inside black, outside white, he can operate more easily in predominately white areas like Stafford." I said, while thinking out loud.

"So where can we find Everton?" DCI Netherbourne snarled while banging his fist on the table.

"Wombourne" the youth nervously simpered with fear.

DCI Netherbourne ordered Carrick and me, to track down Everton, starting in Wombourne, while the youth would remain in solitary confinement. But to get to South Staffs by public transport, would be too slow. WPC Dixie Parker though was on hand after just finishing her revs, so I caught up with Dixie just as she was about to leave the station and got DCI Netherbourne to sanction her to drive Carrick and me to Charlie Foxtrot fast.

"What is it that keeps bringing you and me together?" Dixie asked as she drove out of the city centre and along the A449 to Wombourne via Wolverhampton.

"Fate" I said. "Why? Are you asking me to marry you?"

"Behave." Dixie laughed. "You're already spoken for. I mean they're already taking bets down at the station, about when you and DI Blan McJones are going to name the day. But it seems that every time you need a lift...I'm usually the only immediate patrol car that's available?"

"Well here's another bet for you...we're not going to last." I said before adding "It's a pity they don't equip these panda cars with a CD player...I wouldn't mind listening to some Nancy Sinatra."

"But I thought you and her were...well suited?" Dixie asked while sensing the possibility to kindle a flame of passion.

"What me and Nancy Sinatra...she's a bit out of my league." I replied and to which Dixie gave a puzzled look. "Oh you mean me and Blan. Well how can I put it I'm beginning to realise that I'd made a spontaneous mistake. I still feel restless after Jesty and you're the only one so far that's quenched that fire, I can talk openly to you, while Blan needs someone more like Carrick?" I said, as I looked in the rear view mirror and saw him fast asleep on the backseat and which caused my eyes to suddenly go heavy, before I also fell asleep.

CHAPTER 28

LAZING ON A SUNNY AFTERNOON

Narrated by Frisco Kane

"Streetblade knows streetblade that's what you said. Well now you're my little boy and I'm now going to be your streetblade soul-mate!" Dixie said, as I felt her gently stroke my hair and which caused me to open my eyes for a moment, just as she was speaking.

The words streetblade soul-mate made me smile, as the panda car stopped at traffic lights. But it wasn't until Dixie stopped the panda car to fill up with petrol at Wombourne Trading, the village's only garage that I properly awoke. Then as Dixie used her Police fuel card to pay for the petrol, Carrick and I yawned, stretched and limbered up outside the panda car, until she returned and I whispered "See you later ... streetblade soul-mate!"

"You heard me?" Dixie said with a look of surprise.

"Yippie ki aye cowboy" I said with a wink and a smile.

Dixie then drove away, as Carrick and I strolled down Windmill Bank to the new Wombourne village Police station, to liaise with our female, counterparts

"There's an occasional snout whose, been pretty reliable and there's been a cruiser on the scene. A lot of handshaking with the local kids, whose hands then go into their pockets." Detective Sgt Hazel said and who was a late twenties, Lancashire Lass with dark hair and who smoked menthol cigarettes. While her partner was DC Lez Dawson or 'LD', a sexy 'millennium' style blonde with a cheeky smile and legs up to her armpits

"Dope for cash I shouldn't wonder...anything else?" I asked.

"Well Friday night is music night around here...a lot of the kids aren't local, local, but they go to the village high school and gather at the Maypole on Windmill Bank. It's the late night shop lights that attract them, like moths round a candle. While the trade-offs take part on the community centre car park at the back of the Maypole, as for the Lolitas who earn the cash to trade, there is no one set area. The only other thing is a planning application has been made to put leisure caravans on a field on the outskirts of the village. The applicant is one Dwight Fraser White. I'll get Wolves to check for any links to Everton and Little Winston?" Hazel said

"I'll bet there is. Get the girls off the streets and on their backs in caravans on private property?" I said as I thanked Hazel for the information, but who with LD insisted that we let them escort us during a walkabout around the village.

We explored Wombourne's nooks and crannies like the village sports bar of The Hustler, where we played a steady game of pool. Carrick and I though were not regulars and faintly recognisable to some punters, so we scored a lame duck with the local gossip. Carrick and I were getting hungry by 2.30.p.m. but the local chippy was shut until 4.p.m. when the kids left school and so Hazel and LD promised to meet us outside the Kentucky Mare (as the New Inn pub had been rebranded) at 4.p.m. when the cruiser began his run that took in the school gates.

"Got your badge?" I said to Carrick, as we jumped on a bus that was going to Wolverhampton, but jumped off at Lloyd Hill and crossed over the road to the Dairy Queen Diner. "It only seems five minutes since I was working nights next door and buying Jesty her wedding breakfast here, before we went to see Father Bejazus at Holy Cross in Codsall." I reminisced with a faint hint of a sorrow

Carrick touched my arm and said. "Cheer up mate, gone but not forgotten and all that. You'll have happy times again soon."

"If you're talking about Blan that dog don't' bark." I said as we ordered two Dairy Queen chicken fillet burger specials with coffee.

"Why? What's happened?" Carrick said while seeming rather puzzled.

"Listen let's sit down and I'll tell you more, as we eat." I answered, as we picked up our meal trays and walked over to an empty table.

"I still feel restless after Jesty with Jesty it was very different, they broke the mould when they made her. But with Blan...well?" I said as though I was trying to explain away any guilt in between mouthfuls of chicken fillet burger and fries.

"You've found someone else haven't you? Someone who's got a streetblade history like you...someone called WPC Dixie Parker for instance?" Carrick said, as he munched in to his burger meal.

"How did you guess?" I said, as I supped some coffee.

And to which Carrick laughed and said. "Now I've got some news for you, I've decided to break up with Fiona. I haven't found anyone else, but I think she has a girlfriend and from what I've learned about her unofficial activities, I don't want to be on the wrong side of the fence, in any bunko squad investigation."

"So who's Fiona bunny jumping then?" I asked out of curiosity.

"Trudy, the manager of the Mascara" Carrick replied.

"Well that figures how the Saraband and moreover

Everton knew about the Strike Team rumour." I said surprisingly. "I take it you caught them in the act?"

"Well almost. I found the bed warm on more than one occasion and smelled that old tat tars perfume of Midnight in Paris. Trudy told me it was her favourite when we met the girls at The Slammer...were as Fiona uses Tramp" Carrick said.

"Your own bed...the cheeky cow" I snorted.

Carrick and I, having put our personal worlds to rights, finished lunch and left the diner and steadily walked back to Wombourne, during which I suggested that Carrick should offer Blan a shoulder to cry on. I thought they were more suited and although this may have seemed like 'sloppy seconds', Carrick did have an affection for Blan.

"Cmon there's a bus due" I said as I looked at my watch and we caught a bus on the edge of the village and jumped off at the Kentucky Mare, where we met Hazel and LD who were waiting for us as we crossed the road and cut through the pub car park towards the village high school. I walked with LD on the left hand side of the road while Carrick walked with Hazel on the right, to make sure every angle was covered. It was just after ten past four in the afternoon, the road was very busy with schoolchildren and parental cars, as we budged past, while trying to keep alert. There was nothing unduly suspicious at first, though some of the mothers and six form schoolgirls were rather dishy, like the ones that Carrick saw backed up against the school railings, as they talked to two males in a red Ford Cortina with 'Old School' black spoilers and wheel trims.

The sound of *'Football Soul'* like: *'Monkey Spanner* and *Double Barrel'* boomed out from the car, as Carrick signalled that the game was afoot, as we four detectives kept our heads down and ran at the dodge up to the car. The driver leaned his arm out of the car window to flick some cigarette ash and I recognised a tattoo on the back of the driver's hand. I then grabbed the arm and pulled it back hard against the window frame and which caused the driver to screamed with pain as I said "Hello Everton long time no see...I recognised the star tattoo!"

"Hello Mr Kane!" Everton cried with pain, as the car passenger sensing trouble shouted to Everton to 'Drive, Drive!' Carrick meanwhile was playing tug of war with the passenger door, as Hazel and LD marshalled the girls to stand still and stop screaming. The passenger put his one hand on the doorframe to add some leverage to his pull, but Carrick saw the hand and accidentally on purpose let the door go, before a swift kick, shut the door on the hand and caused the passenger to scream with pain.

Parents began to pull their kids close and drive off, while teachers rushed to intervene in the melee, as we four detectives managed to fumble for police badges. Hazel ordered two teachers to take the scared six form girls inside the school and keep them there, as she and LD helped pull at the car door and used a police radio to call for back up. The car door then opened and the passenger lolled out of his seat while crying with pain at his injured hand, as Everton let the handbrake off and stuck his foot on the gas pedal. The car shot forward and caused me to let go of Everton's arm, but not before it was dislocated by the jolt of the car. Everton tried to steer the Cortina one handed, as his passenger tried to close the passenger door with his good hand. The Cortina jerked around the road like a Dodgem at a fair, before swerving when Everton braked hard at a junction, after crashing in to other cars and people, as he tried to get away.

Everton then spun the car around and hit the gas

pedal and sped back past the school and in to a sea of blue flashing lights that swerved to avoid the Cortina, as it bounced at high speed towards the junction at the Kentucky Mare. The brakes then failed on Everton, while the gas pedal stuck and he drove headlong in to traffic that was coming crossways from Windmill Bank and Station Road. The Cortina clipped and swerved other vehicles, as its exhaust dropped from its mounting and began to spark, as metal hit roadway. The car then swerved on to the forecourt of Wombourne Trading, hitting an old woman, as she filled her car with fuel but as she fell, she kept a grip on the pump handle and spouted petrol from the nozzle, as the car crashed in to three petrol pumps.

Although the garage cashier hit the petrol pump petrol switch off button, it was too late, as sparks from the dropped exhaust ignited the petrol and its vapours and caused a flame to shoot down the pump and in to the petrol tanks. The explosion that followed shook the centre of Wombourne, as the garage fire alarm rang, people ran for their lives, the garage windows shattered and the concrete forecourt erupted like a volcano. Carrick and I chased Everton in a panda car, but we were too late, as the garage forecourt became a fireball and blues and two's screamed, as emergency vehicles raced to the blazing inferno.

"Well what the hell do we do now?" Carrick said as he and I surveyed the scene of devastation and from which a plume of smoke from the fire would soon be seen on the outskirts of Wolverhampton.

"Disappear and leave the goons and wooden tops to it. We've still got those six formers to question, while *Blue Watch* and *Casualty* sort out this mess...anyway we're only going to be in the way" I said.

"I'll tell you this much, it'll be one hell of a report to write up and I don't particularly want to be about, when some idiot Inspector starts asking some awkward questions?" Carrick said, as he and I briskly walked back, towards Wombourne High School.

CHAPTER 29

ROCK WITH A POLICEMAN

Narrated by Frisco Kane

When we arrived back at Wombourne High School, Carrick and I discovered that the sixth form girls had done a bunk. But not before Hazel and LD had collated the names, contact details and any close friends of the sixth form schoolgirls, so the local Bobbies could make the various home visits and station attendance requests.

"Would you two boys like a tour of the school...the caretaker has left me the spare keys to lock up with when we leave?" Hazel said with a glint in her eye.

"Did I tell you I'd studied Modern English and Drama, so how about we re-enact The Graduate?" LD said, as she took my arm and led me to where most sixth formers were christened, on a double mattress, under the school stage.

"You naughty Mrs Robinson" I said as the walkabout began to get frisky and LD ended up wearing, just a long tailed shirt.

Meanwhile in the gym locker room, between the vaulting horses, Hazel after making herself comfortable on a pile of gym mats, revealed all her sporting grace and favour, as she and Carrick practised the Swedish Olympics.

The after school activities lasted until almost 7.p.m. when the four of us used the school showers to wash and brush up. Carrick and I knew the drill implicitly, as we skipped school in the dark and we four detectives strolled back to the Kentucky Mare that was still open for business. It was a safe haven for the nearby residents, as the brigade dampened down the charred remains of the village petrol station.

Carrick and I ordered four pints of lager shandy in the busy pub and listened to all the rumours about the fire from a drunken driver through to a suicide bomber. But the best one was about a member of the garage staff, going berserk and attacking the petrol pump controls with a sledgehammer. While others said it was a shotgun, before deliberately crashing a car in to the pumps and throwing a lighted cigarette or newspaper on to the spewing petrol.

The four of us, also wallowed in the smoky air to give our clothes that smell of burning petrol and rubber, so that our disappearance after the fireball would not raise too many questions. The local wooden tops were still on traffic duty on the Windmill Bank junction, as we returned to Charlie Foxtrot. But as soon as we had or so we thought, managed to escape any intrusive enquiries, a familiar broad Scottish voice laughingly said. "A word if you please... gentlemen."

The sound of DCI Netherbourne's voice made Carrick and I gulp, as we then entered an interview room and closed the door, as the DCI drew on a cold pipe and asked. "When I sent you to Wombourne I didn't expect a re-enactment of nine eleven ...so just what the hell happened?"

"It was like this we were with DS Hazel and DC Lez Dawson when we saw Everton and another male in car, outside the high school, trading with a group of sixth form schoolgirls. We went to speak to Everton and his mate and attempted to apprehend them, but there was a struggle and Everton sped away without having full control of the car. We gave chase, but by the time we caught up with Everton, he'd crashed the car and the garage was ablaze!" I said.

"It's just like Frisco said. So we left the uniform

services to it and decided to follow up the six form schoolgirl line of enquiry." Carrick said backing my version of events and showing DCI Netherbourne the schoolgirls, details in his notebook.

"And did this line of enquiry, physically involve DS Hazel and DC Dawson? Or shouldn't I ask? Right go and put those schoolgirl details on a report and don't flower it up. Luckily the eyewitnesses confirm your story about any Police vehicles arriving after Everton had crashed his car." DCI Netherbourne said with a wry smile.

Carrick and I wrote two short and indirect speech reports that we then left on DS Hazel's desk in the CID office at Wombourne. We then retired to the station bar and we found Hazel, LD, DCI Netherbourne and Dixie who had driven him over, before we followed our partygoers lead and snaffled the cold buffet that was laid out for the uniforms attending the fire. We washed down sausage rolls and porkpie with bottles of Fosters Ice, as DCI Netherbourne proposed a toast. "Here's to Everton and his mate …and a hot road to hell!"

"Well now we've got the Fosters…how about a barbie?" Carrick said.

"OOH…did you have to say that?" Dixie and I laughingly groaned, as a local constable set up a disco, mixing desk for an impromptu party.

"Good evening everyone, my names 'Ice in the Sun and this is the Down the Dustpipe rock n roll road-show. Now my colleagues and I have decided, after all that has happened, to hold an impromptu christening of Wombourne's new Police station Charlie Foxtrot One. And to kick us off we have something rather appropriate…it's *Rock with a Policeman!*"

The constable in order to lighten the mood and lift moral had dressed up for the occasion with a 1970's

Afro wig, star shaped glasses and a T. shirt that said 'The Spirit of the Revolution.' Dixie enticed me on to the dance floor with *'Soul Finger. Nice One Cyril. I love to Boogie* and *'Do, do, do the Funky Gibbon'*. The night then began to sail by with Dixie and I sparking off, dance wise to a variety of music like the old Top of the Pops theme *'Whole Lotta Love.'* Until 10.p.m. when the DJ said. "Okay now we have a special cabaret spot between Detective Frisco Kane and WPC Dixie Parker. It's that man himself… Judge…Dread!"

Dixie and I interacted too *'Come Outside'* and *'Will I what?'* After which Carrick, Hazel and LD joined us for a play fight to *'The Leader of the Gang* and a sing-along to *Viva Suspenders*. It was then that two latecomers arrived in the shape of Blan and Fiona, they had phoned DCI Netherbourne to see where Carrick and I where, as we could not be contacted, when the news broke about the fireball. Then when DCI Netherbourne said we were with him at Charlie Foxtrot One, Blan and Fiona decided to join the party. Carrick then deliberately skanked Fiona when she wanted to dance with him to *'Puppet on a String'* while Dixie in a mischievous mood, put her arms around my neck and looked at Blan and me, as she sang along to the expletive version of *'Don't Marry her…Fuck Me?'*

Police Constable Aaron Wilson was a stout, forty year old, beat officer who, as he was returning to the station, decided to walk through the Maypole garden and where he passed three lads, one of whom made a curt remark "What you fuckin looking at…you nosy fat copper!"

PC Wilson then saw one lad running away, but PC Wilson caught him and as the youth struggled to escape, there was a loud bang and PC Wilson staggered from a stomach wound. The youth yelled for PC Wilson to keep back, at which the gun went off twice more, PC Wilson dropped to floor and crawled to the Maypole. The youth looked terrified, threw the gun in the bushes and fled with his mates, but not before PC Wilson managed to press his radio alarm, as a customer in the village chip shop dialled 999 while another member of the public ran over to the police station.

A klaxon horn then deafened the party music, as Blan was about to march on the dance floor and slap Dixie for trying to get her claws in to me. But the alarm put paid to any cat-fight, as officers poured out of the station and found PC Wilson's body lying by the Maypole. A manhunt then saw every youth on the streets within the village, stopped and searched. This bought some surprising results from drugs to knives to going equipped to steal, stolen credit cards and driving licences, but no gun that was found by sniffer dogs with the revolver being sent to forensics, post haste. Meanwhile amid the mayhem, Blan took me to one side and said "You and me need to talk…if that cat comes near you once more!"

"You'll do nothing, but we still need to talk. I want to end our relationship but not like this…it needs to be more amicable back at the flat." I replied.

Blan then drove back to Stafford with me, while demanding answers, but I was not prepared to start an argument in the car.

Dixie meanwhile asked Carrick where I was, only to be told. "He's returned to Stafford with Blan, to sort things out. Don't worry he'll be in touch, probably first thing tomorrow morning, if not during the night."

Dixie walked away, as Fiona who had been listening in the shadows, walked up to Carrick and loudly asked. "Just what the hell is going on? Is Frisco splitting up with Blan? Why did you skank me back in there and what's it got to do with WPC Dixie Parker? Are you both screwing her is that what it is?"

Fiona became hysterical, so Carrick slapped her face and apologised. "Listen I'm sorry...I found out this afternoon and..."

"And what you didn't say anything? Blan will be in bits!" Fiona cried.

"Why do you fancy her or something? Listen I didn't mean that, what I mean is I know about you and Trudy from the Mascara. I found out sometime back, but now is, as good as time, as any to tell you...I'm ending our relationship. I'll pack my bags and move out by tomorrow morning." Carrick said before walking away.

"Don't you walk away from me Carrick Macross...if you don't come back here now and apologise I'll...humph!" Fiona shouted in tearful anger.

Carrick ignored her threat, as he searched for Dixie who was talking to DCI Netherbourne and begged a lift back to Stafford, before deflating Fiona's tyres so, as to slow down her return to Stafford.

DCI Netherbourne also was in need of a lift, but back to Wolves and only when he had made sure that Dixie was fit to drive after having a drink. Then when Dixie had passed the sobriety test, she dropped DCI Netherbourne off, but not before Carrick confided that he had split with Fiona.

"Right, sort yourself out for tonight then tomorrow morning, bring Fiona in for questioning on suspicion of corruption." DCI Netherbourne said.

'That could be easier said than done!' Carrick thought to himself.

Meanwhile back in Stafford I mused 'Oh what a tangled web we weave?' as I flopped down in an armchair at the flat, as Blan locked the front door and threw her coat over the sofa. She began once again, to demand answers to my decision to annul our relationship, her loud voice falling on deaf ears, as I fell asleep in the chair and which frustrated Blan. But not enough for me to feel her rub my hair, kiss me on the forehead and hear her whisper 'Goodnight'.

Carrick arrived back in Stafford almost forty five minutes after Blan and me, but still ahead of Fiona. Carrick told Dixie that things would be okay, while having second thoughts about giving up, one of the best gaffs, he had ever had, for some scheming cow. Carrick packed Fiona's personal stuff in to a suitcase and crammed the rest into black bin liners. Carrick then waited and when he finally heard Fiona's key in the lock, he pounced and startled her, as he pulled the door open and grabbed her keys. Fiona had expected to find Carrick either in bed or the flat empty and him gone, but as she made a grab for the keys, he knocked her back with the suitcase and then threw the black bin liners of clothes at her.

"And don't come back!" Carrick snarled, as he slammed the door shut.

Fiona hammered on the door and began to cry, before lugging her stuff over to my flat and where after banging and crying at the door, Fiona then collapsed in a heap on the floor and cried herself to sleep.

CHAPTER 30

LONDON CALLING

Narrated by Carrick Macross

I had a restless night and by 6.a.m. was watching the TV news that headlined with the petrol station fireball and the shooting of the Police officer in Wombourne. The sleepy South Staffordshire village was now big news, as I got myself ready and made my way over to Frisco's flat, where I found Fiona sprawled across the plastic sacks and fast asleep.

"Well this as good a time as any!" I mused, as I shook Fiona to wake her up and who in a bleary eyed state, struggled to stand up with my help.

I shoved Fiona against a wall, pulled her arms behind her back and snapped on the bracelets, before spinning her round and searching her pockets for her warrant card, handcuffs and baton. I verbally placed Fiona under arrest and who said nothing coherent, just giggled, as my body search seemed to tickle her. Fiona's face was red from crying while at heart she was vulnerable, not the hard-nosed copper she made herself out to be.

Frisco meanwhile was wide-awake and had been up and about for about an hour, when he heard the commotion and then a knock on the front door.

"Sorry to disturb you mate, only I found Fiona here asleep on your doorstep and vagrancy is, as good a holding charge as any. The DCI wants her bringing in this morning and before you ask, I threw her out of my flat!" I said, as Frisco invited me in for coffee and offered to help escort Fiona to Charlie Golf One.

My arrival awoke Blan who was surprised to find

Fiona handcuffed and half-asleep on the sofa, as Frisco and I drank coffee in the kitchen and said good morning when Blan ambled in to make herself a drink. I related my story over again, while Frisco was all smiles and even gave Blan a good morning kiss on the cheek before musing. "It's amazing how thing's can seem different in the cold light of day?"

"But we still need to talk?" Blan said as she sipped her coffee.

"I agree, but not now. I've got to go out." Frisco said as he telephoned Dixie and arranged to meet her at Stafford station within the next half-hour.

The time was now 6.40.a.m. with Frisco asking Blan if she would mind running him and me to Stafford Central with Fiona, to which Blan agreed, once she had, had a quick wash and got dressed but with the minimum of warpaint. The Custody Sergeant at Charlie Golf One was more than surprised to see Blan, Fiona, Frisco and me, just as the night shift and early shift were changing over.

"Good Morning Sergeant. DS Fiona Netherseal is here under arrest, so we need a spare cell to accommodate her." Blan said.

"The holding charge is vagrancy...and corruption. DCI Netherbourne will want to question her, until then DS Netherseal is to be kept apart from other prisoners." I added.

Then after a courtesy notification to the duty inspector, Fiona was safely locked in a cell before Blan drove Frisco and me to the train station where Dixie, dressed in monkey boots and denims, slouched by the doors. Then, as he got out of the car, Frisco said. "Cheers for the lift, if you see Darna, apologise for going without her to London but two's company and three's a crowd and all that...and Blan don't worry we'll definitely talk when I get back."

Then as he walked away Blan began to cry and so I instinctively gave her a hug and said. "Do you fancy some breakfast at my place then you and I can talk."

Blan graciously accepted my invitation to breakfast, over which, as we talked I unwittingly used a charm offensive that Blan warmed too. One moment we were chatting, as Blan helped to wash the breakfast things, the next we were indulging in mad passion before ending up in bed, where I held her in my arms while she nuzzled my chest.

Meanwhile on Stafford station, as they waited on platform 4 for the train to Birmingham. Frisco gave Dixie a good morning kiss and said. "I meant to tell you, you don't half look sexy in a police uniform!"

"Thank you kind sir" Dixie replied before telling him to behave and playfully slapping his arm when he slipped his hand inside the back of her jeans. Dixie had already bought the tickets for New Street that looked careworn in comparison with the Edwardian style Moor Street Station, where Frisco bought two £30 cheap day travel cards to London Marylebone. It was during this start of the journey that the two of them got to know each other better, as the conversation turned to the 'Hand of Five', a variation of the radio show 'Desert Island Discs'.

Frisco's choice of music was made up of *'Leader of the Gang, Ghost in my House, Tiger Feet, Albatross* and Chuck Berry's rock n roll anthem *Schooldays.*

"I always say that you can tell a man by his music." Dixie said, as Frisco put his arm around her, as she reeled off her top five of *Soul Finger, Cool for Cats, Hersham Boys, Chelsea Dagger* and Blur's 90's anthem of *Parklife.*

"Okay then name five things for your wedding night?" Frisco asked.

"My favourite perfume...Raffles. As for the rest, you'll have to use your bad imagination and guess?" Dixie cheekily replied.

"A two tone bikini, a set of slinky, silk yellow, lingerie? And what colour are you wearing today?" Frisco asked, as he popped two buttons on her shirt.

"Will you behave" Dixie laughed, as she playfully slapped his hand away. "Now it's your turn...lover boy, so what's it to be, essence of old tom cat?"

"Camel 55 if you want to know...all the Arabs wear it." Frisco laughed.

"Well you're not keeping me in a harem." Dixie sleepily said before closing her eyes and resting her head on Frisco's shoulder, as he softly kissed her on the fore head and quickly peeked at her lingerie, before dozing off himself.

Meanwhile back in Stafford, I sat on the edge of the bed and looked at the clock, it said almost 9.30.a.m. I yawned, stretched and put my feet on something that was pearl in colour, nylon and ribbed.

"Here do you want these back? You looked dead sexy in them." I cheekily said, as I tossed Blan's briefs across her face to wake her up.

"Pwgh! You cheeky sod, there my knickers!" Blan answered with a splutter.

My mobile phone then rang with a message from DCI Netherbourne that I related to Blan, as she came out of the bathroom. "The DCI is running late and can we start the interview with Fiona. So I'll meet you outside in quarter of an hour."

"And we need to talk...considering what's just happened?" Blan said

"Talk about what? The whole world's moved on and Fiona's quite rightly out of the equation. That just leaves you and me? Listen we'll talk later and I'll help you move your stuff in to mine...that's if you want?" I replied.

Blan though didn't know what she wanted, she could understand what I was saying and moving in with me was probably the best solution. Blan only hoped that Frisco would understand about this sudden evolution and how she and I seemed to gel, though no one could have expected such spontaneous results. When we arrived at Charlie Golf One, an Inspector was sounding off at the Custody Sergeant that he wanted Fiona released on Police bail, as keeping her in the cells and which should be reserved for criminals, had to be a mistake.

"And you're the one making it!" Blan said, as she then asked for Fiona to be released for interview, before turning to the Inspector and saying. "From one Police inspector to another...if you ever try and interfere in an internal investigation again without proper authority, I'll make damn sure you're the one who'll be sitting in the cells, contemplating your career and pension...okay."

The Inspector stormed off, huffing and puffing as Blan and I escorted Fiona to an interview room that had cameras and a tape machine. Blan asked about her relationship with Billy Bull, the late Everton Smith and her 'Legal Fees'. Fiona tried to bluff it out and even tried the 'sad eye' routine with me, as I then produced the black book that Billy Bull kept of all their transactions. It was Billy Bull's insurance that bit Fiona like a venomous snake and at which point she lawyered up.

Blan then asked for some coffee from the canteen, as she tried to talk, woman to woman to Fiona who tipped the table up, knocked Blan to the floor, where they grappled before Fiona handcuffed Blan and stuffed a hanky in her mouth. Fiona then grabbed Blan's handbag that contained her warrant card, car keys and purse, before looking out of the door and seeing that there were too many uniforms milling about, in order to make a clean getaway. Fiona then hit the fire alarm and made her way to the custody suite where the activation meant the cells had to be emptied of prisoners. This left the custody suite empty, as Fiona grabbed a plastic bag marked with her name, which contained her personal items, before dashing out the backdoor, across the yard, in to Eastgate Street where she hesitated slightly before hurrying left, along the backstreets towards the shopping centre. Fiona looked around, before hurrying across the High Street, up the alleyway at the side of St Mary's Church and stopping in the shadows to catch her breath and search Blan's handbag. She found a set of keys to my flat and donned an improvised disguise of a headscarf and sunglasses that she also found, before quickly walking to Victoria Park, where she got the lift to the floor below my flat and climbing the stairs to reconnoitre the corridor.

I dropped what I was doing upon hearing the alarm activation and raced back to the interview room, where I found Blan trussed up and Fiona gone. I then hit the panic button on the wall and began to free Blan when uniformed officers raced to the interview room.

"Switch that bloody fire alarm off...it's an escape from custody and get me DCI Netherbourne!" I shouted at the uniform officers.

I telephoned Frisco and told him, he may have a bogey on his tail and not to answer any calls from Blan's mobile, since Fiona had stolen her handbag while DCI Netherbourne ordered us to check out Victoria Park.

Fiona used Blan's keys to open the door to Frisco's flat, where she found her clothes stacked in the hallway. Fiona checked that the flat was empty and locked the front door, so that if anyone came back bar Frisco, they would have to get the janitor to use his master keys and she would hear the lift stop on this floor. Fiona sorted out a change of clothes while thinking about where she could hide in the flat, just in case she was disturbed, before she was ready to pounce. Fiona then heard the lift and hid when she heard Blan and me, with the Janitor who unlocked the flat door.

"Okay, it's all clear...apart from Fiona's clobber!" I shouted, as I made a cursory check of the flat before I took Blan in my arms and whispered. "Listen get your stuff together, we'll take it over to my place. I've got Fiona's keys, so she can't get in there. I'll even help you pack your lingerie."

"Behave! You've already had your hands on my knickers once, you'll have to wait till bedtime, for any further trick n' treat." Blan teased.

Blan and I were sharing a passionate kiss when Fiona crept out of hiding and armed with Frisco's baseball bat, hit me, just enough to stun me as I fell to the floor. Blan was surprised by Fiona's sudden appearance and wrestled with her, but Fiona overpowered Blan and restrained us in our own handcuffs and stuffed a handkerchief in to Blan's mouth and pushed her onto the bed. Before gagging and binding me with some of Frisco's ties, to a chair that she brought in to the bedroom.

"Okay then sweetheart...while we're waiting for Frisco and Dixie Parker to return, why don't you and me get well acquainted, seeing as variety is the spice of life...and Carrick can watch." Fiona said with a leering smile.

Fiona gave me a wink and blew me a kiss, as she darkened the bedroom and forced Blan to swallow a date rape pill, before undoing the handcuffs to undress her then once in bed, she was like a bitch on heat.

Fiona's amorous preoccupation in the darkened room diverted her attention from me, as I groggily stirred from the whack with the baseball bat and attempted to bite through the tie that gagged my mouth, so I could breathe. I began to wonder if Frisco had managed to track down Jubilee Christian in London, had he learned the truth about her sudden disappearance and did she have any news about Bathsheba and how was Dixie enjoying her day trip to London?

CHAPTER 31

DOWN IN THE TUBE STATION AT MIDNIGHT

Narrated by Frisco Kane

I awoke from my catnap and caught myself singing in my sleep the words to *'Tom Hark'* by the Piranhas. When my loud and heavy 'telephone bell' mobile ring tone sounded and I received the news about Fiona's escape from custody. Although her flight to freedom did slightly complicate things, it did not pose an immediate problem, as Fiona did not know I was en-route to London or who I was going to see. I let Dixie sleep until the train was pulling in to stylish Marylebone, where we made a pit-stop at the inviting, concourse facilities. Then after feeling rejuvenated, Dixie and I navigated the busy commuter maze of London's underground, railway network to London Bridge and the fresh air of city life.

The Blueberry Spearmint was a blue brick, archways tunnel and situated on the driveway to London Bridge Station. The 'U' shaped building seemed to date to the 1940's, but it was a game to get anyone to open its ornate, white pillared, smoky glass front door when I rang the bell. I then rang the club's phone number and made out that I had a delivery, as I knew that asking about Jubilee Christian over the door intercom would result in zilch. Then when the door opened, I flashed my badge, as Dixie and I barged past a greasy looking and protesting, thirty-something barman.

A pretty girl also came to the door and just smiled politely when she saw Dixie dressed like a boot girl, flashing a Police badge and saying "Be a good girl and go and put the kettle on…there's a love."

"Your badge says Staffordshire and this is London. That badge's not legal around here!" The barman snarled from within a mask of black designer stubble.

"This badge is legal where I say it's legal!" I snapped, as I looked around the interior of the Blueberry Spearmint that had blue brick walls in its central lounge bar and a picture on its wall that caught my eye. It looked like it came from National Geographic, as it was a deep colour picture of diver in a seabed paradise and called 'Coral Reef', as I asked the barman. "You've got a very nice club here, now you can answer a question for me, I'm looking for a female named Jubilee Christian?"

"Try yellow pages?" The barman sarcastically replied.

"Listen sunshine I haven't travelled down to London to play games, so shall we try again?" I snarled as I thumped the bar man in the nuts and pinned him against a wall.

"Okay, okay…but I've never heard of any Jubilee Christian, what does she look like?" The barman croaked

"She's a goth, wears distinctive Union Jack toe cap Doc Martens." I said

"Oh you mean Ruby Red! Try Earlscourt, it's a cellar coffee bar at Tower Bridge." The barman gasped, as I released my grip. .

The young girl then came back with four hot drinks, only for Dixie to say, as we made our way towards the door. "Forget the tea love and get yourself another boyfriend…preferably someone who doesn't readily need a good bath!"

Dixie and I then left the Blueberry Spearmint and quickly walked to London Bridge Station just as the station clock said one oclock. I wanted to stop for a coffee, but I did not trust the barman, not to try and scare Jubilee with a phone call that two cops from Stafford were in town and looking for her.

"Are you normally that masterful when it comes to scroats like that?" Dixie said, as we took the tube to Tower Bridge.

"That all depends on the size and nature of the scroat in question. It's a game, with some you can be forceful, while others you have to use a more subtle approach ...like humour!" I replied while remembering Reno Dunster.

Upon arriving at Tower Bridge, it was Dixie who asked a big issue seller if they knew of a coffee bar called Earlscourt. Dixie slipped the magazine seller a quid and we hurried along the river walkway to a large and gravelled open space that lay in the shadow of the bloody tower. Dixie then pointed to the road bridge and a set of glass doors, engraved Earls Court that led in to a deep red and dated Edwardian style arcade of chip shops and cafes for teenagers. The passageway led to a second set of engraved glass doors, through which I peered in to a shadowy, brick cellar that was blue in colour. My eye was caught by the word 'Manpower' and an, amber coloured advert that showed two girls in black bikinis with buckets and sponges. There was no sign of Jubilee Christian and I told Dixie to keep watch and stop anybody from leaving, when I entered the café from the stairway in the far corner, as I descended the stairs and entered the dimly lit cavern. I saw in the one corner, a girl band taking a mid performance break and despite her new get up Jubilee Christian and calmly said "You alright Jubilee?"

The sound of my voice made Jubilee look up and gabble in astonishment what seemed like a thousand questions. "Frisco, how the hell did you know I was here? How did you find me?"

"Darna and some friendly persuasion at the Blueberry Spearmint, more to the point how are you? You've changed. Look at you, beer towels safety pinned together for a waistcoat and a cheese cutter. You look like a punk rock pearly king." I replied.

"Let's just say I'm an educated girl trying to live a working class experience?" Jubilee replied with a gentle smile.

"And my name's Dirty Harry! But tell me, just out of curiosity, what's the name of the band?" I asked while nodding towards the four girls sitting at a far table.

"Oh that's Sexual Alchemy! They're doing an impromptu gig before they go to Birmingham, so I'm jamming with them...but are you on your own?" Jubilee asked apprehensively.

"No, but you're safe. But that's Sexual Alchemy you say...that's interesting?" I said while trying to decide whether it was divine providence or coincidence.

"But tell me what exactly happened. I know about Charmaine making you look bad, just as though you'd turned native, even renegade. But she's dead now, as is Reno Dunster. I also know about your cousin Fiona Netherseal." I said and beckoned Dixie to join us.

But just as Dixie was about to open the glass doors, a scrawny punk girl pushed past her and descended in to the cellar café. It was Bathsheba Mendalove who had a look of fearful surprise on her face, gulped, spun on her heel and ran out of the café.

Dixie saw me snarl for her to stop Bathsheba, as she barged past, Dixie who raced after her across the gravelled open space and through the shadow of the bloody tower, towards the river. Dixie and Bathsheba skidded on the rough gravel that made Bathsheba wince when it stung the palms of her hands, as she fell over. Dixie saw Bathsheba fall then hurriedly hobble down some steep concrete steps to the riverside walkway, where Bathsheba tripped and fell against a rubbish bin, with her grazed palms smarting and making her cry when she tried to use her hands to steady herself.

Dixie then skidded to a halt where Bathsheba had fallen over, drew her baton to hit Bathsheba across her back and the back of her legs. Dixie then kept Bathsheba doubled up over the rubbish bin, as she snapped on the cuffs, before grabbing her by the scruff of her neck and growling. "You're nicked!"

Dixie then took a steady walk back to the café to catch her breath after all the excitement, while dragging a stumbling Bathsheba whom could do nothing but cry. Dixie banged the glass doors, as she dragged Bathsheba down the passageway to the Earlscourt café where I jumped up from the table where Jubilee and I were sat and who in the meantime, had told me the truth of her disappearance.

I was glad to see Dixie return unscathed, as I knew what a handful Bathsheba could be, while Bathsheba still looked as rough-cut as ever, as I grabbed her by the throat and snarled. "For what you did to Jesty, I ought to scald your bloody face off …you scrawny fucking bitch!"

Dixie then plonked Bathsheba in a chair by the table where Jubilee was sat, while I confided to Dixie about Reno Dunster kidnapping Jubilee, until she made her escape and hid in fear. While her now, dead, murderous and twin sister Charmaine copycatted her in a very bad light.

"Well now the truth's out, there's no need to be scared anymore, you can come home, where Dixie and I will look after you. As for Bathsheba, she's going straight to hell." I said while wishing for a split second that I could sit Jubilee on my lap and gently rock her in my arms.

I then apologised to Dixie for cutting their trip to London short, but we had to get Bathsheba behind bars, before whispering that tomorrow night we would still go to the Eye Candy. As the raggedy looking, girl band of 'Sexual Alchemy' began to play a mix of *'Rebel, Rebel...'* through to *'Postcards and a screaming siren...that's entertainment!'*

I telephoned DCI Netherbourne and Darna with regard to the prize catch, while Jubilee wished that she could throw her arms around my neck and kiss the face off me, before asking a favour. "Listen could we stop off and grab my stuff...it's not much, I only live in 'Mod Row' you know Carnaby Street as they call it...please?"

"How come you can afford to live in central London? I thought property and rental prices, were over the top?" I curiously asked.

"That all depends if you don't mind going down market...within reason and sharing the rent more than two ways?" Jubilee replied with a subtle smile.

"Are you on the game? Second thoughts don't answer that...so where do we change on the underground to get to Oxford Circus?" I said with a gentle smirk

Jubilee smiled 'thank you' while in between songs, I told the Alice Cooper style lead singer that she would need a new roadie, as Bathsheba was under arrest, on an outstanding warrant. Dixie meanwhile warned Bathsheba that if she played up, she and her would shake hands before taking Bathsheba to the ladies and searching her for items of interest like her mobile phone, a pocketknife and a wallet containing £200.

"You been at it again Bathsheba…picking pockets?" I said as I confiscated the money to pay for her and Jubilee's train tickets and other expenses. The three of us then needed to get Bathsheba around London, but without attracting attention and so her hands were handcuffed in front of her and a fiver paid to a street vendor for an old travelling rug. Dixie then cut a hole in it, so Bathsheba wore it like a poncho, as we navigated the tube across London to Oxford Circus.

It was during this excursion to Carnaby Street that I gave Dixie £40 out of Bathsheba's money to spend in the shops, while I helped Jubilee pack her stuff at her flat, above a psychedelic coffee bar called Ruben Canyon and where everyone would meet after half an hour. Jubilee's flat was plain and simple in colour with a stairway that led from the front door to the flat landing, where Bathsheba was allowed to use the toilet, if somewhat crudely. Bathsheba was then tied to a chair, gagged and told to behave and something that nagged at the back of my mind, as Bathsheba was normally disruptive and awkward, so this compliance was something that was totally out of character.

CHAPTER 32

LOVERS ROCK

Narrated by Frisco Kane

Jubilee and I took advantage of being alone and receptively smooched, as she whispered in my ear, before kissing my neck and whining with pleasure as we acted out the story of Jack and Jill and old Cock Robin until I looked at my watch and saw that in just over five minutes time, we were due to meet Dixie in the café downstairs. Then after zipping up my jeans, I checked on Bathsheba who was tied to the chair with two pair of old tights, while a large piece of sticking plaster stopped her from crying out. Jubilee after freshening up, threw her immediate and personal effects in to a large holdall, changed in to her black woollen coat with coloured cannabis leaves that she still had, before leaving her patchwork waistcoat, cheesecutter cap, her door key and a short 'goodbye' note to her flatmates on the dining table.

The three of us arrived at the café ten minutes late, but we were still the first to arrive, as I ordered three coffees and sat down to wait for Dixie to arrive. While the Jubilee I knew and loved was back, as she smiled and squeezed my hand under the table. I didn't relish cheating on Dixie, but I did have a life before her and Jubilee was some who needed some tender loving care.

"Sorry I'm late...but I found a wonderful vintage clothes bargain shop in a side street." Dixie said as she plonked a large bag on the café table.

Then as Dixie got herself a coffee, I looked at what was in the bag and was surprised to find a denim mini and midi skirt, some flesh coloured tights and a pair of moccasin shoes.

"The moccasins are supposed to be the original sixty nine skin-girls footwear according to a recent TV documentary." Jubilee explained

"Oy nosy" Dixie laughed, as she returned to the table with her coffee.

"So when's the fashion parade, start then…sexy?" I replied with a grin.

"Behave!" Dixie smilingly rebuked, as Jubilee laughingly wondered what her reaction would be if she knew what exactly had been going on, while she had been shopping.

I decided that the psychedelic Monkees meets the Banana Splits style Ruben Canyon café was as good a place, as any, to eat before heading back to Marylebone. Dixie took the meal orders to the counter, before nipping to the ladies and changing in to her new gear, as Jubilee and I played the jukebox to reflect everyone's mood with the songs *'For Your Love'* through to *'Gimme Some Lovin'*, except that was for Bathsheba who just ate her food and drank her coffee in silence.

After travelling on the tube across London to Marylebone, I bought two extra tickets to Stafford via Birmingham, before we retired to the station pub to wait for the next train over a drink, care of Bathsheba's money. Then when the train arrived, I explained to the guard about escorting a female prisoner and so the tickets were upgraded to first class for the journey to Birmingham and which left about £20 out of Bathsheba's original £200. Dixie took Bathsheba to the toilet before the train left the station, as she did not want disturbing during the journey. Bathsheba then made her play and being a deft pick pocket, used a picklock that she had kept hidden in the seam of her jacket to release the handcuffs, before returning the picklock back to its hiding place. Bathsheba then opened the toilet door and hit Dixie with the handcuffs, before pushing her aside and jumping off the train and making a run for it.

I heard Dixie shout as Bathsheba made her escape, so I scrambled along the carriage aisle and jumped off the train. Dixie joined Jubilee and together they peered through the train window to see me wave my badge and barge past the ticket barrier after Bathsheba who had snatched some ones underground ticket. Bathsheba then used it to dive down the escalators to the tube platforms, where again I waved my badge, shouted 'Escaped Prisoner' and raced after Bathsheba who was always, just one step ahead of me.

Bathsheba and I jostled through crowds of commuters on the tube platforms and trains, as Dixie called DCI Netherbourne on her mobile phone and explained that Bathsheba had escaped and I was in hot pursuit. DCI Netherbourne then decided that Dixie should escort Jubilee Christian to Stafford where he would meet their train and arrange for a safe house for Jubilee. Dixie and Jubilee then sat back and prayed that I would be safe, as the train sped forth to Birmingham with the two girls falling asleep and dreaming they were in bed together, smooching. Until that was I popped up between the two of them and after which they just fell asleep across my chest.

I found my marathon chase after Bathsheba hard going and I nearly gave up, but dogged determination drove me on, as I hacked my way through packed platforms, stairways and tube train carriages that were too crowded for me to grab Bathsheba. I did stay by the train doors and when Bathsheba did finally make a bolt for the open air, it was at Covent Garden with its notorious, mountainous, green tiled, narrow and winding stairway where we needed Oxygen halfway up and ended the climb to the top, on all fours.

"Geeze that was bloody steep!" I managed to gasp, as Bathsheba and I lolled against the tiled walls at the top of the stairs, feeling sick and winded.

"You're telling me next time I'll jump off where there's, bloody escalators!" Bathsheba gasped, while holding her head down with both hands on her knees.

Bathsheba's words made me summon up the strength to stagger across, pick up the handcuffs she had dropped on the floor and gasp "Sorry love no can do and oh yes...your nicked!"

I then snapped the handcuffs on Bathsheba who was too exhausted to fight back or try to escape again, as I hauled her back downstairs and back to Marylebone while our cross-city dash through London's underground had not gone unnoticed with the Transport Police also finding it hard work to catch up with us. The game then ended when Bathsheba and I waited for a connecting tube train at Covent Garden, with the trains deliberately delayed to allow the Transport Police time to arrive on the station platform. Bathsheba and I were taken to one side, where I showed my police badge and explained that Bathsheba had escaped from custody and why we had run a cat and mouse chase across London.

Bathsheba and I were taken to a Transport Police office and waited for my story to be verified, while I spotted an orange jump suit hanging up and which gave me an idea. I asked a constable who was also using the office, if there was an orange jump suit and a large bag going spare and after a quick search the constable gave me an old but clean jump suit and an old carrier bag. I then asked where the toilets were, with the constable saying that there were no female officers available.

"Don't worry I'm not bashful." I replied, as I walked Bathsheba to the toilet.

Then in a cubicle, I unlocked the handcuffs and stood with my back against the door and ordered Bathsheba to strip, to which she exclaimed. "I think you forget ...I'm not in to men!"

"Listen love, just get undressed and put the jump suit on and throw your stuff in to the bag!" I snapped, as I drew my extendable baton to re-enforce the point.

Bathsheba decided not to argue and begrudgingly got undressed down to some discoloured lingerie that made me grimace, as she put on the jump suit. I then put the handcuffs back on her and walked her back to the office, just as DCI Netherbourne had verified my story over the phone to a London Transport Police Sergeant.

Bathsheba and I were then driven to Marylebone, where we waited for the next train with the upgrades being honoured from the earlier train. I telephoned the DCI to update him, while he told me that Jubilee and Dixie were on route to Stafford by the earlier train and about the predicament that he had found Carrick and Blan in.

DCI Netherbourne had led a Police raid on the Mascara, where an indignant Trudy Godsend was brought in for questioning, with regard to her grace and favour relationship with DS Fiona Netherseal who was classified as an escaped felon rather than as a Police Officer. Trudy after an initial interview was released on police bail, while the Mascara's cathouse licence was suspended. DCI Netherbourne had also been trying to contact Carrick and Blan, but they were not answering the phone and there was no sight of Fiona. DCI Netherbourne initially put Carrick and Blan's non-contact down to high jinks between the sheets, but by late afternoon he began to feel uneasy and so he decided to visit their last known destination.

The Victoria Park Janitor revealed that he had let

Blan and Carrick in to my flat with his passkey, but he had not seen them since and so DCI Netherbourne took no chances and called for backup. Before using a passkey to enter my flat that was in darkness and where Carrick was tied up and Blan was unconscious in bed. There was no sign of Fiona, who after fulfilling her pleasure of sordid sexual intimacy had made good her escape. Carrick told the DCI that the constant ringing of Blan and his mobile phones had infuriated Fiona so much that she had stormed out of the flat with her personal effects. Then as Carrick escorted Blan to hospital for a check up, DCI Netherbourne had the flats searched but to no avail, he was glad he had scuppered Fiona's plans, but where she was now was another matter. What worried me was that Fiona might be lying in wait at Stafford station, so I suggested that we convene at the Pencil Skirt. DCI Netherbourne agreed and telephoned Dixie to tell her about the change of arrangements, before telephoning Amazon to accommodate some late night guests. Bathsheba and I then got on the train and sat back for the long journey to Wolverhampton, while on the earlier train Jubilee and Dixie curled up in their seats and came face to face at 'pillow level' and where as they awoke and smiled at each other, they unwittingly shared a kiss, to which Jubilee said surprisingly as she caressed Dixie's hand. "I didn't know you fancied me?"

Dixie blushed and gently laughed. "To be honest I'm not into females, but I just couldn't help myself...I just had to kiss you!"

Jubilee then gently hugged Dixie who fell asleep on Jubilee's shoulder, while Jubilee held her hand and gave her a gentle kiss on the forehead.

CHAPTER 33

TWIST & SHOUT

Narrated by Frisco Kane

The train journey to Birmingham was long and tedious, so I decided while Bathsheba was asleep, to try and discover how she had managed to escape from the handcuffs. I went through her bag of clothes and searched any pockets and patted down the seams that I also fingered for any loose stitching until I found the picklock, a thin piece of metal that I tucked away in my wallet, as it could always be useful?

DCI Netherbourne meanwhile was enjoying a pint in the 221b Edwardian Bar on Wolverhampton station, as he tried to stimulate some answers from the bar's array of Sherlock Holmes objet dart, the reason for Fiona's actions. But no matter how hard he tried DCI Netherbourne always came back to the same conclusion...DS Fiona Netherseal was amatory aberrant, who it seemed had inherited her late cousin Charmaine Christian's killer instinct!

When the train carrying Dixie and Jubilee rolled in to Wolverhampton station, Dixie took Jubilee to one side and apologised "Listen that kiss...can we just leave it at that. It was just something that happened...I don't want to take it any farther. You see I'm not really in to girls not in that way...so to speak!"

"If you're sure...only you can have a second bite of the cherry if you wish...it's your call love?" Jubilee replied as she gave Dixie a sisterly hug.

"I'm sure." Dixie answered, as she spied DCI Netherbourne who was sucking on a cold pipe, as he was not allowed to smoke on the platform.

Then after a brisk greeting, DCI Netherbourne escorted Dixie and Jubilee to the taxi rank and where they caught a black cab to Chapel Ash, with DCI Netherbourne asking for a receipt for the taxi fare plus tip. So he could claim it back from Police expenses, while Dixie was intrigued to find that the Pencil Skirt was a well polished brothel. DCI Netherbourne told her that the Pencil Skirt was where my wedding day had ended in tragedy, while Jubilee was just glad to see two more friendly faces, that of Amazon and Domino who had adjusted to life as a working, single mother. The hen party then gelled over a drink as the jukebox played *'Nellie the Elephant* by the Toy Dolls.

When the train arrived at Birmingham Moor Street, I jumped off, after fishing the travelling rug poncho out of the bag of clothes and putting it over Bathsheba's jump suit to hide her handcuffs. The orange jump suit attracted some odd looks and cries of 'Guantammano', as I marched Bathsheba through Birmingham city centre to the bright lights of New Street Station. Where we boarded a Liverpool train, but as we sat in an available empty double seat, a drunken scouser asked me if Bathsheba was a member of the 'Taliban' from 'Guantammano.' To which I mischievously, replied "Sorry mate...she was caught working away, while signing on."

The rail journey only took fifteen minutes to Wolverhampton, where I gripped Bathsheba's arm and marched her to the taxi rank. I then boarded a black cab to the Pencil Skirt, where I promised Bathsheba, a hot reception, as I claimed a receipt for the taxi fare plus tip, before bundling Bathsheba out of the cab.

The noise of me banging open the Pencil Skirts doors made everyone look, with at first no one entering the bar. I had taken Bathsheba to one side and removed the poncho, before shoving her down the passageway to her audience and where she stumbled, as she entered the barroom with her head bowed.

"One prisoner" I snarled, the sound of which made DCI Netherbourne hold up his hand to signal for everyone to stay where they were.

Then as Amazon and Domino glared, hissed and barred their claws while Dixie and Jubilee looked on, DCI Netherbourne marched up to Bathsheba who stood with her head still bowed.

"Congratulations" DCI Netherbourne shouted and put out his hand, but instead of shaking my hand, he clenched a clunking great fist and hit Bathsheba hard across her face. The punch sent Bathsheba crashing in to a pub table and on to the floor. DCI Netherbourne then stood with his boot across Bathsheba's throat and glared in anger, before I hauled her to her feet while blood trickled from her nose and lip and tears filled her eyes.

"Listen I'm sorry for shooting Jesty...but it was Jubilee's sister Charmaine and their cousin who arranged the murder. I was only roped in, as I don't like Frisco and used as back up if things went wrong. I didn't have a choice, they threatened to kill me if Charmaine failed to make the hit and I didn't finish the job!" Bathsheba cried.

"And what was the name of this cousin?" DCI Netherbourne demanded.

"Fiona...Fiona Netherseal...she's a copper!" Bathsheba cried, as the jukebox played 'Up the Junction' by 'Squeeze'.

Bathsheba's implication of Fiona in Jesty's murder was enough to save her from the gallows, when she appeared at Wolverhampton Crown Court on March 23rd 2007 and where a high court judge in all his judicial finery, remarked. "The court has taken in to consideration your co-operation with regard to the murder of Detective Sergeant Jesty Dollamore and this is reflected in your acceptance of a plea bargain to second degree murder. A heinous crime, all the same that carries a hefty custodial sentence...Bathsheba Mendalove it is the sentence of this court that you go to prison for a term of not less than twenty five to forty years. Dock officer take the prisoner down!"

As the sentence was passed, I was sitting in the public gallery and felt a hand on my shoulder. I looked around to see the smiling face of Jesty standing behind me, before vanishing like a ghost. Bathsheba's twenty five to forty year sentence had reflected the callousness of the crime, but it was only when Fiona was caught and sentenced that justice would finally be done.

Meanwhile as the nationwide alert for Fiona continued, I was having trouble, sorting out my complicated love life. Blan hadn't been physically hurt by her ordeal with Fiona, but it still gave her a bad enough trauma to take time out from her Police career. While still managing to sit down and talk with me about our relationship and slap me so hard that it stung my face, before saying sorry and giving me a hug and walking out of my life, as a lover and entering Carrick's life, as a common-law wife. While I was torn between two lovers with Dixie being like a little sister or better still a daughter, but without any immoral ramifications, while Jubilee was more like a wife to be. Dixie also regarded my flat as her second home and willingly shared my bed, but she refused to consummate our relationship until she was ready. Dixie had also matured and changed her appearance, she now wore a red leather biker's jacket that was a surprise present from me and grew her hair thicker, while still keeping it collar length. That way it would fit nicely under her crash helmet when she rode the black Vespa scooter, she had bought to mark her promotion to CID, while Jubilee rejoined the force and transferred to the vice and queer case crime unit as Fiona's replacement.

Trudy Godsend was relieved as the manager of the Mascara and sent to run the Eye Candy in Birmingham, but she never took up her appointment and disappeared after leaving Stafford. Meanwhile the Mascara's licence was reinstated in readiness for the club's new manager who we were told was coming up from London and who had glowing, references. However shortly before DCI Netherbourne, Carrick and I were to officially meet the Mascara's new manager, I received a personal invitation to the Mascara that aroused my curiosity. I was shown in to the manager's office and were I saw the back of a woman's head in the manager's chair that was turned back against the desk, as the female said "Hello Frisco sweetheart...long time no see!"

"Babs?" I said in astonishment at hearing her voice, before being pleasurably surprised when the chair swivelled and the smiling face of Babs winked at me.

I could see as she sat back in the chair that Babs had grown tougher in style as she looked sharp and professional in her 'Duchess of York' business style makeover of a new black suit with a black velvet hair band to keep her flowing locks in place. While in the close confines of her new office she told me the reason for her sudden disappearance before Jesty's funeral, as she was scared of being done for attempted murder after her tussle with Fiona.

"Listen I can tell you now that no way would you have been done for anything, it would have been Fiona in the dock and doing the explaining, even it meant using the ways and means act. But your safe now and

231

as safe as you'll ever be, Fiona's a busted flush, it's only a matter of time before she's caught and dealt a life sentence." I said, as Babs locked the office door and took the phone off the hook, before letting me have her warm seat, while she sat on lap for a generous 'old time's sake' smooch.

Babs then celebrated her new job in club management with a karaoke party at the Mascara with DCI Netherbourne and Carrick as surprised, as I initially had been when I introduced Babs as the new manager. Then after answering what seemed like a thousand questions, Babs saw Carrick and I sing *'Twist and Shout'* DCI Netherbourne sing *'My Way'* and Jubilee and Dixie sing *'Substitute'* by the Who. And it was during the party mood that Babs took me aside for a private chat in her office and where, as she leaned back against the edge of the office desk she said. "You and me...we've known each other for some time now and were more than just good friends ...listen what I'm trying to say is...Frisco Kane will you marry me?"

I was taken aback by Babs proposal, with my immediate answer, interrupted by a rock band 'Diatribe' that had been booked for the party that night, making their way backstage. When the noise had then died down, enough to speak I looked at Babs who was standing, first with her arms folded and then with her hands gripping the edge of the desk as she swayed while awaiting my reply. While I took a deep breath and walked up to Babs, took hold of her hands, intertwined my fingers with hers and smiled, as I gave her a gentle kiss and whispered. "Yes but... I need time to work things out with Dixie, let them draw to a natural conclusion."

Babs looked puzzled, as I explained. "You see Dixie's applied for a transfer to the Met. That trip to Carnaby Street gave her a taste of honey, now it seems, she wants a second bite of the cherry!"

Babs and I then shared a passionate kiss and as we smooched, I put my hand down the back of her trousers and which made her smilingly scold 'Behave...you'll have plenty of time...when you come to bed tonight?"

"Now that is an offer a gentleman can't refuse!" I whispered before leaving Babs with a gentle kiss as I joined Carrick on the karaoke for 'Hersham Boys'.

The sound of which made Babs smile, she now had her man and knew it was my way of celebrating my acceptance of her matrimonial proposal. The night though was far from, over and when Babs was just about to leave the office and rejoin the party, Dixie knocked on the office door.

"I believe you've had a taste of honey and now you want a second bite of the cherry?" Babs said with a wicked smile, her words of 'taste of honey and second bite of the cherry' made Dixie smile and think about the kiss Jubilee and she shared on the train journey from London to Wolverhampton.

Dixie gave a subtle laugh as she smiled and said. "I've come to tell you, you can have Frisco if you want him, you see Jubilee and I have got it together and we're transferring to London...but I hope you'll and Frisco will both be very happy."

Babs then subtly laughed and smiled, as she said. "I know he's already told me...but only after he'd agreed to marry me."

Dixie was now stuck for words, as Babs said. "Cat got your tongue?"

Dixie then felt hurt and walked out of the office to look for Jubilee who consoled a tearful Dixie, as they shared a kiss of feminine feline attraction.

It was now Blan's turn to knock on the office door and tell Babs that Frisco was hers for the taking, as Jubilee and Dixie were transferring to London.

"I know femme fatale has struck again and Frisco's already agreed to marry me! But judging by the midi dress your wearing your also dressed to impress...so tell me are you also in to femme fatale?" Babs said, as she and Blan began to share a feminine attraction.

"Well give me a kiss and find out?" Blan unwittingly replied without fear, hesitation or thinking about what she'd just said, as Babs gave her a passionate and enjoyable second bite of the cherry.

Meanwhile back in the nightclub, the band 'Diatribe' sang a range of songs from *'Major Tom* through to *'Zoot Suit'* from *Quadrophenia*. This song made me laugh as the male and female lead singers looked like Jubilee when I met up with her in London, like patchwork pearly kings and queens with cheesecutter caps and safety pinned pop/rock patched jeans and waistcoats. Diatribe also sang *'Gimme some Lovin'* and *We've gotta get out of this place'* that Poppy Lane who was the band's lead singer said. "We believe those two songs should have been in *'Quadrophenia'* to give the film some zest instead of the Lemon Popsicle style *Rhythm of the Rain*."

The party then drew to a close at around 2.a.m. and after a cursory visit to let out what I had put in. I found Dixie enjoying kitten play with Jubilee and discussing how they would soon be sharing each other's charms after they had left for London. While in Babs Office I was surprised to find her smooching with Blan in the swivel chair, while talking about having Carrick and me for constant dessert.

CHAPTER 34

STAND BY ME

Narrated by Frisco Kane

Wolverhampton's greasy spoon quarter is Broad Street, where on the corner of Westbury Street stood Darna's latest venture, a psychedelic rat shack named the 'A Bomb in Wardour Street'. This offbeat rock club had a graphic exterior of ivy clad stonework, encrusted with fake bullet holes and a gruesome, muscle, bone and sinew caricature of a human. That had torn a gaping hole in the stonework with claw like hands, while a long tongue drooled from its mouth as it peered with bulbous eyes from an inner darkness. That tunnelled to the psychedelic, interior of the club, where the chequered dance floor swirled with the scented haze of Coconuts, Bananas and Strawberries, as Carrick and I chatted over a drink.

"So this is Darna's new club? Well it's certainly different from the Black board Jungle." Carrick said. "But have you seen what she's done to Prince Albert, it's now called the Billericay with a funny pub sign of the New York skyline and a pair of black n leopard skin, winkle picker, brothel creepers with silver buckles and a pink Cadillac with a silver signature of Billericay along the wing!"

"Well that's Darna for you, as different as her fortunes in love. I mean who'd have thought that she'd have copped, off with Domino, there like chalk n cheese. Then again I never thought Dixie and Jubilee were that way inclined until I came across them at the Mascara and now look at them shacked up in Carnaby Street...did I tell you what happened when I went down to visit them in London?" I said and to which Carrick shook his head and said no.

"Well I can tell you now, it was fun and games all round?" I said with a grin.

"I got picked up from Marylebone by Jubilee in her psychedelic Mini Cooper and who gave me a great big kiss, as soon as I'd got in the car. Then no sooner had I got in to her and Dixie's flat than they got more than aromatic, before I ended up marrying Jubilee with Dixie doing the honours."

"You what" Carrick said who was gobsmacked at what I had just said.

"Oh don't worry it wasn't for real. It seems that you can get a fake marriage certificate from the Acme Novelty Company and just download it off the Internet. The marriage rites where performed at the Church of The Rose and Crown, but you can use any traditional pub name if want, like the Fox and Goose or the Saint George and the Dragon, while the vicar is the Reverend Pearly Gates." I said.

"Pearly Gates...what the Peter Sellers character in the film *Wrong arm of the Law?* That's rather apt isn't it, being married in a pub with a crook for the vicar?" Carrick mused with a mischievous smirk.

"Aren't they all?" I sarcastically laughed. "No but as I was saying...Dixie did the honours, where the vicar was concerned. It seems that she only wanted to be my girlfriend, while Jubilee wanted the whole nine yards and now she can use the name Jubilee Kane if she wants and I told her that I'd verify it. Then we celebrated at a pub disco to Elvis's *'Little Sister'* and *'Tom Hark'* by the Piranhas... before I spent the wedding night in between Jubilee and Dixie, whose kisses are still sweeter than wine." I replied with a wry smile.

"Then again look at Blan and me?" Carrick said.

"We tried to make a go of it, but it didn't work out and now look at her, our new Chief of Detectives after going on that rapid promotion course. And living over the brush with Babs too boot…it's a bit like *'New Tricks?'* Carrick said.

"In that case, can I be Dennis Waterman?" I asked with a cheeky grin.

"But I bet it must have been daunting, having to undergo a psychological evaluation in order to become a Detective Chief Inspector. Just to see if she was still up to the job, after her drama with Fiona, while Babs softer side of femme fatale, helped cure Blan's flashbacks and now look at them, shacked up together, never mind Blan having to step in to DCI Netherbourne's shoes, after his dickey ticker scare?" Carrick said.

"And now I've got another secret to tell you?" I said and to which Carrick gave me a curious look. "I've married Babs…for real. It was while Blan was on sick leave and Babs divorce had just come through and she'd always wanted to visit the Holy Cross Church in Codsall where Jesty and I had got married. Then after a cup of tea with a drop of scotch from Father Bejazus, he performed the marriage service, before we christened our honeymoon in the back of her car. And now I've got three estranged wives, one living in God's good grace."

"Another living over the brush in Stafford" Carrick said.

"And a third cohabiting in London" I said. "But Blan knows nothing about me marrying Babs never mind Jubilee…and what she, don't know want hurt her."

"But what about Babs wedding ring?" Carrick asked.

"She used her old one, after it had been blessed in

holy water." I said.

"Ah well, as the old Chuck Berry song goes, you never can tell and look at us, shacking up with LD and Hazel at Parkdale Rise in Wombourne. At least if it all goes wry we've got a couple of birds to fall back on and I bet that old Police station has never been such a love nest?" Carrick said, as neon lights reflected images of a Spider, a Crab and a Scorpion dancing to *'Tunnel of Love'* by Fun Boy Three.

The back wall of the club screened an adult entertainment advert, showing two female, masked, Go' Go' dancers blowing kisses and strutting, their stuff. 'Vixens of the Night, Foxglove and Blue Kitten are ready to give you, a home visit of debauchery and domination.'

Carrick and I read the inviting message that was screened on the advert with the two Go, Go dancers looking strangely familiar, as I stood up and walked over to club manager, who gave me a 'Vixens of the Night' business card. The manager also let it slip that the girls operated mainly in the Southwest area of Wolverhampton and it was rumoured that one of the girls was an ex cop, with Carrick being just as curious as me when I told him the information.

"Could it be Fiona and Trudy?" Carrick asked, while draining his pint glass.

"Anything's possible? There's been no sign of them since they disappeared back in February, since when it's done nothing but bucket it down with rain." I said while looking into the night sky, as Carrick and I left the club.

We were then accosted by a tarty looking teenager in a mini skirt and fishnet tights, as she stood on a corner of Broad Street, while Carrick flashed his badge and said. "We're Old Bill love and rag trade, have a catchment area in Wolves...All Saints and Horsely

Fields."

The girl walked away, as we walked towards the bus station and I made a mobile phone call, as Carrick mused. "It's a bit cheeky that, rag trade operating this far in to the city. They should all be pushed back. I mean what next Queen Square a red light area and toms doing business around the Prince Albert statue?"

"That'd be fun...especially if the Wolverhampton sniper returned and stung a few merryman's backsides?" I wryly replied.

"You mean the Ghost of LHO or Lee Harvey Oswald? He certainly gave a few faces the bullet and always at night time...so you never knew where the shots came from?" Carrick answered.

"And they never caught him...or her as the case may be? The killings just suddenly stopped? Anyway, if the Vixens of the Night are Fiona and Trudy then we need a trap. So I've just asked Hazel and LD to join us and what we'll do is use one of the flats as bait, I've also sent Blan a message that we're following up a fresh lead on Fiona and Trudy." I said, as we entered the bright lights of Wolverhampton Bus Station.

We caught the bus to Wombourne and as it crossed over Windmill Bank junction, we glimpsed the fenced off debris strewn and charred ruins of the petrol station that looked like the remnants of a funeral pyre. We jumped off the bus at Wombourne Church and walked around the corner to the 1960's style Parkdale Rise' that stood opposite two village pubs. Hazel and LD where already waiting for us and insisted that we went for a drink at the Beggars Bush and where as we sat outside, the neighbouring Grapevine pub was having a karaoke disco with a range of songs from Elvis, Frank and Cliff through to 'Parklife' and 'Rehab'. We sang along and watched every car and customer that graced the Grapevine car park, with my attention being taken by a plum coloured Volvo. The driver of which sported a razor cut, a blazer and a white polo neck jumper, while trying to look like the Bond villain from *'Russia with Love'*, as he marched into the pub. The back doors of the car then opened and out stepped two debonair vixens in long dark wigs and stilettos. As they stretched their legs, it was obvious they were wearing nothing but black silk stockings and Basques under two long fur coats, while trying to look like Uma Thurman in *'Pulp Fiction.'*

"Is this a coincidence or what? But that has to be Foxglove and Blue Kitten ...the only problem is Odd Job the henchman." I said to LD and considered our next move, as with Carrick and Hazel we moved in to the shadows for a smooch.

"I think we'll just have to bluff it." Carrick said, as we emerged from the shadows and walked towards the Volvo and the two lounging females.

"Good evening ladies...Stafford Vice." I said, as I flashed my badge.

"Is this a bust or are you looking for a good time...officers?" One of the females said in a sultry fashion, while pulling open her long fur coat.

"Cut the crap Fiona or are you Trudy?" Carrick rebuffed.

"Let's find out?" I said, as I yanked at the long dark hair of the female and as the wig came off in my hand, it revealed the snarling face of Fiona Netherseal.

I took the other female to be Trudy, as she fumbled in an elegant evening purse and pulled out a small calibre pistol that she used to keep Hazel and LD at bay. While shouting at Carrick and me, as we tussled with Fiona who found fighting in a long coat and high heels wasn't easy. I grabbed her arm and swung her against the car, before bending her arm until it almost dislocated and she screamed with pain.   Trudy meanwhile kept waving the pistol about while the girls, who had drawn their batons, shouted at Trudy to drop the gun, as Carrick applied the handcuffs to Fiona and I shouted. "Now listen to me, you twisted bitch, you orchestrated the death of my wife...you hard faced little cow!"

The pistol then suddenly went off and Fiona slumped against the car while blood trickled from the breast wound, where she had been shot, as her eyes rolled and she died in Carrick's arms. A sudden, joint swipe by Hazel and LD with their batons at Trudy's hands to try and dislodge the pistol in her grip had caused the gun to go off with devastating results. The shot also brought the henchman running from the pub, but when I flashed my badge, the henchman stopped dead in his tracks, as Carrick stared in disbelief at Fiona's dead body and shouted at Trudy "What the hell have you done?"

Trudy then burst in to tears, as Hazel and LD took the pistol from her and applied the handcuffs. Within minutes the car park became awash with blue flashing lights, as Hazel called Blan on her mobile, to break the news that it had all gone Pear shaped, Trudy had shot Fiona. By the time Blan reached the murder scene, Fiona was at the local mortuary, while Trudy languished in the cells at Wombourne police station. It was manslaughter, open and shut that we four detectives had witnessed and Trudy insisted was unintentional, while their henchman gave a brief statement and was released on police bail.

Then, just as we were all finishing our written statements, Blan who had now taken to wearing trousers suits then entered the CID office at Wombourne and after hearing our side of events, said. "It's like one big viscous circle and someone always ends up getting shot! And we'll have to get that advert pulled...but what gets me though, is that it all started with a bungled armed robbery and ended with a whole heap of murders including three of our own?"

"Four if you include that village bobby who also got shot." I replied

"That reminds me, I meant to tell you they got the lad for that murder, he's fourteen years old and came in to the police station a week or so later with his father and a solicitor. The lad was remanded at Cannock magistrates for sentencing reports on a charge of murder, he's due to be formally sentenced at Stafford." Carrick said.

"Three or four what does it matter, it's a rough end to a funny business but I'd love to know where the lad got the gun? Now I've got some news...we've been asked to oversee Vice in Wolves...it seems the city boys are too lax." Blan said.

"I know we saw it earlier...they've allowed the Saraband and the rag trade to dictate the rules, instead of playing the game." I replied

"So do you fancy it?" Blan said with a beaming smile, as Carrick and I looked at each other with wry smiles and said. 'The boys are back in town!'

It had been a long evening and as Carrick, Hazel, LD and I made our weary way back to Parkdale Rise, the church clock heralded the stroke of midnight, so we stopped for a smooch in the shadows. I put my hands under LD' s long topcoat and noticed she had rolled her midi skirt up to form a mini skirt and when I stroked her legs and saw her cheeky smile. I began to realise that my prayers had been answered, Jesty had returned in the guise of LD.

When we reached Parkdale Rise, the solemnity of the night was only broken by the sound of Ben E King singing *Stand by Me.* While the night's tragic events, meant we could all move on, as Hazel took Carrick to her bed and LD took me to her bed for some amorous passion. I then suddenly awoke in a terrible sweat and thought it was delayed shock, but I soon realised that this time, I wasn't afraid of the dark or scared about seeing ghosts. I was also alone in bed, so I arose and found LD in just her lingerie, standing by the lounge window, as pale moonlight shone through the glass and pierced the darkened room. LD looked out at the night sky with her hands on her hips, mistress of all she surveyed, as I said "I wondered where you were?"

"Hello Tiger...couldn't you sleep either?" LD said.

"I was haunted by a bad dream, I kept relieving the moment Fiona was shot." I said, as I put my arm round LD and we shared a passionate kiss.

"Well I know a cure for bad dreams...so where we going for our honeymoon Paris, Rome, Bay of Naples, Brighton?" LD asked as a fiery passion flickered in her eyes.

"Brighton...do I look as queer as nine pence? But I do like the sound of the Bay of Naples so hold that thought. I'll tell you what though, this time it's not going to be like that flaming James Bond movie...*On her majesty's secret* (bloody) *service!*" I exclaimed, while inadvertently sounding or so I thought like Michael Caine.

LD then gazed at the night sky that blanketed the Wombourne skyline and said. "It's a snipers moon."

Although her observation of the night sky, evoked a strange remark I didn't give it a second thought, as LD gave me a kiss on the forehead before resting her head on my shoulder and turning her face away and giving a wicked smile.

THE END